**"Wha**
**giving him a stunned once-over.**

"It was an awful, botched attempt. A horrible kiss, as far as kisses go. Sorry."

"Never apologize for a kiss." She clutched the front of his shirt, pulling him down to her mouth, and kissed him.

More intrigued than startled—although he was still kicking himself for such an awkward first contact—Certainly stepped in closer and slipped an arm around her slender back. All he'd needed was a test kiss, and an acceptance from her. He relaxed now, and Vika's mouth melded against his. Of course, he should expect nothing less than perfect from her. Perfect looks, perfect life, perfect kiss. And suddenly he wanted to mar that perfection, to imprint his own rough and messy darkness.

"What was that?" Vika asked, giving him a stunned once-over.

# THIS WICKED MAGIC

## MICHELE HAUF

First published in Great Britain 2013
by Mills & Boon, an imprint of Harlequin (UK) Limited,
Eton House, 18-24 Paradise Road, Richmond, Surrey TW9 1SR

© Michele Hauf 2013

ISBN: 978 0 263 90404 8
ebook ISBN: 978 1 472 00668 4

089-0613

Harlequin (UK) policy is to use papers that are natural, renewable and recyclable products and made from wood grown in sustainable forests. The logging and manufacturing processes conform to the legal environmental regulations of the country of origin.

Printed and bound in Spain
by Blackprint CPI, Barcelona

**Michele Hauf** has been writing romance, action-adventure and fantasy stories for more than twenty years. Her first published novel was *Dark Rapture*. France, musketeers, vampires and faeries populate her stories. And if she followed the adage "write what you know," all her stories would have snow in them. Fortunately, she steps beyond her comfort zone and writes about countries she has never visited and of creatures she has never seen.

Michele can be found on Facebook and Twitter and at michelehauf.com. You can also write to Michele at PO Box 23, Anoka, MN 55303, USA.

Believe in something. It doesn't matter
what that something is, so long as you
never stop believing in the magic of love.

# Chapter 1

*Paris*

There are things he had done. Bad things. Dangerous things. Wicked things. He'd made mistakes. Broken rules. He regretted.

And he did not regret.

Everything he had ever done had been to expand his knowledge. Learning was never a bad thing. Most of the time. Sometimes a man needed to sacrifice for the greater good. Or that was how he'd talked himself into his latest disastrous adventure.

Now Certainly Jones desired peace. It was not to be his.

Hands shoved in his jeans pockets and senses alert to the warm summer air and gasoline fumes rising from the tarmac, he hustled toward the glow of a streetlight a hundred yards down from the Lizard Lounge.

The faery club had been inordinately bright—which was why he'd chosen to go there after sundown. He never went out after the world had grown dark, but after months of solitude he'd craved a night away from home. The Lizard Lounge was mind-numbingly weird. He could deal with all paranormal breeds and their ways and manners—but faeries? There were some things a witch who had been practicing the dark arts for well over a century and a half should not see. Situations, illicit couplings and magics in which even he daren't dabble.

Gut muscles clenching, Certainly felt the familiar warning twinge of an internal takeover. Of late, his body was not his to command.

He increased the pace of his footsteps through the dark alley. Fifty strides ahead beckoned the streetlight. His fingers curled against his abs and he bit his lip.

"Stay back," he hissed. The passengers inhabiting his body—his very soul—rippled within his being.

Spellcraft had proved ineffectual to prevent an imminent intrusion. Directing his instincts inward, Certainly attempted to, at the least, identify the imposing entity. It gnawed at his insides and clawed to get out. As his mouth began to water, he pinpointed that it craved a dark, seeping, metallic thing. It wanted…carrion.

"Hell. Not good."

With a rallying dash, he landed in the safe glow and hooked his arm about the black metal pole, swinging halfway about and chuckling in triumph. He'd won. For now. Yet he stood a stranded sailor adrift in a dark sea, and navigating the infested waters always proved perilous.

The next streetlight punctuating this moonless night wasn't for another long block. He stood on a back street, well off the main avenue. He should have gone the other direction, toward the Seine, where the night was always bright with tourists and passing cars. But the thing inside him had been persistent, pushing him this way the moment he'd exited the safety of the Lizard Lounge's peculiar brightness.

The demon inside smelled something Certainly wasn't able to pick out of the atmosphere now that he had a grasp on his own senses, and he wasn't sure he wanted to if his instincts were correct regarding the carrion demon.

Pushing his fingers through his long dark hair, he pulled at the strands, wincing. It wanted control, and the light made it stomp its hooves and bleat to rattle Certainly's bones. Venturing out after sunset had been foolish. Yet he'd needed the escape from the solitude of his loft.

He wasn't sure how much longer he could endure this torture before he gave in and surrendered. Walked away from the light and into the darkness. Once there, the darkness would swallow him whole. He would never make it back to the surface sane. As it was, he treaded the line that tipped over to insanity. But he wouldn't go down that way, would not let the dark passengers he carried inside take him or claim his soul.

He'd stolen from Daemonia, and so yes, this was

his deserving punishment. But he'd find escape to the surface. He always did.

Thinking he could hail a cab and request that the driver keep the interior light on—a feeble and temporary mend to his curse—Certainly scanned down the lonely street, paralleled by brick walk-ups and here and there a limestone three-story, which hailed from medieval times. The street was cobbled, remnants of centuries past when kings and musketeers once paraded before the peasants and Revolutionaries swung sticks instead of swords and lapped up the blood from severed heads. Not so metaphorically, either.

He'd missed that tumultuous time and had instead grown up during Paris's Bohemian phase in the late nineteenth century, *la Belle époque.* A hippie at heart, there were days he pined for the halcyon days of artistry, freedom, absinthe, ether and living from sofa to sofa, wherever his body may fall.

The thought of his wilder youth made him smirk and release the pole. He stepped out onto the street, his well-worn leather boots clicking the cobblestones, and scanned left then right. Cabs generally tracked the main avenues.

The darkness had grown to an inky maw separating him from the brightness of the Lizard Lounge's neon sign and his glowing outpost. Putting up his left hand, he spread his tattooed fingers wide. The entire hand was gloved with spellcraft tattoos used for a multitude of magics. He focused on the electrical connection his body had to the world and tried to see a map of all the streetlights as if a hologram in the air before him. Faint lines formed but quickly puffed away. His demonic passengers weakened his magic. With a huff, he gave up the read and dropped his hand to his side.

Across the narrow street and down the alley, he sighted a vehicle with its headlights on, facing an alcove he couldn't see from his point of view. The long white car was a dash away through darkness, but it was the only action he suspected he'd see on this street for a while. And without firm control of a tracking spell, he would be left to walk home blindly. Perhaps he could hitch a ride?

The carrion demon again scented its target, and Certainly felt his body sway and stumble. Away from the light.

If only he'd mastered the art of fire magic, he could draw up a fireball to lead his way home. Fire was about the only elemental magic witches avoided, for it could bring their deaths. Though some witches had mastered it. CJ hadn't time for it over the decades when he'd been gorging his knowledge on all other magics.

"Hitchhiking it is," he muttered, and made a daring dash for the deceptive safety of the car's headlights.

"Yuck. A werewolf," Libby said.

Viktorie St. Charles walked around her sister Libertie, who stood posed, hands on hips, body encased in a white Tyvek cleaning suit, before tonight's job. Her sister's toe tapped the asphalt in time to the tunes blasting through her ever-present earbuds.

Vika tugged a white mesh cap over her hair, tucking up some stray red strands. With a step, her Tyvek-covered flat shoes squished in a pile of werewolf guts.

No one had ever said financial stability was glamorous.

"Twenty minutes," Vika stated, inspecting the slick mess oozing about her foot. Lemon and myrrh would take out the smell and the blood. "You pick up the chunks. I'll start spraying down the brick."

Giving her the thumbs-up signal, Libby wielded the black zip-up morgue bag with her pink latex-gloved hands and bent over the task. "This guy is still in solid form in places."

"The silver must have worked quickly. Usually what happens in werewolves if it doesn't have time to course completely through the blood."

Vika aimed a handheld spray canister filled with vinegar, water and rosemary, bespelled to remove all trace of DNA, at the brick wall behind the parking lot for a down-on-its-luck bistro. She worked efficiently from top to bottom, directing the stream toward a center point that collected all the refuse for easier cleanup with the portable wet vac that waited in the back of their work vehicle.

They worked in tandem, having done this for years, both sisters knowing the job well. Cleaning was to Vika as music was to Libby.

Years previously, a date with a sexy werewolf had ended in him getting staked with a chunk of silver by a vampire rival. Vika hadn't been attached to the big lug—first date, don't you know—but she had liked him and had been hoping for a one-night stand, with him

in were form, not werewolf, that is. She did not do fur
during sex. The vampire had chuckled and offered to
fulfill her desires, until she'd kicked him in the 'nads.
Didn't matter what sort of paranormal breed you were.
A kick to the gonads would take down any man for a
few minutes.

As the vampire had hobbled away, Vika stood amid
the scattered bits of werewolf and the idea of leaving
behind such a mess had been reprehensible. She'd managed to get the biggest pieces into a nearby garbage
can, and with a run to a nearby supermarket, had pur-
chased some bleach and rubber gloves. The werewolf
had deserved a decent burial. It had been the best she
could offer at the time.

Needless to say, she'd been spied by a Council member while tidying up the crime scene, and the next
thing she knew, she was being encouraged to become
a cleaner.

Her sister Libertie, as good-natured as they came,
had joined in only because she always tagged along
on Vika's coattails. She had never had the adventurous spirit of their sister, Eternitie, who was off in the
wilds of some African nation at the moment. Libby and
Vika were homebodies, and they liked that just fine.

When the area was clean, Vika pulled off her pink
rubber gloves and looked over the wet asphalt and brick
sparkling in the harsh shine from the car headlights.
The warding spell they always initially cast around the
crime scene kept passersby from witnessing what they
were doing, so she worried little about being seen. She

inhaled the lemon scent, smiling. Always felt good to accomplish a necessary task.

Libby packed up the cleaning supplies and bent near the rear tire of the hearse they'd had a mechanic modify as a cleaning vehicle.

"Found something!" Libby dangled the hairy chunk to show Vika. "An ear. Give the tarmac a blast of purifying magic over by the tire, and I think we're good to rock and roll."

"Great."

Vika packed away the wet vac and then grabbed an amulet fashioned from bloodstone and strung on a silk cord from an assortment they kept in a purple tackle box. Just as she was about to speak the purifying spell, her nose tickled—and something brushed her soul.

Noticing her sister's distraction, Libby asked, "One hanging around?"

Vika nodded but found the tickle in her nose would not dissipate. A sneeze strained at her sinuses, entirely unrelated to the wandering soul she felt nudging against her soul.

"Who's that?"

Vika divided her attention between fighting the sneeze and eyeing the dark figure her sister pointed to. He ran up along the hearse toward them. A man with long, messy hair blacker than coal waved his hands at them. One of the hands was blackened with a glove or…maybe it was tattoos? And his eyes…

Vika squinted. Were they red?

He winced and bent at the waist, appearing to fight some inner struggle.

"He can see us?" Libby asked, gaping at the realization. She tugged out her earbuds. "I haven't taken down the ward yet."

The soul brushing up against Vika's soul began to attach itself. A bright glow entered her chest—and she sneezed so forcefully her head bobbed forward and she staggered side to side. She caught herself against Libby's arm.

"Blessed be," Libby said. "That one was a doozy."

"Oh, no." Vika slapped a palm to her chest. "It's gone. I sneezed it right out of me!"

Certainly felt the force of the woman's sneeze enter his core. It was the weirdest thing. One minute he had been racing toward the twosome, fighting against the carrion demon to maintain control of his being, yet baffled at what the two women dressed head to toe in white clean suits were doing in the alleyway with scrub brushes, and then she sneezed, and it was as if the sneeze moved *through* him. Permeated his clothing and flesh and sparkled its way through his innards.

Yes, *sparkled.*

Bright and immense, it was as if some divine force had entered him. And he felt the effect immediately. Because the carrion-sniffing demon urging him toward the rangy scent of dead flesh had given an inner howl—something he'd felt clawing at his insides instead of actually hearing—and then it was gone.

Certainly slapped a hand to his gut. He knew without doubt the demon had been expelled.

By a sneeze?

He shook his head and brushed long strands of hair from his face. Crouched against the brick wall and safely ensconced within the headlight glow, he looked up to see the front doors of the hearse slam shut. The vehicle backed up.

"No!" He ran after the departing vehicle. "Stop. I need you!"

The hearse turned onto a main road near a video store that glared with a multitude of neon lights, and the driver stepped on it, peeling away into the night. Certainly was able to catch only the tiny logo on the back door of the white hearse, a pentacle overlaid with what looked like a vacuum cleaner and the words *Jiffy Clean.*

A patron from the video store walked out, and, staggering, CJ bumped into him. The man cursed him in French and shoved him aside. CJ stepped out onto the street, following the retreating red taillights.

"You are all right, *monsieur?*" the man who had cursed him called, though he was still walking away down the sidewalk.

Certainly nodded and gestured with a wave that he was indeed better than all right. But now he had to find that hearse and the woman who had sneezed at him. She'd worn white from head to toe, so he had no idea what she actually looked like. Her eyes had been green though; he'd seen as much in the glow of the headlights.

"That woman." He slapped a hand over his pounding heart. "She exorcized one of my demons."

# Chapter 2

"Vika, what's wrong?" Libby sorted their cleaning gear in the supply room, placing their hazmat suits in the work sink designated for cleaning away the debris. The pink fringes dancing about her sleeves dusted the air. "I don't think the guy saw anything. We had the whole area cleaned and everything packed up by the time he wandered onto the scene."

Vika glided through the kitchen and pushed through the French doors leading into the living room. A spiraling stairway curled up to the second floor, matching the curved architecture of the house.

Intent on slipping out of her clingy work pants, Vika called down the stairway, "I know that, Libby. I'm just— He saw through the wards. And did you see the way he looked at me?"

"How could I?" Libby soared up the stairs behind

her. "All that long black hair was hanging in his face. Poor guy must have been a derelict looking for a handout. Oh, snap, I should have given him the change in my pocket. Karma is so going to bite me for that one."

Vika rolled her eyes at her sister's worry. Witches and karma? Libby had a broad definition of the practice of witchcraft. On the other hand, it didn't matter what a person called the union with the universe that enhanced their life's path, so long as they respected its awesome power.

Unzipping her pants and tugging off the thin T-shirt in preparation to slip into a nice, hot shower, Vika paused near the open bedroom doorway. A clatter downstairs alerted her. It was a familiar sort of mild booming clatter she and her sister knew well. It announced *his* arrival.

Eyes widening, Libby pressed her fingers to her lips. "He's here already?" She patted her hands over her purple skirt and ran toward her bedroom. "He always just appears! Why can he never announce himself or make an appointment? At least then I'd have a chance to comb my hair and freshen up my lipstick."

"I'll walk down slowly," Vika called.

Tugging her shirt on and zipping her pants along the hip, she padded the high-glossed hardwood floor in the hallway. Thanks to lemon oil, it gleamed. Fresh, clean things made her feel good about herself. Peaceful.

The chandelier lighting the circular living room below glowed softly, yet it also blocked the view of their visitor. It had been over a week, so Vika expected him. Though never actually knowing the exact day or moment he would arrive, she did appreciate what he did for her.

She slid a hand along the white marble railing she kept polished to a shine. The house had been designed by Alphonse Fouquet in the nineteenth century and had been in the St. Charles family since. It was designed with eight walls in a round shape. Half the walls faced the four points of the compass, and the other half faced representative elements. The dwelling was very receptive to the angelic, which was a good thing, as far as their visitor was concerned.

Libby zoomed by her, taking the stairs as if in a track race, *click-click-click*ing in the high heels she'd slapped on. Without welcoming the visitor, her sister dashed into the kitchen. Vika smirked to know what she was up to.

"Reichardt," Vika called in greeting to the stoic man attired in his usual black.

He stood beneath the chandelier, hands crossed solemnly before him. Broad and bold, he looked a misplaced warrior from a previous millennium who should be wielding an ax or some form of roughly forged iron weapon. He wore a goatee this evening, and the thick jot of blackness on his chin gave Vika a smile. The man had never a care for his appearance, though he was always neat, which appealed to her cleanliness fetish, so a little style was certainly a surprise.

"Looking rather chic this evening," she commented.

Before she could ask after his new fashion statement, Libby breezed into the room and stopped beside her in a fury of fringe. Her sister, giddy with anticipation, held out a plate of chocolate chip cookies she'd baked earlier this evening before they'd gotten the cleaning call.

"Cookie?" she offered sweetly.

The soul bringer glanced at the plate as if Libby held forth a stew of rusty nuts, bolts and chirping crickets, and he wasn't certain if one should eat it or build something with it.

Reichardt adjusted his attention toward Vika. "Take off your clothes."

Sensing Libby's pout, Vika tugged her shirt over her head again. "The cookies are excellent."

"I grate chocolate into the mix," Libby said proudly. "It makes them super chocolaty."

Dropping her pants about her feet, Vika was thankful she'd worn a bra and panties today. Often, she forwent undergarments, preferring the sensual feel of fabric sliding against her skin. But when on a job, she wore as many layers as possible. Seemed to keep the unclean away for reasons she knew were superficial yet clung to anyway.

"Step back, please," Reichardt said to Libby, ignoring the proffered treats.

Her sister dutifully complied, though Vika could sense Libby's dismay at not being able to pawn off a cookie on the man.

Reichardt was a psychopomp, a soul bringer whose only job was to deliver the souls of the recently departed to Above or Beneath. The soul bringer put out his hands before him, palms flat, and drew them over Vika's body, without touching. He utilized a form of catoptromancy—his silvered eyes were the mirrors—

that would draw the wandering souls out of her body. He would pass over her many times, each time drawing up warmth to her skin and then pulling up a tickle as each soul left hers in a sparkle of phosphorescent light and attached to him.

Corpse lights, they were called in that moment of release from a body when they gleamed giddily. Yet they were lost and wandering souls not moved on to either Above or Beneath, usually due to a violent death—and an absent soul bringer.

Vika had a sticky soul, and when out on a cleaning job, she tended to pick up the wandering souls. It wasn't purposeful; they attached to her for reasons of which she could never be sure. It was a condition she'd become aware of only since taking on the cleaning jobs.

She had developed an agreement with Reichardt years ago. Once a week he scrubbed her of the souls because they did belong to him, and he could not abide losing one. Which served her well because the idea of walking around with dozens of souls clinging to hers was weird. They didn't hurt her and she didn't notice their presence, save when they entered her soul or left it.

Feeling one last tickle, Vika let out a sigh as Reichardt stepped away from her. The man nodded, his eyes now closed, as he consumed the souls through his skin.

Vika winked at Libby, who winked back.

The man opened his kaleidoscope eyes, and the blade-sharp look he thrust at Vika made her gasp and press a hand over her lacy black bra.

"One's missing," he said in his deep, monotone voice that rattled in Vika's rib cage.

"Missing? But—"

Oh, hell. The sneeze. She'd actually sneezed out the soul that had attempted to attach to her. How that was possible, she had no idea, but she innately knew that is what had happened earlier.

"I didn't do it purposefully," she offered. "It just— You see, I sneezed."

"I need that soul."

Vika felt Libby's arm brush aside hers, joining her ranks in support, the plate of cookies still held in feeble offering.

"You will return it to me by next week's scrubbing or…" Reichardt paused, bowing and shaking his head as if to lament her stupidity.

*Or he'll kill me?* she thought dreadfully, fully expecting such an announcement from so ominous a being.

"I will take your soul in exchange," he finally announced. With the speed of a homeless thief, the soul bringer nabbed a cookie from Libby's plate and disappeared.

Libby squealed. "He took a cookie!"

Vika could but shake her head and grab a cookie from the plate herself. But she didn't take a bite. Instead, she stared at the lumpy brown morsel as if it were her soul, all flattened, cooked and…not in her body.

Bending, she tugged up her pants. "Libby, how am I going to get that soul back? I don't know where it is. It's probably floating all over Paris by now. And he'll know. Reichardt will know exactly which one it is if it isn't in me next time he visits." She took a bite of cookie. "Oh, great goddess, this is good."

"I know, right? It's the best batch I've made so far. I'm thinking of entering this recipe in the annual Witches Bazaar SpellCast and Cook-Off. Vika, don't worry, we'll figure it out. We've got a whole week. We need to return to the scene of the crime. I'm sure the soul is floating about in the vicinity."

"Maybe." She tugged on her shirt. At her ankles, a black cat with a white-striped tail snuggled against her leg and meowed. "Not now, Salamander. I need to think."

Which meant…

"You want me to get out your cleaning bucket?" Libby asked.

"Please."

While Libby retrieved Vika's cleaning supplies, Vika bent and slipped the slender cat into her embrace. Sal nuzzled against her chin, rubbing his soft cheek against her. He'd always been a faithful guy, even when he'd once been human.

"I wonder about that man." Vika's thoughts raced through the night's events as she absently stroked Sal's back. "The derelict. I sneezed directly at him. Could he…?"

The archives in the basement of the Council's Paris base were vast, stretching half a mile in labyrinthine twists and turns similar to the catacombs that surely hugged up against the subterranean walls. The occasional skull even appeared embedded in the walls, of which some had been left in their natural limestone state.

CJ felt at peace here beneath the fluorescent lights he'd had specially installed a few months ago after his return from Daemonia. If it hadn't been for his twin brother, TJ, he may still be wandering the bleak and torturous landscape of the place of all demons. The lights had been a necessity and, he admitted, were out of place in the ancient archives normally lit with soft lighting to protect some of the older books, parchments and manuscripts that lay scattered everywhere.

There were stacks of grimoires—books of shadows—and ancient texts CJ had marked on his mental list to get scanned for easy reference, but he estimated such an arduous process would take decades. He had the time but not the patience or the technical know-how. An assistant was necessary, but a call for job applicants was out of the question. Assistant to the Keeper of All Things Paranormal wasn't exactly a position one could interview for. He had the notion he'd know the perfect assistant when he met him or her.

The Council was an organized body of various paranormal breeds that kept watch over the paranormal nations but notoriously tried to never act in a violent manner to stop wars between nations or petty crimes among the breeds. They suggested, smoothed over and made nice—or so that was their claim.

They'd done plenty to interfere over the centuries, but CJ couldn't think of a time when the interference hadn't been necessary.

Now he searched the computer archives of known paranormals on a shiny silver Mac computer. Before entering the archives he always warded himself against electricity so his magic would not react and burn out the wiring or the fancy new computers. This database had only recently been computerized thanks to Cinder, the former fire demon—now vampire—who did security and IT work for the Council all across Europe.

CJ scanned through a list of cleaners the Council employed nationwide. None displayed the pentacle with the vacuum cleaner symbol. Jiffy Clean? He suspected it a joke on the cleaner's part. The white hearse had been a kick, as well.

"Two women," he muttered as his eyes scrolled down the list. "In Paris."

Most cleaners worked a specific city or country. Paris was large enough and hosted a massive population of paranormals, so it listed half a dozen cleaners—but only one under a woman's name.

"Viktorie St. Charles," he said. "In the fourth arrondissement." One of the oldest parts of Paris in the old Marais neighborhood, laid out in the shadow of the former Bastille. "Hmm, not far from where the vampire, Domingos LaRoque, lives. Quiet neighborhood. Gotcha."

"Hey, CJ!"

Think of the devil, and one of his former minions walks through the door. Cinder strolled in, his height forcing him to bend to pass through the doorway built at the turn of the eighteenth century. He also had to turn slightly to manage his broad shoulders. The dark-haired man patted the top of the computer. "How's the system working?"

"Very well. I appreciate all the work you've done. Makes it easy to find things around here, at least the few lists and files I've been able to enter in the database."

"Great. You need an assistant."

"The right one will walk through that door someday."

"Uh-huh. Don't hold your breath, buddy. How about you? You look…" The former angel, who had long ago been forcibly transformed to demon, and who then centuries later became mortal, and who was now only recently vampire, gave him a discerning once-over. "Not terrible."

CJ smirked. He looked like hell and hadn't been right for months, since his return from that damnable place, Daemonia.

"You have a talent for compliments. I'm learning to control…things."

He'd told Cinder about the demonic passengers that occupied his soul, yet despite having worked at the gates to Beneath for millennia, the guy hadn't a clue how to get the damned things out of him.

"I think I found the one person who might be able to help me. Viktoria St. Charles," CJ said.

"I think you mean Viktorie. Or Vika, as her friends call her," Cinder said, pronouncing it *Vee-ka*. "It's a Russian name. She's the pretty little witch who lives in the round house."

"Round house?"

"That's what some call it. I think it's actually a hexagram. It was designed by a witch to perfectly align with the planets, stars, the moon and whatever else you witches worry about. I've been told it's a cool place to see. Probably comparable to the spectacle you live in."

"My flat is not a spectacle. It's a means to survive." A horrible, mind-eating, depressing means to survival. But his current mode of decorating style was the one bit of luck CJ had discovered to keep back his nasty passengers.

"So you've told me. Still seeking prismatic light?"

"Always."

"What's got you looking up the St. Charles witch? Or I should say witches. They are three sisters, but I think only two live in the round house. Gad, I hate calling it the round house. A hexagram is so not round."

Cinder was some kind of numbers whiz, due to the fact he was originally the angel who created that sort of stuff—the whole mathematics shebang.

"If she is the woman I ran into last night," CJ said, "then she was able to exorcise one of my demons."

"Just like that? Without a hello, how do you do?"

"It was an auspicious sneeze, actually. And no, no introductions. In fact, she fled the scene soon after the accidental exorcism." CJ rubbed a hand along his jaw. "She's a cleaner, eh?"

"Yes. Nasty job." Cinder gave a dramatic shudder. "Especially for two pretty women."

"Speaking of pretty women." CJ closed out the program and leaned back on the creaky office chair. "How's the little woman?"

"You mean my tiny vixen?" The vampire grinned a mile wide, revealing the points of his fangs.

"That good, huh?"

Cinder nodded. "Love is the coolest thing, CJ. You should give it a try sometime."

"So I've been told by my best friend, Lucian."

"Bellisario? I haven't seen that vamp in a while. And what about your brother? Didn't TJ and his little kitty cat just get married?"

"Yep, and expecting a litter, I've been told."

"A litter?"

TJ's wife was a cat shifter, and CJ liked to tease his brother he was going to have a litter instead of a baby, which was unfeasible but still fun to joke about. "You know, she's a cat."

"I don't think it works that way, man."

"Just kidding. No one ever seems to get my jokes. So you in Paris for a while?"

"Parish and I have relocated here for the summer. I will be updating more hardware for the Council. Might even get a fancy scanner in here to scan books without breaking the spines. Bet that would make your day."

"It would. The ancient grimoires are delicate. But I've no time to work on such a project. Now I've got the witch's address, I'm on my way out."

"All right, man, take it easy."

"Say hi to Parish for me," CJ said as he walked Cinder out of the office and headed for the fourth quarter.

Libby breezed into the bright, spotless spell room, swooshing a flutter of purple ruffles in eyesight, as

Vika bent over a mortar of crushed lavender. The spider's eyes listed in the ingredients she doled out carefully. Only needed half a dozen.

"Working on a sleeping draft?" Libby asked, leaning on the cool, white marble counter. She snapped her banana-scented gum. She cocked out a hip, hitting a pose as always. Rock star was Libby's innate M.O., despite her lacking fame and the ability to carry a tune.

"For Becky. She's been sleeping less than a hour a week lately." The vampire, who was Vika's best friend, had a lot to deal with, her dad being the devil's fixer. Becky worried about him constantly. "I don't need help. I know you had plans for today."

Libby's mood perked. On the other hand, when wasn't her mood perky? The dress she wore was vintage, and the cinched skirt with wide white plastic belt reminded Vika of an old baking ad she'd once seen while paging through her grandmother's magazines from the fifties. Always so spiffy, those pre-feminism women, when doing household chores.

"I figured I should stick around," Libby said. "When do you want to head back to the crime scene to look around for the will-o'-the-wisp?"

Will-o'-the-wisp was another name for the corpse light or wandering soul that usually stayed firmly attached to Vika's soul until the soul bringer arrived to scrub her clean.

"Soon as I'm done here. But I can do that myself. Really, Libby, go and have fun."

"I wish you'd come along with me. The witches bazaar is always a riot."

"I know. You've told me about all the eligible young witches."

"I'm sure there's a few to catch your eye. I know you like them tall, muscled and blond."

"The opposite of your thick, brute and dark," Vika answered with a grin. She tapped the last spider eye into the mortar and rolled the marble pestle over the contents with a satisfying crushing noise. "You think Reichardt liked the cookie?"

"Oh, Vika." Libby sighed. "I dreamed about The Taking of the Cookie last night. You don't want to know."

"Yeah, you probably better keep that one to yourself. Would it matter if I said, once again, how wrong having a crush on a soul bringer is?"

"Nope. He's the guy for me. I know it."

Good luck with that. The guy was thousands of years old and hadn't cracked a smile in a millennium, Vika felt sure. His life consisted of collecting souls, all day, all night, all the time. She imagined he did not have a social life, or even a concept of what socializing implied. And to consider love or romance? Forget about it.

"If they've any vetiver for sale today, would you pick me up a pint? I'm fresh out. Salamander got into the plant out in the garden and mowed that down smartly."

"Will do." Libby leaned in and kissed her on the brow. "Talk to you later, sis. Good luck tracking the soul. But if you can't find it, I'll put in a good word for you with Reichardt."

Libby flounced out of the spell room, and Vika sighed. "If only that were possible."

She knew well if she didn't find the soul, Reichardt's retaliation would be swift and just. She didn't particularly favor the idea of having no soul, but she knew she could live without one. A soulless body grew cold and emotionless. Soulless would leave her open to all sorts of untold evils. She would not be the same witch of the Light, and she didn't know if she could live with the consequences.

"Um, Vika?"

She looked up to see Libby peeking into the room, her smile gone. "You forget something?"

"There's someone here to see you," her sister whispered covertly. "The guy from last night."

Vika dropped the heavy marble pestle in the mortar. "The derelict?"

"Derelict?" A tall man with coal hair and an easy stance walked around beside Libby and crossed his arms. He looked only one step up from derelict, with his black clothing hanging on his broad frame and his jeans hems scraping the hardwood floor. He gave the spell room a once-over, drawing his eyes from the walls of glass-fronted cupboards to the inset halogen lights that fashioned the space into the ultimate clean room for concocting and conjuring. "This is your spell room? It's very…"

"Clean?" Vika offered hopefully.

"Sterile."

"Thank you." Pleased with the comment, she stood and gestured her sister to leave. "It's okay, Libby. The problem may now be solved."

Her sister winked and made a kissing gesture behind the man's back before giggling and dashing off to spend the afternoon trading spells and herbs with the local covens at the weekly bazaar.

"Viktoria St. Charles?" he asked, stepping down into the room. His boots clicked the highly glossed marble floor.

The man inserted a void of darkness into the clean room with his presence. He wore black from head to toe, and the room was white upon gray marble. As much as black was her preferred color scheme, Vika always wore pale colors in this room to honor the pure atmosphere. Today, it was a soft heather, fitted to her body from shoulder to ankle in a corseted maxi dress that flared out from the knee.

"Viktorie," she corrected. "As in successful. It's an old Russian name."

"Oh, yes, Viktorie. I'm sorry."

"Why are you here, monsieur…?"

"I looked you up on the Council database. I'm Certainly Jones." He offered his hand to shake, and she did so, quickly, finding his grip sure.

The man recoiled, shaking his hand as if he'd been stung. "What the hell was that?"

She had no idea what he'd felt. Pressing a hand to her throat—ah, yes. "My grandmother's nail." She lifted the leather cord she always wore about her neck. A centuries-old nail was twisted about it as a pendant. "It was taken from her grave after she'd been buried by the villagers."

"Don't tell me." He winced as he studied the necklace. "Nails had been pounded around her clothing to keep the witch down so she would not rise from the grave?"

"Actually, this one, and the one my sister wears, were taken from her jaw." The practice had been a cruel and unusual attribute of the witch-hunt madness of the eighteenth century. "Her magic is contained within this nail. It protects me from dark magic." She lifted a defiant brow.

"It's powerful. I felt it."

"That means you practice dark magic."

"It does." At her silence, he added with a splay of his hands, which revealed his left was covered in a tight assortment of black tattoos, "Someone's got to do it."

Uh-huh. She'd never had a dark practitioner cross her threshold before, and she wasn't sure she liked it now. Best to get rid of this one quickly.

"So, Certainly Jones," she said. "I've heard of you. The Council's resident librarian."

"Archivist, actually. My job involves much more than cataloging books. And you are a cleaner who is also a witch? This spell room is so…"

"Impressive?"

"Sanitary." He looked about as if a dark angel lost among the clean and pure. Rubbing a palm up his arm, he gave a noticeable shiver. "Derelict, eh?"

Vika walked along the marble counter, trailing a fingertip along the cool, curved edge. A means of grounding herself, because she suspected the witch was powerful and wielded much darker magic than she could imagine. It hummed from him, and it felt wrong in the air.

It disturbed her, and she wasn't sure if that was a good thing or not.

"Derelict? You did present a bedraggled appearance last night. As well as now—"

"And you look like a dream. Green eyes. I was right about that." A wink surprised her.

"Ahem." She was not so easy to win over, despite the lucid warmth she felt from his soft stare. "You look as if you've seen better days, Monsieur Jones."

He pushed a hank of hair away from his face. The motion revealed a tattoo on the side of his neck, but she didn't look too closely. He wasn't unattractive, Vika decided, just…not neat. Rumpled and scruffy. Her skin prickled to wonder at how ill-kept his home must be if this was the appearance he presented to the world.

"I have seen better days," he said, followed by a heavy sigh. "And I'm hoping you can return those better days to me. I need your help, Viktorie."

She tilted up her chin. The call for help always tweaked at the protective bone in her body. She strived to be her best, always, to help others, and to do right by the witch's rede. But she was having a hard time relaxing around this man. His presence prickled across her bare arms, and it wasn't an altogether uncomfortable feeling. Persuasive, and yet warning.

She didn't need the warning; dark magic was something with which she refused to associate.

"I don't understand how you think I can help you, Monsieur Jones."

"Please, call me CJ. Last night you did something

incredible for me. I'm hoping you'll be able to do it again."

"I didn't do a single thing for you. I saw you. I got in the car and drove off. But I'm still not sure how you saw me. That area was warded to keep bystanders from seeing us while my sister and I cleaned the crime scene."

"The carrion drew me. Strange, because I'm a vegetarian. But your little ward wasn't powerful enough to blind me."

Little ward? Vika stiffened, putting her hands to her hips. He was wearing out a welcome she'd not granted him.

"You sneezed," he offered.

Vika turned away. That damnable sneeze! It had put her on the soul bringer's most-wanted list and now brought this practitioner of dark magic into her sacred spell room. She said over her shoulder, "And you've come to say gesundheit?"

"How about I offer you a blessed be? Far too late, but well meant, I promise."

His manner was too kind to fit his appearance. And his presence. She didn't like how he made her feel unsure in ways that inappropriately warmed her skin. She slid her hands along her hips down to her thighs.

Did she feel attraction for the man? No, impossible. Maybe the tiniest bit of curiosity. The man was just so...there. Never had she felt another person's energy so strongly. And for as much as it was dark, it also pleaded. Which set up all kinds of warnings in Vika's wanting heart.

"Now if that's all you've come for, I do need to get back to work. I've a spell—"

"I need you to do exactly what you did last night, Mademoiselle St. Charles. Please. You sneezed, and then I felt something *move through me.*"

Vika gaped. She turned to face him. Had the soul she'd sneezed away passed *through* this man? To consider it briefly, it may have been possible, since, if the corpse lights could permeate her, then they could certainly enter another.

She stepped closer to him and studied his deep jade eyes for a lie. "Are you sure? You felt it travel through your body?"

He nodded. Not a flinch or a blink. He was being truthful. "What was it that I felt move through me?"

"A soul," she said softly, and then snapped her mouth shut. She'd said too much. She knew the man not at all. Yet, if she were to find the soul, he was the last person to—not have seen it, but rather, have touched it.

"A soul." He nodded. "That makes weird sense. It chased the demon right out of me." He grabbed her shoulders, forcing her to meet his gaze. "Do it again. Please?"

"I, uh…" She wrenched her shoulders free from his possessive grasp and stepped back, stumbling against the stool. Her hand upset a pile of rosemary, and the earthy scent renewed in the air. Rosemary for remembrance and for a clear mind. She was anything but clear at the moment. Clasping the nail at her neck for strength, she said, "No. I can't. It was a fluke. A demon? And as I've said, I'm busy. Please, I want you to leave now."

He approached her, and the dark menace in his eyes grew apparent. Vika would not cry out like a frightened child. She was strong and had stood against many much more frightening than this man.

"I command you out! Xum!" She pronounced the air spell *etz-oom*.

With a dramatic gesture of her hand, Vika flung air magic at him, and it managed to sway his upper body, but he maintained a firm stance.

The dark witch grinned. "I warded myself before entering your little round house," he said, rubbing the palm of his tattooed hand. "Not as well as I thought. You shouldn't have been able to move me."

"Xum!" She flung more air magic his way, but this time it managed only to swish the hair away from his face. And it revealed the deep violet bruise at the side of his neck opposite the side of the tattoo.

He noticed her hard stare and stroked the bruise with his fingers. "It's a demon mark," he said. "Been there for six months. Ever since I returned from Daemonia."

"You went to…?" She daren't even whisper the name of the foul destination. To do so felt sacrilegious. The place of all demons was not a place she liked to think about, let alone put into voice.

CJ nodded. "On a quest to find something."

"Did you find it?" she asked quickly, so unbelieving he had actually survived to return to this realm in one piece.

"I did."

"And you're…fine?"

"Fine is a subjective definition. It doesn't matter, because all my energy has been focused on one thing since my return. Surviving."

"Surviving what?"

"If I tell you, will you promise to help me?"

Vika had never been intrigued by secrets. Even less so by one involving the place of all demons.

"I promise you nothing," she said. "Tell me, and then I'll ask you to leave."

"You're the only one who can help me, Viktorie. I've not had any luck expelling these demons in six months."

"Have you spoken to an exorcist?"

"Many. No luck. When I returned from Daemonia, I unknowingly brought along a few passengers. About a dozen, as far as I can determine. These demons are firmly affixed to my soul. Or so I thought until last night, when with a simple sneeze, you did what I haven't been able to accomplish."

She did not wield such power. A witch had to study for years, decades, to learn exorcism. "It was a fluke."

"I'm sure it was. Yet even my brother, TJ, who has mastered persuasive exorcism and releasement, couldn't get these bastards out of me. And believe me, we've tried many times. You know what is tried after all else fails?"

"What?"

"Physical beatings. But the pain demon inside me enjoyed that too much so we ditched that method. Fortunate for my aching ribs."

The man had subjected himself to beatings in an attempt to clear out his demons? "I can't help you—"

"Yes, you can! Listen, the demons that cling to my soul take over my body when the light does not hold them back. You expelled a carrion demon last night. The bastard was on a quest for raw meat."

"The werewolf," she whispered in disbelief.

She clutched her arms to her chest at the notion this man had been seeking the bloody and scattered remains of what she and her sister had cleaned up.

"Is that what you were cleaning? The demon smelled it. It wasn't me."

She shrugged, noncommittally, not knowing the man and not wanting to believe he could have been compelled to such a disaster. What would he have done had he arrived before they'd cleaned up the mess?

He approached, and Vika hustled backward until her spine hit the wall of lighted drawers in which she stored herbs and potions. "Stay back!" She put up her hand, and CJ stopped, his chest against her palm. She could feel his heartbeats against her hand. Frantic. Excited. Nervous.

Desperate.

And beneath the desperation hummed his darkness, like a hive of trapped insects seeking escape.

"Powerful magic," he said softly of the nail at her neck, yet he didn't move from her touch.

Instead of pulling away from him, Vika spread her fingers, staring at her hand as her palm took in the beat of his life beneath the wrinkled shirt. What witch purposefully journeyed to Daemonia? Gaining access must have proved a monumental feat. And to have survived?

He must be so powerful.

"Tell me what you went there for."

"I can't. It was selfish. Vika, please."

She met his eyes, her mouth falling open in a startled gasp. She was pretty sure Libby had not called her Vika in front of him. How could he know about that nickname? Only her family and friends called her Vika, a Russian shortening of her name.

Breathing out, she shook her head. "I don't understand what you think I can do for you. So I sneezed. I shot a soul through you, and it expelled a demon. Do you think I have souls to hand? Do you think it's a process I can duplicate again?"

"Possibly. How were you drawing the soul into you? Was it from the body you'd just cleaned up?"

"Yes, it was the werewolf's soul. But I didn't purposely draw it into me." She slid to the right to get away from his intense closeness and paced toward the door. A shiver traced her spine. Against better judgment, her innate magic was attracted to the man's power. "I have a sticky soul. It tends to catch lost souls that linger after death."

"I've never heard of that before. That's cool. So you're full of stray souls?"

"No, a soul bringer scrubs them from me every so often."

She turned and saw he looked over her work and the mortar but kept his fingers interlocked behind his back. It was polite not to touch another witch's work unless invited to do so. As he leaned over her book of shadows to scan the spell, his hair dusted the paper, and she flinched because it was as if she had felt his hair brush her skin.

"You should increase the belladonna," he suggested. "It'll jack up the potency, and you'll need less lavender. For nocturnals to rest, yes?"

"That's a wise observation." She strode to the counter and wrote it down on her notebook. "Thank you. I will try that. You said you practice the dark magics. I can't imagine a simple sleeping draft would be of interest to you."

"I'm noctambulatory myself. Though I haven't utilized any spells against it. I've come to terms with the night, and it me. Spellcraft is a particular expertise, both dark and light. Though, since I've taken on these demons, my power has decreased measurably. I can barely throw air. It's pitiful. Please." His hand clasped over her forearm, a warm touch that belied his bedraggled appearance. "If you can replicate the process, I beg you to try. I can't go into the dark. I need to stay in the light to keep them at bay. I rarely sleep. I fight them daily. These demons inside me…they'll kill me."

It was an awful thing to endure, she felt sure. When even one incorporeal demon occupied a soul, it could overtake the person, drive the person mad or kill him or her. And he said many lived within him?

If the soul had moved through him…

"Are you sure the soul I sneezed at you moved through you? What if it's still inside you?"

She could get back the missing soul!

"No, I definitely felt an exit."

"Could have been the demon leaving."

"No, that followed immediately after I felt the brightness pass through me."

Ah. The brightness. Yes, that was the indefinable feeling.

"It was...wondrous," he said softly. "As if a divine presence had, for but a moment, brushed against my soul. Trust me, there's no way I'm carrying a wolf soul around inside me. Just a lust demon, a war demon, menace and grief, and a few others."

"I need that soul back," Vika said.

"Because of the soul bringer?"

She nodded. "He's particular about receiving all the souls in his territory."

"Then let's make a deal, shall we?" He tilted a hip against the counter and eyed her up and down, for the first time showing some interest in her for more than what she could do for him.

She liked when men looked at her with blatant desire. Made her feel sexy. Never a wrong feeling. But Certainly Jones made her uneasy. It was the darkness surrounding him. Much as she trusted her grandmother's nail would protect, she didn't want to step too close to him without a shield ward to protect her own soul. Nor did she trust her impulsive desire to touch his power.

"What did you have in mind?" she asked.

"I must have a connection to the werewolf soul. Maybe?"

"If it's still in the vicinity of its death, it may be

compelled toward you. On the other hand, it may try to reattach itself to me. I was headed there now—"

CJ clasped her hand. "Let me go along with you. If I can help you locate the soul, will you agree to expel another demon from me?"

"But I don't think I can."

"It's the only thing I've got going for me right now. You. Please, Vika. Help me."

She dropped open her mouth because never had she heard such a sincere plea. And while her neat and ordered heart cringed at the idea of letting this unruly, bedraggled mess into her life, the part of her that squealed over creating order and establishing calm wanted to take the man in hand and clean him up, body and soul.

She nodded, and replied without reservation, "It's a deal."

"Thank you."

"But just this once. If we don't find a soul, I'm not obliged to help you further in any way, shape or form."

# Chapter 3

In all his long life, never once had CJ sat inside a hearse, and he hoped to never repeat the experience when dead because he intended to prolong his life with the classic witch's immortality ritual—consuming the blood from a beating vampire heart once a century.

Setting the morbid thought aside, he admired the car's beige leather interior. It was surprisingly clean for an old model. Vika said it was from the seventies. It looked brand-new and smelled like lemons. Certainly was afraid to touch the dashboard for fear of leaving behind the slightest oils from his fingers.

Viktorie St. Charles's round house and the spell room had been equally as immaculate. He had gotten a chuckle over the little plaque inside the front door that had read A Clean House Is a Happy House. The woman was all about cleanliness. And her appearance reflected the same motto.

Her bright red hair was pulled into a tight braid down the back of her head, not a strand out of place. Her face was like porcelain, her narrow brows perfectly arched and her lipstick red. All contrasted exquisitely with her inquisitive emerald eyes. And the dress she wore was a tight sheath wrapped about her slender figure in a dusty purple color, as if a bunch of roses bound with ribbon.

She was gorgeous, in a tidy way. He shouldn't think to muss her. But oh, to unloose that hair and watch it fall over the purple satin and down her narrow back. CJ's oft-ignored sensual desires hummed for attention.

"What are you looking at?" she asked as she turned the hearse down the alley, their destination.

"Perfection." He turned and faced forward, not sure if he'd meant it as a compliment. "Was that your sister who answered the door when I arrived? Libertie?"

"Yes, Libby left for the witches bazaar. You ever go there?"

"The one behind the Moulin Rouge? No, it's a bunch of old hags selling mandrake and love spells."

"Times have changed, CJ. Now they're into cyberspellcraft and digital conjuring. When was the last time you've been?"

"Decades. Digital conjuring?" What the young witches wouldn't think of next. He hated to admit he didn't know about a particular magic.

She nodded and pulled the car over to park. "You said you know many magics. Is digital one of them?"

It would be as soon as he could dig up some information on it. Cyberhacking, he'd heard of, but to use the computer to digitally conjure magics? Truly, he'd been stuck in the archives too long.

"I'm adding it to my arsenal soon. So this is it? How does the Mistress of Neat like you find herself on the cleaning end of a spattered werewolf? And are you always dressed so elegantly for such a messy job?"

"When I've a call, I wear simple clothes under my hazmat suit. And this isn't elegant. It's my normal dress. Cleaning is my passion," she said in a tone that invoked more sensual means to passion for CJ. She opened the car door. "Come on. Let's see if your dark and weary soul attracts anything."

"Certainly won't be an uptight witch," he muttered as he stood up from the car and closed the door.

"What was that?" She pursed her gorgeous lips and eyed him narrowly over the top of the car. "Did you call me uptight?"

He braced his forearms on the top of the car and smiled at her. "I did, oh, Beauty of the Bizarre and Unnatural Cleaning Jobs. But now you're going to cut me down for the comment and make me feel like the dirt you think I am, right?"

She tilted her head, considering. "Not worth it. I haven't made up my mind about you."

"So not a derelict."

"That's apparent. You've a job working for the Council. I assume you've a home. Derelicts can't usually claim as much."

"Your home is a fascinating study in white and

roundness," he said, moving around to the front of the car to lean against the front quarter panel and watch her walk the bricked-in area in small paces. "That spell room of yours. It was so…"

"You said sterile."

"To a fault. Tell me why someone who is so into cleaning chooses white? I mean, wouldn't it be easier to keep a darker color clean? Or even wood or steel?"

"It appeals to me," she said without looking at him. Arms held out, she walked the area as if trying to capture something in an invisible net held between her arms. "It gives me satisfaction to do a job well."

"I can say the same."

"What does your job involve, CJ? I've always thought librarians—"

"I'm an archivist, and I handle all the records for the Council. That includes all grimoires written throughout the ages, all spells and potions, objects of magical means and nature, contained creatures of mysterious origin, etcetera, and so on. I also keep the database on the paranormal nations."

She paused, bent over, the gorgeous lines of her body playing deep shadows in the folds of the dress at her knees and hips. Mmm, the woman needed to be bent over the end of his bed…

"All of us?" she prompted, whacking him out of the sudden and illicit fantasy of foreplay on his big, comfy bed.

"Witches, werewolves, vampires, demons, familiars, mermaids, trolls, imps, shape-shifters. The whole lot."

"No faeries?"

"Absolutely not. The sidhe can take care of themselves, and more power to them."

"That's quite a monumental task, keeping track of us all."

"And I do it well." CJ spread a hand over his gut and cast a glance skyward. Daylight waned due to what he suspected would be rain before evening. A twinge in his elbow confirmed the weather prediction. "That is, when I've not a soul full of demons trying to take over my body and fucking with my magic."

"Are those spell tattoos on your hand?"

"Yes." He tucked his hand along his torso. "I've quite a few all over. You ever hear of Sayne?"

"Yes, he's an ink witch who travels Europe. I've never thought it an effective form of magic."

"My tattoos are powerful. Much like your grandmother's nail."

"Sure."

He sensed Vika wasn't warming to him in any way. And why should he care? He only meant to use her to see if another exorcism was possible. And yet, CJ's interest continued to stray to the woman beneath the sexy gown, and her sure voice and the confident tilt of her head. Tidily gorgeous. Not his type of woman at all.

*You don't have a type, Certainly Jones.*

True. But it was high time he got a type. One of the things he realized he'd been missing after his return from Daemonia was a life. A life shared with others. And if on his bed? Hell, yes.

"So, you feel anything?" he prompted.

"No, but you could walk around and help. See if the soul is attracted to you."

CJ wandered the enclosed area, focusing, eyes closed, to see if he could sense or feel the same brightness he had last night. What he did sense was the demons inside him chuckling and writhing in accusatory glee. Idiot witch, they screamed at him. Just wait until nightfall.

Perhaps by nightfall Vika will have exorcised another demon from him. It had to be possible. He wanted nothing more than freedom from the bastards inside him. And if he needed a stray soul to do so, he'd stand here all day waiting for the little bugger to attach its intangible essence to him.

"So when you're in the light the demons don't bother you?" she asked over her shoulder as she strolled along the brick wall blocking in the small parking area.

"Mostly. The incandescent stuff only works for so long. Daylight is iffy when the sky clouds up." He glanced skyward. Many gray clouds. Should he be here? "A few months ago, I discovered prismatic is the best kind of light to deter demons, keep them back, if you will."

"And what happens when the demons take over? Do they do it all at once?"

"Fortunately, no. Usually there's an inner struggle I feel, as if the lot of them are ripping at my insides, and then one comes to the fore. Takes over my very being. I'm aware of what it's doing and not. Depends on how strong it is. The damned lust demon took me out to a nightclub last month and I ended up—"

Yeah, he wasn't going to finish that one. He'd never had sex with a dryad before. Wasn't sure how it had gone down, and he didn't want to think about it now. At the least, it had broken his dry spell with women. If she had been a woman. Yes, she'd been female. It was too wrong to think any other way.

"So you're not in control of your body when the demon comes to the fore?"

"Not one hundred percent. It's different each time. Some are more powerful than others. I can fight the demon, but it looks like I'm spazzing out, and sometimes it's easier to surrender. I never stray too far from home."

"Which is where?"

"In the fifth. I live in the DeMarck Building."

"I know that place. Gorgeous iridescent tile work on the outside?"

"That's the one."

"You said it's been six months since you returned from…that place?"

She didn't want to speak the name Daemonia? Probably for the better. Smart woman.

"Yes. I do have one good demon in me, though. It's a protection demon. I let that one out because it has a tendency to paint protection sigils on the walls and floors of my home. Haven't noticed they'd done much good, though. They're wearing me down." He stopped and put his head into his hands. "It's getting so hard, and I'm tired. I want them gone."

"Maybe you shouldn't have gone into the place of all demons in the first place. Why did you go there, and

what did you do? You must have pissed off someone
or something, or apparently, a whole host of demonic
somethings. Whatever it was, you probably deserve
the punishment."

"I don't need the admonishment right now."

But she was right; he deserved any bad karma coming to him because of what he'd done. But as long as
he'd gotten there before Ian Grim, that was all that
mattered.

It was always about Grim.

"I'm sorry, I— Well, no," Vika said. "It's what I
feel. A guy goes into the place of all demons, he's got
to expect retribution."

"Do you always follow the rules, Vika? Live by the
book? Make sure your life is as clean as it can possibly be, from outside to soul?"

She lifted an indignant chin and nodded minutely.

"You ever have any fun?"

"Of course I do." She cast him a glance through
her lashes, which stirred CJ's passions again. "But I
suspect my idea of fun and your idea of fun are vastly
different."

"I suspect so. We're very different souls."

"That's no understatement," she agreed.

He gave his arms a waver across his chest. "Not
feeling anything."

"You haven't gone over there." She pointed toward
the end of the hearse. "You know, there are other meth-
ods to casting out demons."

"Tried them all. Even ventured into a Catholic
church and had the priest lay his hands on me. I sus-

pect he got frightened when the chaos demon starting chewing on his cross. I was spitting out marble for hours after that one. Think I chipped a molar."

"So the demons inside you are impervious to exorcism? That's remarkable. I've never heard of that."

"I suspect because there's a whole gang of them inside me. They're not particularly friends, but I think they band together to hold the fort, if you know what I mean."

"And they've come directly from Dae—er, the place of all demons, instead of being summoned here through a conjuring, so I suspect that makes them stronger, as well. A witch can only control a demon they have conjured personally."

"Exactly. Yet they can't access my magic, which is a good thing. Just wish I had more control over it."

"There must be something. Some spell?"

"I haven't had a lot of free time to research in the Council archives, though I wonder if the answer isn't there."

Vika stopped before him, crossing her arms over her chest. The position emphasized her small breasts and revealed the hard peaks of her nipples beneath the thin fabric. Sexy, yet controlled, and perhaps a little curious. CJ entertained mussing her up. She would be a challenge he wasn't prepared to take on because his record with women—well, he hadn't established much of a record over the decades.

*You need to change that, buddy.* But probably not with a witch who called him a derelict and couldn't even utter the name of Daemonia. Much too uptight for him, though he'd seen glimpses of the sensuality she probably tried very hard to keep under control.

On the other hand, he needed intimacy, plain and simple. Dare he imagine he could find it with this beautiful creature?

"You're staring at my breasts," she said drolly. A shadow passed over her face as the sky darkened.

"I am." He spread his hands before him. "They're nice and neat. Just like you."

"That's the strangest thing a man has ever said about my breasts."

"You prefer suckable? Lickable?" Her eyebrow lifted. "Sorry, that was vulgar. I'm not up to speed with accepted comments on a woman's anatomy. But isn't that what most men think? Hell, it's what I'm thinking, but I thought we were still on polite terms."

"I think you've moved on to lewd and tasteless."

"Woman, get off your broom."

"Seriously? Did you just say that?"

Before he could retract the callous comment, she marched to the driver's door and opened it. "We're finished here, Monsieur Jones. Do not return to my home, because I warn you, it will be warded against asshole witches from this day forth."

And she drove off, leaving Certainly shaking his head and laughing. Yet deep inside, he felt the gang of demons curl their fists and shout triumphantly.

Once the hearse reached the end of the alleyway, Vika stepped on the brake and slammed a fist against the steering wheel. "I will not let that arrogant man get to me. He doesn't know a thing about me."

So why did she feel as though the dark witch had peeled away a layer from her, and what he'd exposed beneath was still as pin-neat as the top layer? Uptight? She was not. And she was hardly a prude. Men had spoken much more vulgar things to her, and often she warmed to the dirty talk. Let it not be said she didn't enjoy a lusty make-out session with a sexy man.

But she was not aroused or interested in Certainly Jones. Because he was wrong. Tainted by devious demons.

"Someone has to keep a tight grasp on sanity around here."

She checked the rearview mirror. The dark witch stood at the end of the alley, hands in his jeans pockets, looking her way. She couldn't see the expression on his face. Was he waiting to see if she would back up? Or was he laughing that he'd sent her running with her tail between her legs?

Maybe it was the demons? Had it been a demon spouting crude comments about her breasts back there?

"He said he was fine in the light." Most light, anyway. Prismatic light protected him best? "Interesting."

Everything about the man tweaked at her curiosity. He was scruffy and pale, while she preferred her men neat and sun-kissed. When she looked in his eyes, she couldn't see beyond the flat jade there. Most men's eyes gleamed and gave away their thoughts before they had them. And his unabashed willingness to say what he thought offended her, but only because she was taking offense.

If she did not take offense, then he had no power over her.

Vika shifted into Reverse but didn't take her foot off the brake.

Certainly Jones. What a name. Must be English. He did have the slightest hint of a British accent. Accents did appeal to her carnal passions, as they did Libby. Yet she was calm and cool when around an attractive man. A wise woman never let loose and gave away too much too soon.

She didn't need him to find the missing soul. She could attract a wayward soul on her own, thank you very much. Not that she'd been successful at it thus far.

He'd turned, and the silhouette of him, head bowed and arms slack at his sides, looked pitiful. A lost boy trying to fight off the real demons in his life. The Catholic Church couldn't help him? She was surprised he'd set foot on holy ground. She didn't know for sure, but she guessed he must have worked extremely foul magic to have been able to set foot in Daemonia.

"He deserves whatever he's gotten," she whispered.

And yet, he'd pleaded for her to help him. He was desperate. The man couldn't go into darkness for fear of a demon taking over his body.

"There must be some spell," she mused. "And if there is, I want to find it." She eyed him in the rearview mirror. "You ready for me, CJ? Because I always accomplish what I set out to clean—I mean, help."

Uh-huh. She'd meant clean.

Vika took her foot off the brake and backed down the alleyway. Shadows glanced off the white hood of the car sandwiched between three-story buildings. When the hearse sidled alongside the man, she rolled down the passenger window.

"Get in. I have a lot of work to do, and the day isn't getting any lighter."

He slid inside but didn't offer a gregarious *I've won* smile, as she had expected. Instead, he winced. In fact, he struggled to keep his jaw from opening, or maybe he was fighting a shout. And when he turned a frown on her, his face looked different. Not so slender.

And his eyes glowed red.

Vika heard the lightning crackle the air before darkness swept the sky.

CJ grabbed the steering wheel and slid his boot over on top of her foot. "Let's go for a ride, sweetie."

*Chapter 4*

Vika struggled to control the hearse as it careened down the street and toward the main avenue, where there would be hundreds of tourists in danger should CJ manage to steer against her—so far—firm grip. His foot pressed over hers on the accelerator, and though they were going only about twenty kilometers an hour, it was too fast for the looming touristy area.

And it wasn't CJ. Some kind of demon controlled him. Didn't matter. She had to fight them both to maintain control.

The demon hissed and slid closer, cramming her body against the car door as it tried to take over the seat. It gripped the steering wheel and wrenched the car sharply to the right. Vika kept her eyes on the road, and both hands were still on the wheel. So far, they'd hit nothing.

A hot tongue licked up the side of her face, and CJ chuckled in a breathy, evil rumble. "Strong witch. But driving down the middle is not fun at all. Obstacles must be crushed!"

CJ jerked the steering wheel to the left. With her vision blocked because his body was in the way, Vika didn't see the parked car. The hearse's bumper scraped along the side of the vehicle, the noise crunching and loud. She elbowed CJ in the gut, connecting with hard muscle, and he flinched. His foot left hers, but his hand remained on the wheel.

If she could find a well-lit area, the demon may flee. It was day. Though the sky had suddenly darkened, there was no rain, and no streetlights had flickered on yet. Ahead lay the main avenue and, beyond, the River Seine.

Attempting to brake was impossible because the demon-possessed witch tugged her out of the seat and, switching places with her, shoved her onto the passenger side. Now she lost track of where they were headed. In a last effort, Vika scrambled upright, grabbed hold of the shift and shoved it into Park.

The hearse squealed and spun, the engine making an awful hissing noise. The back of the vehicle swung around. A car horn honked. Vika braced for impact against the chest of the man, who hooted and beat the ceiling of the car with a triumphant fist.

The hearse stopped with a dull, crushing metal noise. Stretched across the front seat, Vika landed flat upon CJ's chest. She winced, anticipating a crash from another car. What a horrible way to die, sprawled across a man she barely knew and trusted not at all.

When the impact didn't come, she immediately opened the glove compartment and took out the flashlight. Clicking it on, she shone the bright light at the dark witch's eyes. "Get out, you bastard!"

Crawling backward and kneeling, yet keeping the light aimed on the witch, she shoved at his knee as he struggled to untangle himself from under her. When he was free and gave a hefty exhale, she did not relent with the light.

CJ put up a palm to block the light. "It's okay now. It's gone. I'm me again, thanks to your quick thinking with the light."

"Yeah? Well, get out! Right now, dark one. I don't need your kind of trouble. We could have harmed innocents!"

"Vika, I'm sorry, I had no control—"

"Damn you!" She slapped his shoulder with the flashlight. "My car is probably totaled. Get out!"

"Okay!" CJ opened the car door, which slammed against the concrete barrier fronting the river. He had to ease his way out through the narrow space.

Around them, a crowd had started to gather to assess the situation. Smoke hissed from the hood of the hearse.

"It was the menace demon," CJ said, bending to offer the weak explanation. At his temple a streak of blood glistened. "The shadows in the alley were enough to give it control. Vika, please, let me help you with this. Can you start the car? Let me drive it off the street and deal with the authorities."

"I said to get away from me," she said firmly, directing the light at his eyes again for the annoyance factor. "I don't want your kind of mess in my life. Please, walk away. I can handle this myself."

He put up his hands and stepped back. A bystander approached him and asked if he was hurt.

Vika settled in the passenger's seat and blew out a breath, anticipating dealing with the concerned mortals outside. She could hardly tell them a demon had been in control of the car.

"Goddess, I hope it's drivable. I do not need a repair bill right now."

Opening the door, she nodded she was fine, but when the ambulance arrived on the scene, she realized it would be better to submit to their triage than try to walk away, as Certainly had.

He was out of her life. And life would be better off without his danger.

So why, then, did she search the crowd in hopes of spying his dark tangle of hair and regretful eyes?

Ian Grim looked up from the crushed raven bone he was preparing to burn along with rowan bark and amber in the mortar. Perched over his spell table all afternoon, daylight had slipped away from him. His lover for centuries, Dasha, was away to Venice photographing a piece for a Gothic magazine. When the cat was away, the mouse did like to play.

Candlelight flickered, yet he had to blink a few

times to adjust his focus on the tracking spell set before the windowsill.

It was moving.

"Finally."

Dropping the steel pestle in the mortar, Grim rushed to the windowsill and leaned over the brass pendulum. It was suspended from a fine chain above a map of Paris. Paris being the most likely place to find Certainly Jones. It was his home, after all, and a man rarely strayed far from home. But since Grim had become aware of Jones's return from Daemonia six months earlier, he'd been off the grid. The dark witch had warded himself into a literal black hole. And only Jones was capable of concealing himself with such powerful magic.

Grim had been patient. This vita spell utilized a strand of hair he'd gotten off Jones and had been saving for decades. It sniffed out Jones's DNA.

"So you've been injured," he muttered, studying the map below the pendulum. It pointed to a spot along the Seine and didn't move from there. "Just a drop then. Not trailing blood in your wake."

Unfortunate, because it would not ultimately lead him to Jones, unless of course, he'd been injured where he lived. He doubted the witch would allow that to happen. But having his blood would make it easier to break through the wards, perhaps even conjure a battering spell. No matter, with the witch's blood he could concoct a successful tracking spell.

"I will find you, Jones. And then whatever you took from Daemonia—" and he had his suspicions "—will be mine."

\* \* \*

Vika had the hearse towed to a local car repair shop. Other than the broken headlight and a wicked scrape in the metal down the passenger's side, everything was in working order. The brake pads needed changing soon, the repairman suggested, but could probably go another few months if she needed to save for such an expense.

Vika thanked him and drove away. The sun cast a thin pink ribbon along the horizon as it dipped below the dark silhouette of a city park. While waiting for the repair work to be done, she'd sat in a café across the street, nursing a pumpkin mocha latte. She was hungry now but felt antsy. Heading home to make dinner was not tops on her list. She wasn't ready to explain her harrowing experience to Libby and get the big sad eyes from her or the admonishment for hanging out with such a dangerous man.

CJ wasn't dangerous; it was the demons infesting his soul who harbored the danger.

"Infested," she muttered.

It sounded wicked and not at all appealing. And yet, he could not control the demons. And she couldn't get the sight of his sad jade eyes out of her thoughts.

The man could be a perfectly nice, kind soul if she'd give him opportunity to prove that. Not to mention his compelling sensuality. When he'd been in her spell room, he'd seemed so grounded, comfortable in his skin. She'd been attracted to his power, against her better judgment.

"What are you doing?" she whispered. "Don't try to talk yourself into liking the guy. Just move on."

Right. She could find the missing soul by herself. Didn't need a witch who knew every magic in the book to help her. Much as she'd like to delve into his magical knowledge, she knew that way lay disaster.

"So his intelligence appeals to you," she reasoned out loud as she navigated the streets, taking a bridge across the river to the Left Bank. Not the side of the city she lived on. "Because it certainly isn't his looks. Dark, wicked, evil-looking man."

And yet his hair was so glossy it gleamed like hematite in the light, and despite that odd tattooed hand, his fingers were long, graceful and full of expression. A man's hands told so much about the owner. And his eyes—goddess, but he was attractive in a sad, pleading way.

"I was hard on him after the crash. He could have been hurt. Oh, I wonder if he was?"

The emergency crew with the ambulance had told her she checked out, and then cautioned her to have someone stay with her tonight and keep an eye on her in case of a concussion. But what about Certainly?

"If he was hurt he could be lying on a street somewhere, bleeding out. If he lays there too long, it'll grow dark and then—"

Her heart sped up at the thought of CJ's demons rampaging the streets of Paris. It would be her fault, too, because she'd dismissed him so quickly and so angrily.

"I shouldn't have taken my anger out on him. It wasn't his fault."

Stopping at a sign, Vika remembered he'd told her

his address. It was a nice neighborhood in the fifth, and she wasn't far from there. She turned the hearse toward his building.

"Just a quick check. I need to know he's not dying."

Then, she could put away her worry for Certainly Jones and be done with him.

Certainly trampled down the stairs from the building's roof and into the brightly lit hallway before his flat to find Vika poised to knock on his front door. In a flash of red hair and heather skirts, the witch turned to him and offered what looked like a forced smile.

"This is an unexpected pleasure," he offered. "Or is it?"

"I couldn't rest without checking to see if you were all right."

"Thoughtful of you." Yet he was leery. She'd raged at him after the crash. As she'd had every right. The trouble he could give her was not something he wanted to unleash on her quiet, perfect life. "I'm good. Not even a scrape."

"Then you haven't looked in a mirror. There's blood on your forehead."

He touched his forehead, feeling the crusty trail of blood and examining the crimson flakes on his fingertips. Damn. He'd been cut? He hadn't felt it or realized it until now because he'd gone straight up to the roof. Had he bled at the accident sight? Not good. Extremely not good if he'd left behind even a single drop of blood.

"Are you all right?"

He nodded absently, not wishing to let on to his

alarm. This was something in which he must never involve Vika. It was too dark for her brightness. Thanks to the menace demon, he'd already rubbed a black mar along her life.

"I'm sorry, Vika. There's nothing I can do to change what happened. And I can't claim no fault because it was me doing the bad stuff, despite my body not being completely my own during that awful moment."

"Yes, but it wasn't your fault. It was the menace demon who made you do it."

"It was, but that you believe me means—wow. Thank you. Just, thank you. That means a lot."

"I've had a few hours to think it over while I was waiting for the car to be repaired."

"You got it in already?"

"Yes, well, a little persuasive magic never hurts, does it?" She winked and then touched her lips, as if rethinking that impulsive act. "I stopped by because I needed to know you're not hurt. How are you?"

"Shaken and stirred, but all in one piece."

"Same with me. I think we both need to get some rest. Can you…sleep? If a cloudy day brings up your demons, I can't imagine what night does to you."

"I've trained myself to sleep with all the lights on. Not the most relaxing, and I'm lucky if I doze for three or four hours a night. Noctambulatory, remember? Spend a lot of time bent over my workshop table, crafting spells that never work. Lately, I can't manage more than allotriophagy or scrying. Don't give me that look. You know someone has to practice dark magic to balance the light. I bet I seem a real basket case to you."

"You do."

He rubbed a palm down his chest. "Demonic possession tends to leave me a bit worse for wear. But I clean up nicely. Will you come in and let me make you something to eat? I can do amazing things with fresh veggies. I promise you will be impressed."

"No, I—"

"Right. It's not safe with me," he added, stepping back from her defensive posture. "Probably it would be better if you drove to your little round, white home and put your spice rack in order."

"It is in order. Alphabetized, too."

"Naturally. Have you eaten?"

"No." She sighed. Resisting the offer, surely. Scanning the tiled walls and ceiling, she avoided eye contact with him. He knew his eyes went red when a demon was in control, and he hated she'd seen him like that. "The lights are very bright out here," she offered.

"I've replaced them all with the highest wattage possible. The residents bitch about it, but I've put a shock spell on the fixtures so if they try to change them— zap!"

"That's cruel."

"It's called survival." He clutched the doorknob. "Give me a few minutes to try to win back your trust after our harrowing experience this afternoon? Dinner and then a sip of chartreuse?"

"I am a bit peckish. And I prefer crème de violette. But I won't stay long. You feed me, then I'm out of here."

"Excellent. I happen to have crème de violette. I

should warn you before going inside. There's no real way to prepare a person. What I've acquired since returning to this realm, what I surround myself with, is a means to survival."

She gave him a hopeful gaze, and his heart thudded hard. Those huge emerald eyes. He wanted to kiss them and savor them. Apologize to them and be worthy of their admiration.

"So try me," she said.

"All right. But take it all in before you say anything. Promise?"

She nodded, and when he opened the door, the red witch stepped over the threshold and gasped, clutching her throat, as her eyes veered skyward.

## Chapter 5

Head tilted back, Vika wandered into the huge loft apartment that mastered the sixth floor. Marveling, she took in all the busy wonders suspended above her.

"Prismatic light," she whispered, her footsteps moving her slowly forward across the hardwood floor.

Everywhere hung chandeliers. Clear crystal chandeliers, colored and black crystals, all strung, attached and hanging upon silver, brass and black iron and steel fixtures. The entire rainbow dazzled. And bewildered. There were massive structures stretching over six, seven, even eight feet across, and smaller ones hung as if fruits laden heavily within an orchard.

Overwhelmed by it all, she clutched her arms about her and looked to CJ, who still stood in the doorway, ankles casually crossed and thumbs hooked in his jeans pockets.

"My home," he offered.

"There are so many." She spread her arms as if to take them all in, but it was impossible. "And all of them on all the time?"

"Yes, I never turn them off. Have a backup generator up on the roof in case the power goes out. It's disconcerting at first."

"I'll say."

She moved down the aisle toward the kitchen. The loft was spread across an open floor plan. To her left, a huge four-poster bed mastered what must be the bedroom, with a Chinese screen offering little privacy, save perhaps to stand behind to dress. The kitchen sat plopped in the center of the vast hardwood-floored area, the chandeliers above it all clear and casting a rainbow upon the counters and fixtures. Way over to the right a comfy gray couch and a few easy chairs gathered about a massive granite coffee table.

Behind her and around a long counter forming a half wall along one side of the entry looked like where CJ might do his spellwork. A scatter of magical accoutrements sat beneath crystal clouds of dazzling light.

Stumbling, she stepped aside a heap of jeans mounded on the floor and noticed other things lying about. An empty box here, a pair of boots over there. A tangled electrical cord and various screws and bolts, perhaps from the installation of a chandelier. Sigils had been drawn with what looked like white spray paint here and there on the hardwood, and she noticed some on the brick walls, as well, but had no clue how to decipher their meanings.

The place was a mess below, but above? Some kind

of crystal heaven. And she didn't subscribe to the idea of a physical heaven.

"You take a look around," he said. "I'm going to start something for supper, as promised. You like the tiny tomatoes?"

"Love them."

"Caprese salad, it is. I've fresh mozzarella and capers and a delicious red wine vinaigrette from a local artisan who lives just down the street."

Reaching up, Vika touched a particularly low crystal hanging in the center of a chandelier that spanned five feet in diameter. Tucked among the behemoths were smaller, more personal light fixtures one might see above a dining room table. There must be hundreds.

She walked down the aisle along a wall of floor-to-ceiling windows where old wooden shelves harbored dusty vials and pots and vases of herbs and potions. A gorgeous ruby crystal chandelier captured her attention, and she stopped below it and caught the red reflections dancing on her palm.

The overall result of chandeliers filling every space in the air above her was both gorgeous and terrible. It was as if Versailles had been slapped together with a cheesy Las Vegas casino. Kitschy. Disturbing. Strangely sexy—like the man himself.

She hadn't seen anything lovelier. And at the same time, never had she seen something so monstrous. These light fixtures had been hung in an attempt to fend off the demons infesting CJ's soul. And the man slept with them on all night?

"I would go mad," she whispered.

More so, if she lived in this place, the disorder would

send her to madness faster than the cacophony of light. The urge to tug on some rubber gloves and mix up an herbal cleaning solution tweaked at her sense of order as she ran her fingers over the light coating of dust on the well-pocked butcher-block worktable.

Behind a curtain of crystals strung on thin wire that served as a sort of veil instead of cupboard doors, sitting on the shelves were dusty bottles of vampire ash, faery ichor, angel dust and bat brains. Standard spell ingredients. And then the less standard, such as a newborn's cry, demon scales and the air from a corpse's hollow skull.

Distracted by an open grimoire, she checked over her shoulder to ensure CJ was still in the kitchen. Flipping back to look at the cover, she saw his book of shadows featured the three faces of Hecate: snake, dog and horse.

"Without death there can be no new life," Vika whispered, recalling Hecate's teachings.

Leaning over the red leather-bound book, she inspected the page that put out the slightest odor of chicory when touched. The spell name, *In Which the Dark Is Stopped,* was scrawled in tiny ink marks.

Most grimoires promised the impossible. Only a truly powerful witch could achieve something so grand. He'd said he had mastered many magics, yet was weak. Perhaps CJ would be powerful had he not a soul weighed down with so many hitchhikers.

She perused the required ingredients. A few common herbs, and some less common: rat's spine and troll blood. The process was something else entirely.

It required the name of an angel who had extinguished heaven's light. Angel names were not easy to come by.

"Impractical, yes?"

Jarred from her intent study, Vika spun around and squeaked out a distressed cry.

"Sorry." He stood before her, a kitchen butcher knife in hand. "Just checking you didn't fall under the spell of bedazzlement some do when they stroll under the lights."

"They certainly do have the power to dazzle." She pressed her fingers on the top of the blade he held and directed it downward to his side. "Be careful. If you want my help, you'll need to keep me intact."

"You'll help? I thought I'd frightened you away for sure. Or that Menace had."

"I'm much tougher than you believe. Most certainly wary, but also fascinated for reasons beyond my ken. I trust you are different from the demon who has shown itself to me."

"Thank you for that trust."

"You have earned my cautionary trust."

"I'll accept that." He nodded toward the grimoire. "You think you can work the spell?"

"I don't know. It is impractical. To erase darkness from the world for twenty-four hours?"

"True. And what good would it do me to gain but twenty-four hours? I want these bastards out, not merely pacified." He pointed to his chest with the knife, which made Vika cringe. "It was just a consideration. I've many more grimoires to go through, but not a lot of time in which to browse them."

"Your job at the archives keeps you busy?"

"That, and trying to stay in the light and alive."

Such a simple goal—to stay alive. One she took for granted daily. Surely, a grander challenge than merely protecting one's soul from an angry soul bringer.

Pleased she'd decided to stop by and had gotten a glimpse into this fascinating man's life, she took the knife from him and walked toward the kitchen. "Do you need help? Oh."

A bowl of salad waited and two plates had been set out on the round, glass-topped table. A sexy purple bottle of crème de violette sat in an ice bucket. It was a quaint, romantic scene, one that stirred her heartbeat faster. Totally unexpected, and yet it prompted her wariness about the man's intentions.

But overall? Nice.

Certainly reached around and grabbed the knife from her grasp. "Dinner is served, *mademoiselle*."

It felt too easy. A little bit right. And not at all wrong standing next to Vika and washing dishes like an old married couple. Graceful in her movements, she did not set a plate aside for drying until it had been scrubbed sparkling. She was easy to talk to now they'd gotten past her mistrust of him. Not completely, though. CJ knew she wasn't going to let down her guard around him, and he expected as much.

When they'd finished, she washed out the sink and dried that, too. Was he supposed to do that after dishes? Whoda thought?

Vika folded the drying towel and placed it neatly on the counter, then straightened the chairs before the table and blew out the beeswax candle, squeezing the homemade wick to a fine point. When she blew, her lips pursed and CJ had to lick his lips at the sight. So kissable.

"Have you a broom?"

"Huh?" Snapping up from his stupid stare, CJ twisted his thoughts around her strange question. If he let her go much longer, she might start picking up the clothes on the floor, and he did own a vacuum somewhere in this mess.

Vacillating on the pros and cons of letting the witch go to town on his disaster of a life, Certainly decided he couldn't let it continue. Not on the first date. That was for making a good impression, not tricking the woman into manual labor. And yes, he was calling this a date for his own personal fulfillment.

He didn't do dates. One-night stands, casual encounters leading to sex and no returned phone calls, were his standard. Busy with work, always, and never inspired to seek consistent companionship, Certainly had lived up to his best friend Lucian's nickname for him, Brother. It implied a monkish lifestyle, and CJ could not deny it.

Though he did desire. And since returning from Daemonia, his aspirations and life outlook had changed. He wanted—no, craved—closeness with a woman. And standing not ten feet from Vika, having watched her smile and chatter about the spells she and her sister were practicing over supper, and now feeling her wonder as she inspected the chandeliers, he felt the desire rise and the need to explore the tender and wanting emotions he'd ignored over the years.

"No broom, and I insist you stop trying to clean the place. Let's have an after-dinner drink."

He poured a small narrow glass of the crème de violette for her. It smelled of violets, but he preferred the spicy chartreuse, which he poured for himself. They clinked glasses, and Vika sipped hers, while he swallowed his measure in one tilt.

"Isn't chartreuse made by monks?" she wondered. "And so many herbs in it. I think the taste would get lost."

Pouring another draft, he offered her his glass. "Smell." She leaned in, closing her eyes, and drew in the aroma. It took all his control not to reach for her porcelain cheek and brush a finger along it. *Not yet.* "Each time, you smell something different, taste the tarragon, and then the anise, or even the mountain lavender."

"I'll stick with my sweet liqueur," she said, curling her wrist toward her as she sipped the violet concoction. "I like things sweet. Now, you are a little bit sweet yourself."

"Me? Sweet?"

"You've a decidedly cedar scent that rises above a mix of many other herbs. I like it."

"Must be from the herbs I use for spellcraft. I don't pay much attention."

"It must be difficult for you, if you're such a powerful witch, to have that power depleted by the demons."

"It is, but they cannot deplete the greatest of my powers."

"Which is?"

"Well, it's been said a witch's greatest power is not theirs to wield. Rather, it exists in the minds of others."

"Oh, yes. What someone believes you are capable of may be the power that holds them back, whether or not you possess such power. It is the power of the mind."

"Belief," Certainly chimed.

"I agree with that." She smiled freely, tipping her glass to his in a bright *ting*.

Paused in the center of the kitchen looking about—for more cleaning work, he presumed—Vika set her glass aside as he reached her. He moved in for a kiss. It was quick and a little off her mouth. A hint of violet liqueur hushed out at her startled gasp. He'd screwed it up, and he pulled back with a wince.

Mouth open, she gave him a stunned once-over. "What was that?"

"It was an awful, botched attempt. A horrible kiss, as far as kisses go. Sorry."

"Never apologize for a kiss." She clutched the front of his shirt, pulling him down to her mouth, and kissed him.

More intrigued than startled—although he was still kicking himself for such awkward first contact—Certainly stepped in closer and slipped an arm around behind her slender back. All he'd needed was a test kiss and an acceptance from her. He relaxed now, and Vika's mouth melded against his. Of course, he should expect nothing less than perfect from her. Perfect looks, perfect life, perfect kiss. And suddenly he wanted to mar that perfection, to imprint it with his own rough and messy darkness.

Hand gliding up against the back of her head, his

fingers diving into the soft garnet braid, he deepened the violet and chartreuse kiss, clutching her tighter and teasing her to answer his force if she dared. She didn't balk. The witch wrapped her sorcery about his intentions and pulled tight, taming his sudden wildness until he moaned into her mouth. Her hair, silken and slick under his exploring fingers, pulled free from the updo and tumbled over his face and neck. It spilled endless streams over him, ensnaring, capturing, tying him up in her delicious net.

The body melded against his was long and lithe, soft and hard, hungry and undulating, pressing against him, daring him, meeting his challenge. He grew hard. He pulled her hips forward, crushing her against his aching want. It had been too long. Until he'd gone to Daemonia, he'd not had a relationship with a woman that lasted longer than a night. He'd never felt the desire to make a lasting connection.

Everything had changed. He wanted—no needed—someone. All his life he'd fended on his own. Family was close but distant. He didn't even know where his sister, Merrily, was right now, yet he sensed she was safe. He didn't know the concept of family in any other terms, but he felt something was missing. Life was precious. He wanted to experience romance and love, and to know the feeling someone cared about him and waited for his return, no matter where he should wander.

Vika pulled away and stumbled backward, catching her palms on the counter behind her. Her eyes wide and vibrant, she brushed away strands of hair from her cheek. "Wow."

"No kidding." He chuckled. "Mistress of the Unexpected Kiss, you are filled with surprises."

"You're pretty spectacular in your own right." She touched her lips, reddened from their kiss. "I, uh… Wow."

"I could feel the nail hum in that kiss."

"I could feel your power, dark yet restrained."

They exchanged laughter and goofy grins. It was a moment of utter wowness, and all they could do was share some shy glances.

"I've never been kissed like that," Certainly offered. "So brazenly."

"You haven't been around much, have you?"

"Much as I'd like to lay claim to a certain macho prowess, I've been busy studying magic over the decades."

"Decades? Seriously? You're a handsome, virile man, Certainly Jones. Have you been so busy you haven't taken the time to kiss a woman?"

"Pretty damn close. I get it when I need it." That had been a vulgar confession. She didn't seem to mind. "I just…" He touched her lower lip, wanting to remember the shape of it, to imprint its seductive power upon his flesh. "I think you just touched parts of me that haven't seen light in a long time."

"Really?" She glanced above their heads. "Even with all this prismatic noise going on?"

"Vika, there are places inside me that will never see the light."

"That's awful to say." A stroke of her fingers along his jaw, and he closed his eyes to focus on the exploring touch, to memorize it. "We'll get the demons out."

"You've suddenly become my cheerleader for demon expulsion."

She gestured with a shrug of her shoulders. "Guess I figured out you might be worth the trouble." She kissed him again and, spreading her fingers through his, entwined both her hands within his near their thighs. "Between fighting for my life with the menace demon earlier and walking beneath this amazing constellation of light, my world view has altered in a way not even magic could manage. I've always liked things a certain way, neat and tidy. You disperse disorder, chaos and menace with every footstep you make."

"It's not something I can control."

"I know, you explained that. But, well…" She smiled a blushing smile, and her thick lashes fluttered coyly, like butterfly fringe. "I think I understand now why my sister is always falling for the bad boys."

CJ's shoulders straightened proudly. "Are you saying I'm a bad boy? I'm just me. Certainly Jones. Boring ole archivist and occasional adventurer to places no human or paranormal breed should ever venture. Fearful of the dark, and keeper of prismatic light."

"And the best kiss I've had."

He tilted down his head as if to say "really?".

"Ever. And that's saying a lot, trust me."

"Guess I'm not so rusty as I think." She strolled past him toward the door, and Certainly's heartbeat stuttered. "You're leaving?"

"Yes." She twisted an end of red hair about her finger. "I feel compelled to leave the night where it stands, kind of wondrous and new. To save some anticipation."

Really? That's what women wanted? Anticipation?

"I want to spend some time browsing through my grimoires tonight, see if I can find something to expel demons." She paused at the door, hand falling onto the knob. "You didn't expect me to stay?"

"Oh, no. I mean, not unless you wanted to." At her raised brow, he rushed out another forced refusal. "No. That would be forward. I'm not that kind of guy." He winced. "I've never been that kind of guy."

He wanted to change that, though, to somehow fit into Vika's idea of anticipation.

She smiled, and her emerald eyes beamed brighter than the crystals overhead. "See you tomorrow, Certainly. If you happen to feel a stray soul brush up against you, grab it, will you?"

"How do I contain it?"

"With a mirror. You know catoptromancy?"

"Of course." The practice involved catching souls with a mirror. He should be able to manage that, even with his lesser powers. "Good night, Vika, Purveyor of Anticipation."

She tilted her head and blew him a kiss.

And he felt it land in the vicinity of his core, there in his center where the demons roiled, anticipating the night. The darkness. Yet something bright and bold had touched their incorporeal carcasses.

And they didn't like it one bit.

Vika spun beneath the chandelier in her living room, only to crash into her sister. Libby held her back, her eyes wide and a silly smirk tickling her lips. "What is up with you, sister mine?"

"Don't ask," Vika rushed out. "You'll just laugh."

"I have never seen you dancing in the middle of the room as if you were at a Samhain festival frolicking naked through the coltsfoot. And no music. You are in a good mood. What's up? Oh, tonight's Friday. Are you and No-Name Titan headed out to the clubs?"

She and her best friend, Becky Titan, held Fridays as sacred. "You can call her Becky. Just because her dad didn't give her a name doesn't mean we can't make one up. We use Becky most often. And she's in the States with her father, visiting friends."

"Then what is it that's brought the color to your pale, perfect cheeks? The last we spoke you were going to find the soul— Ohmygosh. The derelict?"

"He's not a derelict, so stop calling him that. His name is Certainly Jones, and he's the archivist for the Council."

"A librarian?"

"Not exactly. He catalogs more than books. We went looking for the soul."

"And found it! No wonder you're so happy."

"We didn't find it, and in fact, one of his demons made a horrible showing and crashed the hearse."

Libby's eyes widened.

"Just a broken headlight, which I've already had fixed. Sorry, had to dig into the household account, but I promise to concoct a few spells for you to bring along and sell at the next bazaar to make up for the expense. I plan to return to the area tomorrow and spread out the canvass periphery. How can one soul hide? It's got to want to go somewhere, don't you think? Oh, no, I wonder if it attached itself to someone else? I may never find it."

"You'll find it. You need to be vigilant, and I happen to know you do vigilance well. But that's still not the reason for the happy dance. You know I will break you down, Vika. It would be wiser to speak now than have me go at you until you talk."

True. Libby never let anything go if it was a secret or mystery. She had once badgered Vika about an All Hallows' Eve present for six days. Vika was expert at holding out information. It gave her satisfaction to do so.

"I can't say."

"I won't laugh. Promise. I'll tell you my news if you tell me yours."

"You have news?"

Libby pulled a red glass witch ball out of her tote bag. "Got it at the bazaar. Isn't it gorgeous?"

Vika studied the handblown glass ball. Long glass strands dashed from side to side within the globe. "This is amazing."

"The strands are supposed to trap souls. I thought to hang it in the garden above the white heliotrope."

"Perfect. Though, I hope it won't interfere with the souls that stick to me."

"Oh, I didn't consider that. I was thinking to catch a few butterfly souls to use in my spells. I'm so sorry. We can't put this up."

"No, do. I'll let you know if it causes a problem."

"If you're sure, then I will. Now tell." She went dead serious. "Or I'll have the vines in the garden rise up and meet you next time you go out back."

"I'd blast them with nightshade. Libby, you know you can't go up against me when it comes to spellcraft."

Her sister's shoulders wilted.

Vika started up the stairs, gliding her fingers along the railing and looking down over the chandelier. It dazzled, but it was as if a speck in the universe compared with CJ's amazing constellation. She wanted to return to his loft and lie on the floor and lose herself in the terrible beauty of it all.

"I kissed him," she called down, and then dashed into her bedroom and closed the door behind her.

"What?" Libby's footsteps trampled up the stairs in record time. She pounded on Vika's door. "The derelict?"

"He's not— Libby!"

"You kissed him." On the other side of the door, her sister turned and leaned against it. "Was it good?"

"We both said *wow* after we kissed," Vika called through the door.

"Oh, wow. But he's the complete opposite of everything you find attractive. And he's so…messy. How did you two manage to get your lips in the vicinity of one another to make a kiss happen?"

"I'm taking a shower now," Vika called out, and smiled all the way to the bathroom.

# Chapter 6

Paging through a few grimoires in search of a spell to help CJ, Vika was worried she wouldn't find anything for casting out demons. Her grandmother's magic had been focused on earth spells, and it was the rare spell that dabbled with the dark. Though certainly she would associate demons with the earth and the lower realms.

"What do you think?"

Libby spun into the room, purple crocheted skirt skimming the air. The concoction was tightly knit and hugged her sister's ample curves in all the right places. It stopped scandalously high upon her thigh with a wave of crocheted ruffles as Libby did a guitar-strumming rock star move.

"Uh." Vika pushed aside the spellbook and vacillated on the truth or the embroidered truth. "I love the color. It's perfect with your hair."

Libby pouted. "What's wrong? Is it too tight?"

"No, it's just right. You've such nice breasts. I always wonder why I wasn't gifted that attribute," she said of her smaller assets.

"Because you got the bright hair."

"Is this wild red flag of hair I have a better trade-off than sensuous breasts? Some days I'm not so sure." Vika twisted the strands of jade mala beads wrapped around her wrist.

"Wow. You rarely feel down on yourself. And after the high you were on last night? What's up, sis?"

"Nothing. I…" She tugged the natty, cloth-covered grimoire closer. "I've spent hours going through grimoires but can't find anything for expelling demons that hasn't already been tried."

"For CJ? You must really like him. Have you tried to comb his hair for him yet? I can't imagine that mess is something you could stand to look at for more than a few minutes."

"His hair doesn't bother me. And it is combed. It's just long and in need of a trim." And it usually covered the bruise on his neck, which she hated looking at. A demon mark. Awful thing, that. "He doesn't have time for a visit to the barbershop because he's stuck in a literal struggle for survival against the demons inside him."

"How many?"

"I'm not sure. I'm thinking it's an infestation. The light keeps the demons back. Most of the time. But it must be a specific kind of light. Prismatic," she said, remembering with a shudder the terrible constellation that had hovered in CJ's loft. "Yesterday when the menace demon reared its nasty head, the clouds had come out and it was merely an overcast sky."

"You have to be careful around him, Vika."

"I am wary." Wasn't she the chick who avoided dark magic? So what had that kiss been about?

That kiss.

After CJ's initial awkward kiss, she'd been compelled to answer, and he'd quickly gotten over his nervousness, and their contact had stirred her from the tips of her toes to the ends of her eyelashes. A truly wow moment. And as a woman who prided herself in sensuality and knowing exactly what it took to turn her on, it had surprised her in a good way.

"It's not so much I like the guy—though he is growing on me…."

"It's that you want to clean him up. I know you, Vika. I can see your fingers twitching to get into the mess of Certainly Jones and sort him out. He's got a strange, sexy vibe going for him. Nice broad shoulders, darkly handsome. I'm sure there's more tattoos under those clothes, too, and the goddess knows I do love a man with tattoos."

Her sister blew out a surprised breath and, with a sheepish smile, curled her fuchsia lips. "Did I just say that? Anyway, do you think you can focus on cleaning him up, literally exorcising his demons and also kissing him? Sounds like a conflict of interest."

"It does?" Vika sighed. "I don't know. Does it have to be?"

"Wow, you've got it bad."

"I do not have *it*. Nor is anything bad. Yet. I had hoped to have something solid to bring him today when we meet later."

"Ooh, the second date."

"It's not a date, it's a— Okay, it is a date. So I'm stepping out of my comfort zone with the guy. What's wrong with trying something new?"

"Nothing at all, as long as you're careful. And I know you will be. As for exorcising the man's demons, familiars bring demons into this world from Daemonia. And you know how they do that."

"The familiar must be sexually sated, open to provide a bridge from the demonic realm to the mortal realm," Vika said. "Then the witch casts the spell and summons the demon. These demons weren't planted in CJ via a familiar, Libby. They hitched a ride on his soul when he was tromping around the place of all demons. And I wish you would refrain from giving it its proper name. I don't wish to accidentally invoke anything by speaking it."

"Sorry, I'll be more careful. So what if you do a little reverse engineering?"

"I'm not following."

"Well." Libby sidled up to the spell counter and toyed with a jar labeled For Use in Daylight Only. Inside, something luminescent fluttered about. It had been half price during a blowout sale at the witch's bazaar. "Sex is a common means to summon a demon to this realm. What if, in turn—" Libby's green eyes glittered and her smile fixed at the corner of her lips "—sex could be used to send one back? The sex part opens the familiar to be a conductor to the mortal realm. What if sex relaxed and opened CJ to enable you to go in and tear out those demons lurking inside?"

"Are you suggesting I have sex with the man in order to clean out his demons? Wait. You did say that. Libby, I'm sure Certainly Jones has had sex since he's returned from—that place. As well, I suspect more is involved beyond getting one's rocks off."

"Yes, like having sex with a witch who knows an expulsion or exorcism spell. There must be something in one of these grimoires. And combined with grandmother's magic?"

They touched the nails at their necks.

"There is, but…" Vika gave her sister the most incredible look. She didn't care anymore her skirt was too short. "Seriously? You think I should— With the dark witch? No. I barely know the guy."

"You've kissed him. That's a lot more knowing than some of us have lately."

She alluded to her crush on Reichardt. If the day ever came Libby afforded a kiss from the soul bringer, Vika would not only be startled speechless, but also have to check outside to ensure the sky had not fallen.

"I don't mean jump his bones the moment you lay eyes on him again, but you know… It's an idea. Something to keep in mind." Libby winked and flounced around toward the door. "I'm going to do some shopping. I'm in the mood for some new shoes."

"Put a skirt on!"

Libby tugged at the dress hem. "Really?"

Vika nodded. "You don't want to flash anyone."

"Fine. I've got a cute white knee-length number that should look good with this."

"That's perfect. And Libby? Sex? Seriously?"

"You know you want to." With a wink, Libby skittered away.

And Vika caught her forehead in a palm. All focus on finding a spell vanished. Libby's suggestion raised all sorts of images to mind. Kisses and sensual caresses. Clothing falling at their feet. Bare skin touching and rubbing in a symphony of discovery. And CJ's interesting tattooed hand gliding over her skin. She sensed it would stain her indelibly with his darkness, and she shuddered at the thought. But it wasn't an entirely horrified shudder, more so, one of anticipation.

Dashing out her tongue to lick her lips, she considered Libby's suggestion. CJ had called her a purveyor of anticipation....

"No." Vika sat up straight, dismissing the images of the dark witch's hands skating over her skin. "It's irrational. Nothing in the texts mentions sex will work to send a demon whence it came."

At least, that she'd found so far. She hadn't searched beyond the few volumes she and her sister owned. There was an incredible database of grimoires worldwide. The answer must be recorded somewhere.

"The archives."

The Council kept copies of every grimoire ever written. Not to mention the *Book of All Spells,* which did the same, magically. Every time a spell was created— no matter where in the world, or by whom—it was magically recorded in that book. But she didn't know

Dezideriel Merovech, the witch who kept the *Book of All Spells*. CJ must have a means to contact her and look through the book. And if not, he did have the entire library at hand.

"I wonder if he's gone through them?"

When had he the time?

"Would he let me take a look at the archived grimoires?"

Her spine straightened. The idea of getting to look over the Council's collection of what should be *all* grimoires ever written was too exciting. Almost on line with the prospect of engaging in sex to see whether or not it could prove a useful tool in exorcism.

"I should go fix my hair. Gotta look right for this afternoon. So he'll say yes."

And then she caught herself grinning madly. Yes to the grimoires, or yes to sex? A positive answer to either would please her. A girl couldn't survive on spellcraft and cleaning alone. One must tend the sensual demands her body craved.

Did she crave CJ?

"No. Yes. Maybe? Oh, yes, I do want another taste of his chartreuse kiss."

The sky was fast growing dark. CJ did not like this. The weather service had predicted rain all week. Not the most favorable conditions for him to spend any amount of time with a gorgeous witch whom he'd like to kiss again. But he refrained from an inward chastisement of his demonic hitchhikers, knowing his emotions regarding the woman would only feed their determination to overtake him. The sun was still high in the sky, albeit slipping behind clouds every few minutes.

He'd hope for the best.

He strode to the place where the werewolf had died. He and Vika had agreed to meet here. He kept an open mind and heart for the feeling if any wayward soul may inadvertently brush against him. If the soul were anywhere in his vicinity, he should sense the brightness again.

A corpse light. Shouldn't he be able to see it? They usually glowed phosphorescently. Not that he'd ever seen one before.

The white hearse was parked near the brick wall, the opposite side from where the incident had occurred. Vika had wanted to broaden the search today. He spied her brilliant red hair, curling over her narrow shoulders and down the center of her back. She must always wear long dresses, which he liked, because they fit tightly and emphasized her slender curves. She had a bit of the Morticia style going, while he had noted her sister was Retro Rocker Chick.

Either way, Vika looked amazing. Like a porcelain doll standing on a natty Paris street, she looked as if someone had plucked her out from their collection and set her against an urban backdrop for a high-fashion photography study.

She waved as he approached. A goofy grin spread on CJ's face, and he surprised himself because he couldn't remember the last time he'd felt so unfettered with worry. He felt great, and if being around Vika did that for him, he planned to spend a lot more time with the witch.

He walked up to her, threaded his fingers through hers and spun her into an embrace so he could kiss her. Just going with his feelings. And she responded in kind, affixing her body along his and melting into the kiss like a sweet Sunday treat.

"Well, hello," he said. "Feels like you're happy to see me."

"A girl could never have enough of those kisses." She tucked his hair behind his ear. "I don't know what it is between us," she said on a breathy tone, "but whatever it is, I like what's happening so far. You ready to do a little soul hunting?"

"I am."

"Will the cloudy sky interfere?"

"Probably. You prepared for that?"

"I'm not sure. Are you?"

He shrugged.

She stepped from his embrace and smoothed her palms down her unwrinkled skirt, worry shifting her eyes from his to all about them. "Don't you have some kind of safety measure? A flashlight? It worked in the car."

"Yes, well, Menace was winding down already when it worked for you. When I've attempted the same, the demons usually break the flashlight in half and toss it at the nearest passing human. I've found if a demon does break free and takes over, its steam runs out quickly. Usually no more than ten, fifteen minutes tops."

She absently clutched the nail at the base of her

throat. "A war demon could do a lot of damage in that time."

"I know. And I happen to have one inside me. Maybe I should do this alone while you wait in the hearse for a speedy getaway?"

"We're both needed. You might feel the soul, and I need to draw it into me. And…I thought if we could find it, and if the timing was right, I might try…"

"Another sneeze?"

"I don't think I could make myself sneeze, but I do have air magic. A forced gust would produce the same result a frenzied sneeze would."

"But then you'd lose the soul again."

"No, this time I'd keep an eye out for it. If it moves through you, I just need to track it. Right before it enters or exits a body it glows brightly."

"I sensed that brightness, but I didn't see it."

"You didn't know what to look for. If that happens, I should be able to snag it. Well, I'm not sure about anything, really."

"That you are willing to try is the nicest thing anyone has ever done for me, oh, Nightingale Nurse to My Dark Infestation."

He kissed her again and felt the stirrings of lust grind roughly against his bones. Or was that warning vibrations from her grandmother's nail? No, the lust demon inside him purred and lifted its incorporeal head. It was that harsh reaction that warned CJ he had best keep his distance from Vika.

He tapped the nail wound about the leather cord at

her neck. "This should be strong enough to keep the demons away from you."

"Or attract them," she said.

"True. They are unable to access my magics from within me, so they would seek to obtain power elsewhere. Hell, Vika, you should ward yourself. Just in case."

"I've a white light ward on always."

"Yesterday?"

"Yes, but the demon didn't attack me. It took control of the car, which was not warded. Probably explains why I'm still in one piece."

He ran his fingers over the mala beads at her wrist. Jade for immortality and the search for truth?

"Don't worry, I'm a big girl. I know to run when running is necessary."

He hated to think anything he did could make her run from him, but in his next thought, CJ was glad for her street smarts.

"All right then, you start over there. I'll go this way," he said. "I'll keep you in sight, should I feel anything."

The witch methodically tracked along the sidewalk, arms out and head lifted, while CJ wandered around behind the brick wall for a tour of the crime scene. From here, he could see the top of the Eiffel Tower, and he remembered the years during its construction. The city had been in such an uproar over the iron monstrosity. A mar on the landscape! It must be torn down immediately following the World's Fair! He always got a chuckle to look back through history. That had been about the time he'd met Lucian Bellisario, a new vampire, transformed against his will, with whom he'd become fast friends.

But enough mental wandering. He needed to stay sharp. Tapping his left index finger against his neck where a vita tattoo would enhance his senses opened him to the minutia skimming the edges of reality.

An insect fluttered near his ear, and he brushed it away. CJ twisted his head about but didn't spy anything with wings or hear a buzz. Had it been the soul? He didn't use this spell often, so he was out of practice. Drawing in a breath, he calmed his anxiety to enhance focus.

Where was Vika? The shift of her black taffeta skirt didn't sound.

Thunder rumbled overhead and the sky darkened.

*You want the red witch. She's tasty.*

CJ's heart dropped. The stirrings within him increased in intensity. This was not going to end well.

*It will be what you make it. Are you strong enough to protect the girl? Prove it.*

It was hard to determine if the inner voice was his or if it belonged to something darker and incorporeal. But he was strong. He could protect the girl. And he would.

CJ set back his shoulders, opening his chest, and inhaled the clean, tangible air charged with the foreboding of rain. The electrical sensation of the altered air shivered over his skin and made him feel alive. Hungry. And open for anything.

"You find anything?"

He swung his head around. Vika stood there in a pose that silhouetted her slender figure against the darkening sky. Her breasts were small but high, and his fingers tingled to touch them, to mold against her heat and squeeze until she moaned and pulled him closer.

*Want. Can have.*

Bowing his head and running his hands down his chest, CJ eyed the pretty piece of flesh. She'd tasted good. Her mouth fitted to his in a blissful connection. Wonder how sweetly she'd cry out should he find her core and bring her to orgasm? The fingers on his left hand twitched. The protection ward on his palm, used to prevent things from entering him, burned. It hadn't been effective in Daemonia.

He crooked a finger at the witch, and she stepped toward him, tilting her head in question. That perfect bow mouth set beneath bold emerald eyes was like a cat's face, only sexy and as curious.

*Just a few more steps, witch. Come to me.*

"What did you find?" she asked. "The soul?"

The earthy scent of her coiled about his head and into his senses. His skin prickled with want. Inside he growled, a long, moaning noise vibrating within his rib cage. So easy to take her.

*You need to take her. We need her. Touch the nail at her neck. Feel the power.*

She studied him, and he swept out a hand and grabbed her by the wrist, slamming her against the brick wall and pinning her there with ease. He dragged his tongue from her jaw, up along her soft, smooth cheek and to her temple, where her pulse thumped and her salty sweetness tempted his taste buds.

"CJ, what are you—?" Ineffectual fists beat at his chest. "You're not CJ. Let me go!"

"No, no, sweetie, you're mine. I get to taste you now, because he spends far too much time thinking about how you'll taste rather than indulging in you. Yes, you will be delicious."

He dove to her neck and licked her vein. It pulsed hot and thick beneath his tongue. He could bite it, but unlike the vampire, he hadn't fangs to pierce the skin. Stupid dark witch. So ineffectual. This body provided little advantage to the game.

Vika kicked, but her long, tight skirt wouldn't allow her effective defense. Though her heel smashed the top of his boot, it hurt, yet only Pain quivered within—in joy.

"I like it when little girls struggle," Lust growled. "Stirs your pheromones to a delicious soup of fear and anger. You, you little thing, have some aggression bottled up inside this gorgeous trapping. Let's lick it out, yes?"

"Xum!"

A blast of something hit him in the chest, and he lost his grip on her and stumbled backward a few steps. What had that— Ah. Air magic. When he had control of the body, the dark witch's defenses were not so strong, and any wards he'd put up or wore on his skin were ineffective. Lust slapped a palm to his chest and grinned at the red witch with the fiercely defiant expression. She did not wish to be trifled with; he didn't care.

She pointed through the air, slightly above his head. "It's here. The soul."

What was she talking about?

"Hang on, CJ, I'm going to get rid of Lust for you."

"You are foolish—"

The witch recited a Russian incantation, and with a gesture of her hand, directing some invisible energy toward him, a blast of brightness entered the dark host's chest.

Lust clawed at the insides of the stupid witch who'd had the audacity to venture into Daemonia and steal. Lust would not be expelled without causing as much damage as he could to the thief. Clinging to the muscles, plasma and bone that fashioned the feeble witch, the demon fought against the dazzling corpse light moving through skin, sinew and the witch's very heart. One intangible claw hung on, and then...

Brightness exploded upon him and pushed him out of the body. Unable to survive in the mortal realm without a host, and not having been summoned to this realm, Lust was immediately sucked to Daemonia.

Certainly fell to his knees, catching his palms on the tarmac. Sweat beaded his brow, and he gasped in exertion. He'd felt the soul enter through his chest and leave out his back. The lust demon had torn at his heart, unwilling to relent. His muscles felt shredded, damaged inside.

Barely aware of his surroundings, the brush of fabric dusted his arm. Vika moved about him. Looking for something. And then she declared, "I got it!"

He rocked to the side and sat, legs sprawling before

him and arms falling forward to rest his hands on the ground. Exhausted from the expulsion, Certainly could but nod and manage a loopy grin.

"The demon is gone from you? Yes, I think so. I knew it was a demon when you pushed me against the wall. You're not that kind of guy."

He winced. Wasn't he? Shouldn't he strive to be some kind of guy?

"Your voice was different, too. Deeper, kind of raunchy."

"Lust," he gasped, and smirked regretfully. A demon had attempted to seduce the woman he was only just warming up to. "The demon wanted to do things with you. Things I…"

Wanted, but wasn't sure how to ask for.

She kissed him on the cheek and pressed a finger to his lips. "I don't need an explanation. All that matters is it worked. I expelled the demon from you *and* I managed to capture the werewolf's soul again. I have it inside me. The soul bringer will get his due."

She hugged him, and he pulled her onto his lap and nuzzled into her silken hair, losing himself in her eager excitement. She'd done it again, had now successfully defeated two of his demons. He couldn't let this woman go. He had to keep her.

Because she made him feel light amid the weird absence of darkness.

His fingers curled about her hips possessively and he pressed his lips to the nail at the base of her neck while the demons inside him cackled.

"Let's head to my place," she said. "Reichardt usually senses when I've souls for him. He'll be there, I'm sure."

"Do I recall seeing a chandelier in your living room?"

She gave him a reassuring squeeze. "You did."

The prismatic light from the elegant chandelier mastering the center of the St. Charleses' living room was just enough to send the demons prodding at CJ's edges cringing into the dark nooks and crannies pocking his soul. CJ relaxed and blew out a breath. Safe here. For now.

Alone while Vika had disappeared up the curving marble staircase, CJ watched as a black cat curled about his ankles, and he bent to scratch the critter behind the ears. The cat's tail was interesting, striped with thin white bands, while the rest of its body was grayish-black.

"Oh, hello, Monsieur Jones." The sister sallied into the room in a flirty white skirt and purple top. "I see you've met my sister's ex-boyfriend."

CJ straightened, the cat in his arms. "Her what?" Pausing midscratch, he turned the cat to study its intent gold gaze.

"This is Salamander," Libby said, giving the cat's tail a tug. "Vika's ex."

"Vika used to date a cat?"

Libby nodded negatively.

He held the thing out at arm's length. The feline stared accusingly at him, flicking its tail angrily. Seriously? "A familiar?"

"Nope."

Well, that only left— "You mean he was once human? Isn't that kind of cruel?"

Libby laughed heartily. "Don't worry. We don't believe he remembers anything from his former life. It wasn't Vika's fault. Sal ran into a nasty warlock, and that's what you get when you play with the big boys, isn't it, you silly thing?" she said in baby talk to the cat.

The cat flicked its tail and would not look at Libby, showing her its disdain.

"Vika dated a man named Salamander?" CJ didn't know what disturbed him more. The name, or to learn the cat used to be— No, he wouldn't think about it.

"His name was Sal," Libby explained. "But it felt weird to call him that, so Salamander it is."

"Right. Because there's nothing whatsoever weird about naming a cat Salamander." He tried to hand the thing off to Libby, but it wrapped its tail around his wrist and clung like a…lizard.

Libby managed to snag the cat and sent it scampering. "So, you're looking fine today, CJ. And not so desperate."

"Thanks. I think. Not desperate, but tired. Your sister exorcised another of my demons."

"Ah, so that's why she's beaming. Good for you. I bet it's a real riot inside there, eh?" She tapped his chest. "But more important, did she find the soul?"

"She did, and it's stuck to her soul right now."

A man suddenly materialized in the living room near the kitchen door.

Libby clutched CJ's hand. "He's here. Vika, Reichardt is here! And for once I'm not holding the toilet plunger. Can life get any better? Hello, Monsieur Reichardt." She shook her hand from Certainly's and made a nervous little curtsy to the soul bringer. "My sister will be right down."

The man, silent but seeing all, CJ suspected, gave him a nod and waited, hands calmly folded before him. He'd never met a soul bringer before, but he knew they were not conversationalists or social. They lived to ferry souls. Day and night, all hours of the day. Must be a boring life. Yet, being angelic in origin, they were some of the most powerful beings to tread this realm, and he respected the man's silent strength.

Vika sailed down the stairway and greeted the man. "CJ, this is Reichardt, the soul bringer."

"A pleasure to meet you." CJ offered his hand, but the stoic soul bringer merely nodded as if a bored bouncer standing guard before a nightclub door.

The soul bringer looked to Vika. "Remove your clothing."

"What?"

Vika cast CJ a sheepish glance. "It's a requirement."

"I don't think so." He stepped before her, putting himself between her and the soul bringer.

"Is there going to be a problem?" the soul bringer asked.

"No problem." Libby tugged CJ away from her sister, and he only reluctantly followed. "You two go into the kitchen."

"Yes, the kitchen." Vika shook her head admonishingly at CJ and directed the soul bringer through the swinging kitchen doors. "You stay under the light," she called back to CJ.

"Uh-huh. The light." The French doors swung shut with a snap. CJ looked to Libby. "What the hell?"

"It's routine," Libby said, still holding his arm, as if she had enough strength to hold him off from storming the kitchen and making sure his woman did not strip for the brutish stranger.

His woman? Far from it. But wouldn't he like to make that claim, and mean it? Not if she got naked for every man who passed through her front door, or her ether, as the situation was.

"Is that how it's always done? She gets naked for him. Every time?"

"Well, she usually has on her bra and undies—which I'm sure she's wearing today. Maybe. Rarely is she completely naked. Though there are occasions. It's all cool. Reichardt is…" Libby sighed heavily. "Emotionless."

"Doesn't mean he's not copping a feel."

"Oh, I think it does. He doesn't actually touch her to scrub the souls. He uses a form of catoptromancy, but the mirrors he uses are his eyes. They go all silvery when he's performing the scrub. I'm not sure he sees the nude body in the same manner a normal man would." Again, another sigh. "I wouldn't let it bother you. Trust me. It'll only screw with your head."

Less than five minutes later, Vika breezed through the kitchen doors, followed by Reichardt. Vika tugged at the neckline of her dress and flipped her hair over a shoulder. CJ eyed the soul bringer warily. He didn't look overly satisfied to have just felt up his girlfriend.

*She's not your girlfriend!*

Still.

"Libby," the soul bringer said.

Libby perked.

"Have you another of those cookies?"

"Really? Yes!" With a delighted squeal, Libby headed toward the kitchen, grabbing Reichardt's hand as she did and tugging him bodily through the swinging doorway.

Vika approached CJ with a smirk. "She's a crush on the guy."

"That explains the wistful sighs."

"Sighs and fantasies that will never come true. Poor girl. Of all the paranormal breeds in this universe, she had to fall for the one completely lacking in emotion. I'm not sure his glass heart beats. How sad is that?"

"The sad part is, he just got to see you naked, and I did not."

"I was wearing panties. And he doesn't see me. He goes into some weird trance and I think he only sees the souls. He got the soul, by the way. I'm safe."

"Safe, but still not naked," CJ said teasingly. "Just panties? So he saw your...?"

"Is that all you men think about? Getting a woman naked?"

"It is a favorite thought, but not exclusive to the male brain. We also think a lot about food, entertainment— usually of the sporting kind—sex, cars, magic—in my case—sex, and yes, more naked women. Tell me you ladies don't undress we men with your eyes?"

"Well." She let her eyes travel down his chest, and CJ suddenly felt very naked. It was not an undesired feeling, either. "Yes, I suppose we do."

She turned and walked off, turning to crook a finger at him. "Want me to show you my spells?"

Thinking he'd rather see her panties, CJ cast a look to the chandelier above. Out the window the sky had brightened, and the clouds had moved away. Safe, for now. He followed the witch into the spell room.

*Chapter 7*

Inviting CJ into her spell room was putting her trust out there as far as she dared. This room was personal to Libby and her. Most witches did not eagerly invite others to peruse their spell rooms, but she had snooped over CJ's domain. This wasn't so much an "I owe you a peek" offer, as an "I need to get to know you better" show of trust. And he had once already been inside, not at her invitation, so to now wrest control put her in a place of power.

Vika stood in the doorway, arms crossed and hip against the door frame, as Certainly strode about the room, studying the glass drawers for ingredients. She liked the contrast now of dark and light. Wherever CJ went he insinuated darkness. Not purposefully, but merely by being. His was a complicated darkness, woven with strands so twisted and complex Vika wondered if he could ever become untangled.

"Did you ever not want to practice dark magic?" she asked.

"No. My parents practiced the same." He ran a long finger over the front of a glass door, behind which sat her mortars, one of which had been hand carved by her father in sandstone. "My brother and sister and I have never known anything different. Dark magic is not evil, Vika."

"I know that."

"But it's not clean, either," he added, turning and leaning against the counter, opposite the room from her.

His implication was loud and clear. She liked things clean. What was wrong with that?

"Have you a book of shadows?" he asked.

She nodded to the book open on the marble table that mastered the center of the room. "Been working on it since I could hold an ink pen and recite spells. Do you have a copy at the archives?"

"Probably. The *Book of All Spells* generates a page every time a witch creates a new spell. Dezideriel Merovech allows me access to the book frequently to keep things up-to-date."

Dez was a nearly millennium-old witch who was married to vampire Ivan Drake, who served on the Council, along with his parents, Nikolaus and Raven. But they lived in the States, so CJ must travel to view the book.

"I'd love a peek inside that book," Vika said.

"Even with all the dark magic lurking within its pages?"

"Even so. Curiosity doesn't imply I have to practice it."

"True. I do admire a curious heart."

He placed his tattooed hand over his heart. The dark ink work blended against his black shirt. How painful to have endured the needle on what Vika guessed must be one of the most sensitive places on the human body.

"What are you working on at the moment?" he asked. "Anything I can help you with?"

Vika strolled to the spell table and tugged her book toward her. Normally she never shared her works in progress, but knowing CJ's vast magical knowledge bolstered her eagerness to show him. And she wanted to share with him. It felt conducive to learning more about his life.

And anything that allowed them to converse closely appealed to her desire to have him near her.

"This is my latest interest."

He slid onto the clear Lucite stool beside her and leaned over the book. Tugging a pair of foldable glasses from his shirt pocket, he put them on and read. That he wore glasses ratcheted up his sexiness level to a new degree. Smart men targeted Vika's libido like chocolate and oysters did to some women. And though she knew glasses did not imply smartness, the look worked for her.

And his closeness stirred her senses to ultra-alert. He was so…there. Warmth rose from him in tangible waves. A solid entity she could not disregard. And he smelled like her herbarium, a wild mix of scents she could pick out, such as thyme, basil and bergamot, and then the scent would dissipate and allow another to rise, such as the dry sweetness of cedar she'd noticed last night. He wore the world on his skin. And she wanted to explore that world.

"Fire and water fusion. I like it," he said, tapping the page in her book with a finger. Taking off his glasses, he tucked them away. "Show me?"

"I'm still in practice mode, but I can do little tricks." She pulled a beeswax candle set in a silver holder to her and, with a breath and the thought *lumiere,* brought the wick to flame.

"You've mastered fire?"

"No, all witches know that simple trick."

He leaned his elbows on the counter, which rubbed his arm against hers, and Vika stood there a moment, staring at the candle flame, while her attention was focused on the intimate contact. Skin on skin would feel better. Cedar and bergamot permeating her flesh and warming her senses to a heady desire.

But she was getting ahead of herself.

Gliding her fingers above the flame, not touching, she recited the spell. "Earth, fire, bone, water." With a tap of her finger to the flame, the red heat transformed to blue water and continued to flicker in flame shape.

"Nice," CJ said.

"You can probably reduce an entire burning building to water," she said, catching her elbow on the table and her chin in her hand. "Am I right?"

He shrugged. He could, but he was nice enough not to say so after her small accomplishment.

"Draw it out," he said with a nod to the watery flame.

"I haven't gotten that far in my study yet."

"It's all in the hands and intention." He took her hand and she spread her fingers wide, accepting the intense heat of their connection. CJ smoothed his palm across hers with the untattooed hand, indicating she should hold it flat before the flame. "Mirror the flame, and feel its movement in your palm."

With a twist of her mouth, she concentrated on the watery flame, and the dazzle of undulating light within the clear surface. She could feel the movement against her palm. The water flickered softly, as if touched by a breeze.

"I feel it," she whispered. "I think I can control it."

CJ slid his hand down to her wrist, where the jade beads were wrapped, and touched her lightly there, not breaking contact. She sensed he bolstered her magic with his own, and in fact, her intent felt most strong at the base of her throat. Grandmother must approve, she thought suddenly.

The flames spattered up tiny water beads, and then, with a lift of her finger, the beads darted toward her palm. She gave her finger a twist, and the beads spiraled in the air between the candle and her hand in a trill of suspended droplets. Her heart speeding, she sucked in a breath. She wasn't about to announce how thrilled she was because that would break her concentration.

"Coil them into a weapon," he instructed. "Use your whole hand."

Frowning, because the first thing that came to mind would never be what he suggested, Vika balked. "Why a weapon?"

"Doesn't have to be. But make it a projectile of some form."

That was easier to accomplish. She folded her fingers inward, one after the other, and the water droplets spun into a tight, long chevron. With a thrust of her hand, she sent the watery dart across the room to splash against the glass doors.

They held gazes in silent triumph. "I did it," she whispered.

"You pick up things quickly. You have great skill. And this." He tapped her grandmother's nail.

"That, and a good teacher. Show me something else?"

Their faces were but a handbreadth apart. CJ's eyes darted between hers, saying more with his gaze than she felt he could speak. She adored his soft smile, a little unsure, but even more willing. He touched her jaw briefly, and she wondered if he would kiss her, but too quickly he nodded and stood back, shaking out his tattooed hand as if he'd been burned.

"It's your grandmother's magic," he said, when he noted her wondering lift of brow. "Sometimes it snaps at me, as if a warning."

"Good ole Grandma. She's watching over me."

"And she doesn't entirely approve of me."

Vika shrugged. "She doesn't entirely dismiss you, either. Maybe the nail also senses the demons."

"Not a bad protection to have." He nodded once, accepting that. "So. Something else. How about this?" With a sweep of his hand, he lifted the extinguished candle, and it soared about the room in a wide circle to parallel the movement of his hand.

"Transprojectionary dislocation!" It was a strong magic that required decades of practice. And he performed it with such ease. "I thought you said your magic was weakened by the demons within you?"

"It is. This is but a silly display. I could move buildings if I chose to do so. But not with my passengers holding down the fort."

"It will be a marvel to see you at full strength. I hope to see that someday." And more. Exploring the world of Certainly Jones was an adventure she wanted to take. "You've spent a lot of time studying magic?"

"Too long." The candle settled with a clink on the marble counter. "To my detriment."

"How so? I should think it incredibly helpful to have such a vast arsenal of magic to hand."

"Yes, but something must be set aside to make room for all the study." He leaned in again, and this time he brought his face so close, she prepared for the kiss. But it didn't come. "Relationships," he said, "have suffered."

"This one is doing well so far," she tried.

"At your grandmother's discretion."

And then he did kiss her. A sweep of his hand tilted her head to meet his mouth with hers. A tender, soft touch, lingering, not pressing, more drawing in her breath and basking in her. The not-touch occupied her core and swirled in her being as if water droplets dancing at his command.

Never had a kiss so thoroughly grasped her, as if she'd been put under a spell. Dark magic? Perhaps.

"Is that okay?" he whispered against her mouth. "I think about kissing you all the time now, but I know I've done nothing to deserve your kisses. If anything, I've only repulsed you with my demons."

"You think too much." She kissed him. His throaty moan pleased her. A man's surrender at her instruction. "You can kiss me whenever you please."

"Mmm, and you can touch me whenever you please." He tilted his head against her fingers. "I've never had something so soft touch my skin."

His broad hands stretched across her back, and he leaned in closer, not quite bringing his hips in contact with hers. Still polite, yet delving deeper into the kiss and coaxing her further into his darkness.

"You make me view the world differently, dark one," she said. "And that's a good thing."

Touching his smile, she then teased the tip of her tongue under his top lip. He answered with a dash of his tongue along her lower teeth. The dance dared her to surrender to any apprehensions she'd had about him—and she did willingly. Strolling her fingers down his shirt, she traced the hard plane of his chest and felt a sudden zing, as if she'd been shocked.

"Ouch!"

"Oh, sorry." He tugged aside his shirt to reveal a

large mandala-shaped sigil over his left nipple. It was intricate and filled with boxes.

"Sak yant?" Vika guessed.

"Yes, a form of Thai magic, by Sayne, as well. Each box is a different spell. This one repulses other magics. I should have turned it off before touching you. It usually doesn't respond, but your nail must have glanced over it."

She clasped the necklace. She never took it off, not even for a shower.

"You don't have to remove it. I can block the ward with a few taps." He touched his tattooed fingers to one of the boxes within the sigil. "But it is getting late and soon will be dark. I can't stay," he said. "Unless you want me to stand beneath the chandelier through the night."

"Well." She made show of considering just that, then shrugged. "I'm going to practice the water displacement some more. Thanks." She kissed him, then without touching the sigil on his chest, studied it some more. The man was a map of spellcraft, and she had donned her explorer's hat. "See you tomorrow?"

"I'd like that. I'm going to sleep well tonight, thinking of your mouth." He traced her lips and she kissed his fingers. "Something to take with me into dreams."

CJ crossed the loft threshold under the violent glare of the prismatic light. His world had been reduced to imprisonment within his home, and he'd learned to hate the constant minute tinkle of overhead crystals and the flash of color across his skin, when it should have given him marvel as it had Vika when she first viewed it.

Stomping across the painted protection ward, he paused in the center and tilted his head, closing his eyes. A strange judder moved the floor beneath his boots. He knew it wasn't an earthquake or the building settling, as sometimes upper floors felt wavery.

"Someone is trying to breach my wards."

The protection demon's wards, to be exact.

Racing to the sofa, he found the remote control he'd designed to turn off all the chandeliers with one click or in specific groups, such as in the bedroom or kitchen or only over his spell room. Hastily returning to the ward, he knelt and, bowing, spread out his arms to each side, the remote held in one hand.

Of all the demons within him, he had a sort of alliance with Protection, and he had actually summoned it to the fore on two previous occasions. Now, he needed the demon's help.

"Ada ada io ada dia."

His gut churned, the infestation awakening and battling against one another for reign. And when he felt the warm glow beneath his skin, familiar and welcome, CJ clicked off all the lights.

The loft grew so silent he heard the hum of the electricity buzz through the wires. And then, palms slapping the hardwood floor, he was overtaken.

He'd found exactly what he'd hoped to find on the concrete railing before the Seine in the fourth quarter. A minute, dried speck of blood above a gash in the concrete. Apparently the dark witch had been in a fender bender and hadn't walked away without injury.

Ian Grim had carefully scraped the blood into a vial with the tip of a pocketknife blade, and now, in his lab, he had prepared the mixture and laid the bead of processed blood onto the same map he'd used with the pendulum.

Immediately the bead, small as a dragonfly's eye, had began to travel the streets on the map, at first following a main road and then veering down an alley.

Grim stood patiently over the map, hands clasped to his gut, his muscles tense and jaw tight. It had been six months. Finally he would learn where Certainly Jones was hiding.

Over the decades they had matched each other in magics, always trying to one-up the other. They had never been allies or even friends. Always enemies, but not quite, for they employed a gentleman's conduct for all duels and magical showdowns. They were always generally aware of the other's location and doings, and if something struck one as interesting then the challenge was issued.

Dasha tended to put up with his macho grandstanding. He loved her for her quiet acceptance.

He hadn't realized Jones had a clue what he was up to until the man had returned from Daemonia and Ian had sensed what his nemesis had returned with. Something he'd wanted to lay his hands on for decades.

"You haven't won yet," Grim muttered as he tracked the slowly moving bead that veered toward the fifth arrondissement and then scattered in a powder across the map, as if blown away by explosives.

"No!"

The dark witch must have been on to him and blocked his approach with protective magic. To be expected. If Grim were able to easily sneak up on Jones, he'd be disappointed. But he was closer than ever now.

"The fifth." Only one of the largest quarters in Paris. "I will find you, Jones."

# Chapter 8

This cleanup was weird.

Pulling on her gloves, Vika looked over the piles of ash. Normally, she was rarely called in for a vampire cleanup. The vamp was staked; he ashed, leaving behind just bits of clothing and personal items. Usually. This time, one particular pile of ash was only half-formed, sitting before the legs and hips of what had yet to ash.

"A young one," Libby said, joining her side with dustpan and broom in hand. Clear goggles, that covered her nose as well, wrapped her head because the fine dust tended to fly up one's nostrils. "That's too sad."

The young vampires didn't ash as easily as those who had perhaps a few decades of vampirism to their arsenal. And the heat generated during an ash didn't get hot enough to destroy clothing. Hence, the cleanup call.

"You grab the feet," Vika said. "I'll get what's left of the hips. This shouldn't take long."

Libby handed her the black body bag, and Vika zipped it open as her sister inspected the shoes on the feet. "These are Louboutins."

"Don't think about it," Vika warned.

"I know. Really bad karma to steal the dead's belongings. But do you know how much those things cost? And they're purple. I think they're my size, too."

"Libby."

"All right, all right! Lift."

They succeeded in getting the legs into the body bag without having to remove the shoes to lessen the weight. Libby tossed the bag into the back of the hearse.

"So he liked the cookies, eh?" Vika asked. She began to sweep the ash, Libby holding the dustpan and dumping it frequently in a hazardous waste disposal bag.

"He took two this time. Said he'd never had anything like them before."

"Soul bringers don't usually eat, do they?"

"Not sure. They're from angel stock so they don't have to eat, but they can. And he did."

"That's remarkable. That Reichardt had a sort of conversation with you. Well, two sentences, but still."

"I know! Remind me to always have a fresh batch of chocolate chip cookies available."

"Something tells me I won't need to remind you. But seriously, Libby, you are dating other guys, right?"

"Oh, no. What if Reichardt finally gets it into his

head to ask me out and I've got a date with someone else? That would so not be smart."

Vika pushed a small mountain of ash toward the dustpan. "I suppose not." He wasn't going to ask, because the guy could have no concept of what a date even was. "Maybe you should come out with me and Becky next weekend. Friday girls' night out? Just for kicks."

"You've never invited me along before. Would Becky mind?"

"Not at all. I think I should ask her about those shoes. She runs with the glamorous crowd."

Vika suddenly couldn't erase the feeling something more than a routine vampire slaying had gone on here. "I know most vamps are pretty well-off, but, I don't know. Are they all females? Does this feel odd to you? I'm sensing some latent witchcraft in the air."

Libby paused from brushing up the ash and closed her eyes, studying the air about her by opening her instincts to the electrical energies in the ether. She nodded. "I do, too. Most spellcraft would have faded by now. Must have been a powerful witch in the vicinity, and recently. That is weird."

"Witches and vamps are on neutral grounds now," Vika added. "And a witch would have no reason to take out vampires like this, not even for a source—"

"CJ is a powerful witch."

She twisted a look to her sister. "What are you implying?"

"Huh?" Libby stopped playing with the tip of her

purple glove and released it with a *snap*. "Oh. Well. I'm not implying anything. Sorry."

Vika nodded and turned to her work.

"But he does practice dark magic," Libby added.

Why her sister couldn't get on board with her being interested in the ultimate of bad-boy witches was beyond Vika. He was exactly the sort Libby fell for. It was a good thing Libby wasn't attracted to CJ. He was hers.

*Really? Already claiming the guy, and you're still not sure if you're safe around him?*

"Oh!" Vika gasped as a few corpse lights suddenly entered her body, one right after the other, as if rushing to the front of the line. They burst inside her and then faded until she felt not a thing.

"How many?" Libby asked.

"Three or four? I can never be sure. Probably all of them. I think there's at least five dead vamps here, though I'm not sure that ash pile is one or two."

After she'd taken on a soul, she felt nothing more. No sign from within that she harbored lost souls. The first time she'd realized she was actually collecting souls was when Reichardt had been at the scene of a cleaning. He'd watched as she and Libby had done their work and then pointed out the souls he'd come for were stuck to her. She had no problem agreeing to a regular scrub, while Libby had swooned and hadn't been the same since.

"That smaller pile there." She pointed out one moist with dark liquid, which she guessed was blood. "I'm going to make a call and say that was a heart. And why would it not have ashed at the same pace as the rest of the body?"

"Because someone had reached in and pulled it out to drink the blood," Libby said. Witches had to consume the blood of a beating vampire's heart once a century to maintain their immortality. "But why five vampires when one will do? Do you think all the hearts got grabbed?"

"I don't see how it's possible. Someone would have fought back. Unless there was more than one perpetrator."

"Or the witch had the other vamps in thrall while he methodically went from heart to heart. We have to report this to the Council," Libby said. "We're not detectives."

"I know. I have no interest in getting involved in whatever *this* is. I have so many other things with which to concern myself at the moment."

"Like the dark witch with the tattooed hand?"

"Who kissed me again."

Libby gaped and pressed her gloves to her mouth, but her eyes were all glee.

"He's invited me to the Council archives this afternoon. We're going to search the grimoires."

Libby's glee dissipated. "Sounds like a real exciting date, sis. And you think *I* need to get out more?"

"It's a work date. I'm determined to—"

"I know, clean him up. So what happens when all his demons are gone? You two go your separate ways? Because I so cannot see you hooking up with him,

even if you two have kissed. He's completely opposite your type."

"You keep saying that, but I don't have a type." Vika
zipped up the hazardous waste bag, and the two of
them hefted the ash-filled container into the back of
the hearse. "Do I?"

"Tall, blond and Nordic. You like them looking like
Thor, not Thor's evil nemesis."

"Who is Thor's evil nemesis?"

"Not sure, but I suspect he'd look like CJ."

"Who has a look that bears a remarkable resem-
blance to your type."

"I know." Libby tugged off her gloves and took out
the spell-sanitizing spray from a rubber container in
the back of the hearse. "And yet, I'm not at all attracted
to the guy."

"Which, I have to say, I appreciate. You should see
his home. It would amaze you. I told you he needs prismatic light to keep the demons at bay? He must have a
hundred chandeliers hung overall."

"Seriously? Like some kind of Tiffany's on crack?
Yet another weird feature about the dude that totally
doesn't add up to Vika material. You be careful, sister
mine. I know your need to help and clean things up is
the biggest compeller in this situation. Don't fall so far
you can't see the light for his darkness."

"That's a bit dramatic, Libby." Sounded like a line
from one of the country music songs she was always
singing at the top of her lungs.

"Yeah? But who's the better judge of character between the two of us?"

Vika sighed. The answer was unnecessary; they knew it was Libby. Vika was too caught up in herself at times to notice the foibles of others, while Libby's extroversion made her a people reader extraordinaire.

Was she taking a wrong step with CJ?

He had threatened her safety twice. Not him, exactly. The lust and menace demons had done that. And he'd been genuinely upset and apologetic. He was misunderstood, that was all. And so what if he didn't look like her standard dating material? Maybe it was time she tried something new.

A walk on the dark side.

Her skin flushed in anticipation. Memory of his gentle kiss slowly growing bolder until her skin had felt like liquid fire, as if it was the watery candle flame. Yes, she wanted to delve deeper into Certainly Jones's compelling darkness.

The archives were appropriately Gothic and stuffy, tucked into the basement of a building the Council had appropriated centuries earlier for storage. CJ had showed Vika around on a tour. Iron walls supported tunnels dug out of the limestone, and doors were operated with high-tech digital codes. Dry stone and mildew mingled with dust and what she sensed was burned wiring from decades gone by. Bats skittered in the rafters, and a chill enveloped her ankles as if walking over a fresh-packed grave.

She liked it.

Now they sat at the library table beneath a massive Swarovski chandelier fashioned with iron fixtures and crystals that gleamed in all colors. One of the first the company ever made, CJ explained. And it was haunted.

Vika kept looking toward the crystals, expecting to see them move or tinkle in the stillness. If the chandelier was indeed haunted, the spirit or ghost attached would surely sense the presence of ultrasensory entities, such as she and CJ.

Certainly cast her a grin from across the table. "We're safe here."

"I know." She propped an elbow on the table, the black lace on her sleeve sweeping a stack of books. "But *how* is it haunted? I don't know much about ghosts, but I'm ever curious."

"My knowledge of the spirit world is on level with yours. And I adore your curiosity."

She tilted her chin up pridefully. She felt his look glow upon her skin in a warm flush.

"I've been told a duke who hailed from Revolutionary Paris was tossed up on the chandelier by peasants and landed on the iron stakes. He was left there to bleed out. Supposedly you can hear a dying groan echoing down, but I've yet to hear it. Tea?"

"Oh, yes, please."

He turned on a tea service at the cupboard against the wall, above which a long fluorescent light had been hung. He'd explained his lighting precautions since returning from Daemonia. He'd not divulged to the Council his sudden need for better lighting, but Council members rarely visited the archives, so his secret was for now quiet.

Vika paged through the ancient book of shadows

she'd selected from the archives, hoping for words like *demon, exorcism* and *Daemonia* to jump out at her. When CJ had brought her into the special humidity-controlled room where they stored the grimoires, it had taken away her breath. The room was half the size of his loft apartment, and it had been stacked floor to ceiling with books of all shapes, sizes and bindings. No wonder they'd not been ordered and scanned. Where to begin?

"You need an assistant," she said, standing and reaching for another from the stack they'd carried out as the most likely to contain what they were looking for since their covers depicted demons or had been fashioned from human skin.

"So I've been told. You in the market for a job?"

"I already have one I enjoy. And I don't think I'd get to the grimoires because all this dust, well…"

She sighed at the sight of every surface dulled with dust. The old, rich woodwork screamed for a good oil polish. Should have brought in her cleaning cart from the hearse. She could still go out and get it….

"What if I had the place cleaned up before you arrived?" he suggested from over a shoulder.

"Would never work. I'm far too busy with my business."

"Jiffy Clean," he said with a chuckle.

"That's Libby's joke. I didn't notice the sticker for weeks, and I have no idea how to remove it from the hearse without ruining the paint job."

"Something the Martha Stewart of witches can't clean?"

She tried to think of a comeback, but the sudden sweep of CJ's hand across the nape of her neck made her stand up straight. It was followed by the warmth of his breath. The nuzzle of his nose tracing the length of her neck stirred her heartbeats.

"Wh-what are you doing?"

"Your hair spilled away from your neck, and I had to touch it. To learn this little space of skin." A kiss tendered below her hairline. It branded her softly. "Is that all right?"

She nodded. "Don't ever ask me again if your kisses are all right, dark one. They always are."

Her fingers brushed the surface of a grimoire bound in violet suede and then curled over the edges to tickle the pages.

CJ's mouth barely touched her skin. She felt him enter her pores and heat her being. Her fingers curled tightly, her nails cutting the edges of the brittle paper. He touched only her neck, not his hands on her arms or his body against hers. It was deliciously erotic and frustratingly confounding. She wanted him all over her, and she did not. This subtle tease wakened her sensory longings and brewed them to a slow, wanting purr.

Pressing her palms to the softbound grimoire, Vika tilted back her head and her hair swept over CJ's face. He brushed it aside and over her shoulder and then dashed his tongue down her neck. A touch right there at the base where it curved into her shoulder, and then he retreated, as if testing her, tasting her.

Vika sighed. She shifted her hips, tilting to the side, and found his solid form strong and sure as she glided against him. One of his hands swept around and about her waist, pulling her closer. Slowly but surely, as if demanding and he would not allow her to resist, but yet so measured she couldn't be sure she wasn't agreeing to all this herself.

The teapot whistled and he managed to reach behind—his other hand still clutching her about the waist—and remove the pot from the burner. "We'll let it cool."

His voice tickled her senses with a deep baritone. So manly. She couldn't imagine refusing anything he should request. And she had not thus far. Perhaps he worked a subtle magic on her? A wicked magic for sure, because she could not figure how she was falling for this man. This positively dark man who held no qualities that attracted her. Save for the way he touched her.

"You are the Mistress of Subtle Yet Insistent Distraction," he murmured against her skin.

His tendency to give her silly titles thrilled her. Another point to his favor.

A kiss traveled to her dress neckline, which was wide, cresting at the curves of her shoulders. His palm moved up her stomach, gliding over the black lace, which married the fabric to her suddenly warm skin.

She pushed the book away on the table.

Gripping her possessively below her breasts, he pressed his teeth to her shoulder, not biting, not digging in, but hard enough to make her gasp and grasp at the air, yet finding nothing with which to anchor herself. He'd grown daring since their encounter in her spell room, this man who had confessed a preoccupation with magics and not relationships.

Head falling back and aside his, Vika whispered, "Hold me tightly, CJ."

With his teeth he tugged at the neckline of her dress and managed to slip it off her shoulder. Hand firmly at her chest, he pressed his hips against her derriere, and she felt his erection, his long, wicked hardness, hug against her body. A wanting murmur hushed across her lips.

Moving lashes of tongue and bites along her shoulder and neck, CJ avoided the necklace with the nail that may warn him away. Instead, he tempered her faltering patience with lingering pauses and silences or a careful touch to her flushed skin that made her shiver in anticipation. Her breasts rose and fell with need. His hand was so close, yet he'd not moved to touch her there, where her nipples tightened and tingled.

A momentary glance above verified they stood well beneath the chandelier's glow. *Safe.* For as much as she wanted safety. Or what if she did not, and instead she decided to remain open to anything he should offer, attempt to take from her? Not so tidy then, eh?

Vika clasped his hand and moved it higher, squeezing her fingers over his. He pinched her nipple through the silk-backed lace. Her moan dusted the tea-spiced air, and it felt good to voice her desire. To speak to him with the sound of her want.

"You like my touch?" he whispered.

"Oh, yes. Touch me everywhere, dark one."

He swept a hand around her and pushed the grimoire across the table, clearing a spot and then lifting and turning her to sit before him. She stared up at him, a man who could command her with but his breath. Mouth open and eyes arrowed on hers, he asked her for something, daring her to relent.

Vika grabbed the front of his shirt and pulled him in for a kiss. A hard, bruising connection that opened his darkness into her and spilled down her throat in a lush sigh. He tickled up her skirt, taking his time, inching it slowly, his fingers tapping and sliding at her thighs, and all the while, feeding her hungry kisses with his.

CJ's kisses poisoned her need for control, to make order. She wanted him to mess her up, to ravage her clean spirit. She nibbled his lower lip, tugging not too gently. He groaned and shoved her skirt high to her thighs, where the ruffles collected with a *shush* in her lap. Exploring fingers lightly traced the inside of her thigh, as if the ghost from the chandelier had managed to substantiate touch.

A sensual alchemy of her sighs blended with CJ's groan as he opened her mouth with his tongue and bit the inside of her lip. It hurt sweetly. She clasped her thighs about his hips and clung with her fingers to his shirt, pulling, clutching, needing so desperately to fall.

Falling, falling, deep into his mystery. She spread her arms wide in her mind and let the moment sweep her to oblivion. He gripped her chin and held her head so she could not look away from him. His lips were reddened from their kiss. She imagined her hair must be mussed and her cheeks and lips as stained with passion as his. Oh, but her skin needed him to deepen its color all over, stain her with his magic.

"I can't stop touching you," he said. "You're the one magic I haven't yet explored, and I need to learn it now."

He lunged for her neck, roughly kissing at her vein and moving up along her jaw. And he slid a hand between her thighs. Her panties were tiny, sheer and black, and he snagged the thin elastic waist and tugged. The airy fabric slid over her aching mons, and she shifted her hips expectantly.

"I'm going to touch you everywhere, Vika. There are no demons in this world who can hold me back."

"Just as long as you can hold them back."

"We're in the light. Trust me?"

"Yes."

He lifted one of her legs, gliding his hand along her sinuous length, and propped her ankle against his shoulder, kissing the inside of her calf and drawing his tongue to her anklebone. Ultrasensitive there, Vika wriggled. Her bare skin soaked up his heat with every kiss, every lick.

He gripped the hard black leather shoe, and when she thought he would pull it off, he slipped his tongue between the space under her arch and the leather. The electric touch scurried through her system, and she tilted her shoulders against the stacked grimoires. She lifted her breasts, and her head landed on a thick book as pillow. Slowly, lazily, he stroked her arch, playing her arousal to a glowing, pulsating peak.

Gliding a hand down her bare leg—the tattooed

hand shimmered across her skin with magic untold—
he followed with kisses to mark her flesh, as if a witch
hunter searching for the telling sign. None would find
it, for Certainly's kisses were indelible; only she could
read and interpret them with her sighs.

His fingers played over the sheer panties, each stroke
slow and sweeping. He held her gaze and she his beneath the dazzle of crystals constellating above them.
Hot breath seeped through her skin and skittered delicious tingles through her groin and up and down the
insides of her thighs. His jade eyes, bold and sure,
asked permission.

Biting down on her lip, Vika closed her eyes, waiting, anticipating...

A hot kiss pressed against the black panty. Breaths
hushed over her folds. He kissed her there, through the
sheer slip of fabric, tonguing along the delicate, elasti-
cized edges and finding her skin hot and moist.

Vika clutched the tumble of her skirts at her hips.
Soft breaths were punctuated by teasing lashes of
tongue traveling the length of her entrance. His hands
clung to her ankles, each one propped at his shoulder.
His hair tickled her stomach. Spiced tea perfumed the
dusty air, and above, the crystals tinkled as if a caval-
cade processional to a faery march.

He tugged her panties with his teeth, slid them down
her legs and quickly over her heels, and then knelt before her, positioning the spike heels of her shoes at his
shoulders.

She thought she heard him whisper, "Fuck, yes"
when she dug in her heels, but her mind reeled with the

clatter of crystal, the perceived whispers of the ghost and the shift of papers as her movements unsettled the books stacked around her.

She clutched a book and dragged it to her chest because it was all she had to hold, an anchor, a means to keep from floating off on a blissful wave. As CJ's tongue mastered her trembling loins, her fingernails dug into the leather cover, surely carving divots in the ancient tome. Her core jittered, as did her entire being. So close she soared to the edge, to crying out at the command of her lover. Her legs quivered, her heels digging into his shoulders. Muscles in her belly tightened, anticipating the storm.

And when she came, her body arched upward and her hips bucked. Her cry was soft and kittenish, a top note to the satisfied moan roiling from CJ's throat.

"Yes, so perfect," he muttered, biting her thigh gently. "My perfect little witch has been undone."

Vika felt the heat redden her cheeks, and her sigh exhaled delicious exhaustion. That was what she had wanted—for him to redden her. To undo her.

## Chapter 9

Certainly leaned back against the counter, the tea service behind him. He turned and poured a measure into a clear glass cup. Turning, he watched Vika sit up on the table, tug down her skirt and fuss with her hair.

"No, don't do that," he said. "I want to look at you just as you are. Mussed."

She put down her hands and gave him a little smile before self-consciously looking aside. Her garnet hair was tugged from the updo, and one sleeve shrugged off her narrow shoulder. Her skirt was bunched above her knees, revealing long, pale, gorgeous legs that ended in those sexy shoes that had dug into his shoulders. He would find marks there later. He hoped.

Her mouth was red, and she sucked in a corner of her lower lip and looked up at him from under a swath of bright hair. It was a kittenish look, like a sexy come-on from one of those *Playboy* models to which no man could deny an attraction.

Certainly swallowed a sip of tea—hard. "Great Hecate, where have you been all my life?"

She twirled a strand of bright hair about her forefinger. "Living in my little round house. Studying magic. Casting spells. Cleaning up piles of werewolf and other assorted creatures."

"I've never met anyone quite like you. Conflicting in so many ways, yet each bit of you complements all the other bits. I like you undone, Vika. But I like you all tidied up and perfect, as well."

"If we're going to analyze what we like about the other, I have to say you're not the kind of man who has ever attracted me."

Another sip of tea went down the wrong way, and Certainly managed to croak out, "Thanks a lot."

"It's true. But I can't seem to stay away from you." She took his left hand and stroked a fingertip over the tattoos on the back of it. "You're everything I never thought I'd want. When you look at me like that over the rim of your teacup, I want to tear away my clothes and let you stare as long as you like. I'm normally pretty controlled around men. You bring out the vixen in me."

"Tear away. I'll look as long as you want me to."

She fingered the neckline of her dress, her long black lashes dusting the air as she apparently considered doing some clothing removal. He wasn't even close to coming down from the incredible sexual high they'd shared, and if she wanted to go round two, he was right there, hard and ready for action.

But she shook her head and stood up from the table, her skirt shrugging down to hide her sexy gams. "Is there a bathroom down here?"

He gestured to the left, and she walked out. That was either the quickest fall from arousal, or she needed a few minutes alone. Some kind of woman thing. He hoped.

He was dreadfully out of practice with women, but she had seemed to enjoy his fumblings.

Tilting down the remainder of the tea, he eased the front of his jeans down to make room for the hard-on that would not soften, he felt sure, until long after he'd parted from Vika's company. Might have to rush home for a long shower.

He gathered the grimoires they'd shoved aside during their heated coupling. A page had been torn, and he cursed his carelessness. These texts were ancient. Great care must be taken with them.

The title of the spell on the page read *Seducing Demons from the Body.*

If the universe wasn't knocking him over the noggin, he'd guess he and Vika had an innate magic when together and had conjured this spell to the surface. Either way… "I can dig it."

He read through the ingredients, of which there were only two: a man and a woman (one must be possessed by a demon), as well as the usual accoutrements: candles, athame, herbs, blood. If he understood the gist of the Latin spell, it seemed to work in reverse of a demon summoning normally performed by a familiar and his or her assistant. Having sex would open the one possessed by a demon and allow his partner to conjure that demon forth and cast it to the demonic realm—but only after having sex with said demon.

"So simple as that?"

Yet it involved sex. Only then could the body release the incorporeal demon from within. And then to have sex with that demon to lure it toward final release?

"Trickiest means to an exorcism I've ever heard of." He wasn't so sure about allowing one of his demons the rein to have sex with Vika.

Would Vika approve? He'd had almost sex with her. She had been willing, unflinching and receptive. But they hadn't gone all the way, and he suspected if he suggested sex as a demon-exorcising skill it would spoil the mood and make the experience suck.

"Not for the first time. But maybe the second?" He folded the spell, and when Vika returned at that moment and asked what it was, he said, "A recipe for preserving mouse hearts. Could come in handy. You okay?"

She'd tidied her hair and adjusted her dress. Almost as pristine as when she'd arrived, but he knew beneath the surface the woman was a wild tangle.

"Yes. But I got a cleanup call while we were…entangled. They left a text. I have to leave. It's faery related, which is always disturbingly weird and requires immediate attention to keep the evidence from mortal discovery. Once that faery dust hits the ether, strange things start to happen, trust me."

"Of course. I think I'm going to hang around here, page through a few more grimoires."

"It's getting late. Shouldn't you get home before dark?"

"The Metro station is just outside the door, and it stops right across the street from my building. A completely lighted journey home. I'll be fine." He kissed her, tasting the sweetness of cherry lip gloss she must have just put on. "You could come over after the cleanup if you like. I'll cook for you."

"Between you and Libby cooking for me, I'm a very spoiled girl. I'll see you then." She spread her palm over his heart and nodded, as if deciding that yes, he was okay, and then kissed him quickly on the mouth and sidled off without so much as looking back.

"The Queen of Subtle Indifference," he decided. "So interesting, that witch."

Certainly ran through the rain blasting the world with cold, hard droplets. Though the Metro stairs were literally across the street from his building, his clothing was soaked by the time he landed in the lobby and nodded to the doorman, who informed him the electricity in the building had gone out. Not an uncommon occurrence during storms. The electrical wiring in the building dated to the early twentieth century.

"Thanks, Jacques. Good thing I take the stairs, eh?"

"Power should return in an hour or two," the doorman called after him.

Also a good thing he had a generator. But first, he

had to make it to his front door via the dark staircase. This was not going to be easy.

Taking the stairs two at a time, Certainly was already beginning to feel the stirrings inside as his passengers awakened to the darkness they fed upon as if ravenous beasts. It took him less than thirty seconds to make six floors—and not a moment too soon.

A growl escaped unbidden as he opened his front door and rushed inside.

To darkness.

"The generator?" He dashed into the hallway and to the roof access doorway. Inside, his muscles clenched and he fought against the demon that sought to control him. Through sheets of rain, he spied the smoking generator. "What happened?"

Had it been struck by lightning? It looked okay. No burn marks on the metal cabinet. He pulled the ignition cord, and the motor sputtered. It had to work when wet. It had before.

Lightning slashed the sky and frightened the emerging demon so that Certainly felt the actual cringe within his body. From the rooftop, he scanned the streets below. A neon sign flickered three blocks away. The entire neighborhood was dark.

With renewed urgency, the demon thrummed through his veins, pulsing to the fore. Bent double, CJ fell to his knees. "Who is it this time, damn it!"

A throaty chuckle spit out raindrops. "Hungry for some pain?"

Vika dropped Libby off at the witches bazaar and told her to be careful of the weather on the way home.

The worst had passed; she could feel it in her bones. But that had been some crazy lightning earlier. Must have taken out power in parts of the city, for they'd driven some streets dark for the lacking streetlights.

Since she was close to Certainly's home, she decided to abandon caution and go for it. She'd been abandoning more than caution when around the man. This afternoon in the archives had been—scandalous. Sexually, it had rocked her world. The instant connection they had developed was downright combustible. And mercy, but she wasn't wearing any panties now due to her quick change before heading out to the cleaning job. She wondered if the dark witch would be up for round two.

"I know he will be."

And yet, reluctance twanged deep in her gut. It was evening. Dark and rainy. She knew she had no reason to fear. His home was well lit with the prismatic light required to keep back his demons.

That still didn't erase the unease clinging to her skin.

She found a parking spot down the street from CJ's building and decided a walk in the sprinkling rain wouldn't make her hair any less appealing than it already was. Tugging off the Tyvek shoe covers and stashing them in the back of the hearse, she made a note not to forget the bag of faery dust they'd swept up. It must be returned to Faery unless she wished to risk mischief and malice. Vika didn't like dealing with the sidhe, so she would contact a freelance liaison she regularly hired for jobs such as this.

The concierge in the lobby tipped his hat to her and

informed her the electricity was out and she'd have to take the stairs. He offered her a flashlight, and she accepted it while her heart sank to her gut.

Taking the stairs, she could not anticipate what she would find on the sixth floor. No electricity meant no light. But CJ had said he had a backup generator.

"Whew." Allowing her nerves to get the better of her was so out of character.

Quickening her steps she made the top floor, but she didn't try CJ's door when she saw the roof door open and swinging from the breeze blowing down from above.

She listened before taking the three steps up to the roof, clinging to the slick iron railing. The rain had picked up again and it poured over her shoulders, soaking the thin white T-shirt she wore above skinny black jeans. Shivering against the heavy droplets, she ventured across the pebbled roof, her flat heels finding slippery purchase. A few tin vents jutted up. The stairwell was bricked in so she walked around it, expecting to find the generator on the other side.

Vika walked around the brick wall and spied a dark stream of water. It trickled over her shoes, and she saw it was blood. "Certainly?"

"Heh, heh, heh." He sat against the wall, a serrated piece of metal in hand. His arm bled from inner elbow to the wrist, and at sight of her he smiled a macabre grin before banging the back of his head hard against the brick wall behind him.

"What happened?" She lunged before him and CJ growled, setting her back and stumbling away. Red eyes. Not CJ. A demon controlled him. Had it forced him to draw the metal down his arm? "Let me have that, please?"

CJ viciously slashed it toward her, and she avoided getting cut only by dodging and landing hard on her elbow. Throaty coos of pleasure sickened the demon's laughter. He slammed his fist against the wall and dragged his knuckles slowly, peeling away the flesh.

"Stop it! You're hurting him."

"And so I must," the demon growled. "It feels so good, yes? Ah, delicious pain."

"Pain," she muttered, wincing that this man must be tortured by something so hideous.

"Torn flesh is orgasmic," he intoned as if in the throes of wicked pleasure. "Come closer, red witch. Me want to share the witch's pain with you."

"If you kill him, then what will you do? No one to torture with your sick games."

"Me won't kill him. He's a healing spell tattooed here." The demon snapped out Certainly's arm, displaying the bloodied tattoo on his biceps, the shirt-sleeve torn away from the shoulder seam. "He used me to get to Daemonia. Now I shall use him well."

"What does that mean? He used you?"

"Pain inflicted upon others."

The demon cackled and slammed the metal piece across CJ's leg, cutting through the heavy jean fabric. CJ's body reacted, stiffening, and he howled, but the cry was accompanied by the demon's macabre smile.

He felt everything, Vika knew, but could only witness, not control.

"Blood must be shed to enter the place of all demons," Pain said. "This dark witch shed much." He leaned forward, his wet hair hanging like black oil across his face. "You don't think the vampire goes painlessly with the stake, eh?"

"Of course not, but I have no idea what you're talking about. Certainly would never harm—" Vampires? Staked? Had CJ—

The demon's laughter exploded, as did CJ. He leaped up, hooked an arm in Vika's and swung her about, then pushed. She tumbled toward the stairwell, yet grasped the railing before soaring headfirst down the steps.

He lifted her as if she were but a doll and kicked open the roof door.

Vika grabbed the iron rail and managed to hold long enough to tug the demon off balance. He clattered down the stairs, releasing her to fall onto the top step. The demon cursed her and scrambled up behind her. This time he tossed her over a shoulder.

"Slippery little witch. Let's try the next stairs together. Your bones can break my fall, and my fall will break your bones!"

Through the inky darkness, he charged toward the stairway. His boots slipped from the wetness, and he stumbled, slamming them both against the wall at the head of the stairs.

Vika kicked—clutching the nail at her neck—and connected her heel with the back of his knee, and found her freedom. She grabbed the doorknob to his home and said blessings it was open. Inside, she dashed toward the center of the loft. All was dark. The crystals tittered with her frantic movement. There would be no safety here unless the electricity returned.

But there were the sigils placed on the walls, floor and counters by the protection demon. She raced to a wall where a red spray-painted sigil depicted something she couldn't translate. What the hell did it protect?

The pain demon tracked the dark room with Certainly's eyes, sniffing, clutching the air with his fingers in anticipation of finding her. He could use only the witch's senses, and those were not as heightened as those of a corporeal demon who could assume his own form in this realm.

Suddenly the lights flickered. Vika slammed against the fridge, searching the constellation above. It had been only a flicker.

"Lumos!" she tried. Stretching out her fingers to connect with the latent electricity in the air, she scoured the ether.

Nothing.

She couldn't see CJ or hear his demonic passenger lurking, but he must be close. Despite the floor-to-ceiling windows, the loft was dark. It clattered with crystals that shivered as if as fearful as she felt right now.

Stupid to have come up here after the concierge had told her the electricity was out.

"Asking for trouble," she muttered, and made her way along the kitchen counter. Her fingers glided before the knife stand. She considered arming herself but decided the demon would have the weapon out of her hand and to her throat in but a blink. She had a more powerful weapon.

Whispering a command and forcing her earth magic through her fingers, she sent a stream of phosphorescence before her. It whipped through the loft, snaking below the chandeliers and illuminating, if but for a moment, its surroundings.

Her jaw snapped shut and her chin tilted up. He held her from behind, painfully wrenching her head. "Sneaky," the demon growled. "Let's take that magic to the streets. This dark witch won't let me tap into his magic. He's strong. But I know his bitch isn't as strong. Come on."

An arm about her neck, he tugged her from the kitchen. Vika would not go peacefully. She dropped her body weight, forcing the demon to drag her. And she grabbed for everything they passed, clutching a stool and slowing his progress.

"I like you, red one. You're a fighter! You'll bring lovely chaos to the streets of Paris."

"You'll never make it to the streets!" she yelled, finding her anger gave her strength and determination.

As he dragged her over the threshold, she gripped the door frame with both hands and strained to keep hold. She shouted, "Harrahya xum!" A spell to focus her power.

That repulsed the demon and sent him stumbling toward the stairway. He gripped for the wall, his fingers sliding, and Vika winced. If he fell, it would be CJ's body that took the damage, and she didn't want that.

Sending out her air magic, she swept it around and behind the demon, teetering him on balance as one of CJ's boots slipped off the step. He fell forward, landing on his palms. Flipping back his hair, he grinned menacingly and crawled toward her, red eyes narrowed.

The lights flickered again. Vika shouted, "Lumos!"

Inside the loft, all the chandeliers lighted. And stayed lit.

She scrambled across the threshold just as CJ grabbed her about the ankle. Out in the hallway the bright lights flickered on. The demon howled and let go of her. Shuffling beneath the safety of the prismatic lights, Vika waited to see what would appear around the corner.

CJ's hand slapped the threshold and clawed to drag his body forward. "Sorry," he muttered.

Vika's heart fell. "CJ?"

"I'm back." He crawled over the threshold. His fingers bled, as did the cuts on his face and his biceps. Reaching her, he looked her over, his hand sweeping up her body and to her face, where his shaking fingers barely touched her. "*Mon Dieu,* did I hurt you? Please forgive me."

She grabbed his hand and pressed his palm to her cheek, feeling shivers overwhelm her now she knew safety. Cold and wet, her heartbeats pounded. "Hell, CJ, I don't think I can do this anymore."

He dipped his head to her lap and wept.

# Chapter 10

"You're shivering," CJ said to Vika.

He tugged off his shirt, which clung to his body and felt like a dirty shroud after being controlled by the pain demon. His blood soaked the shirt and his pants, but thanks to numerous healing spell tattoos on his body, his wounds were already scarred.

"Take off your clothes and I'll put them in the dryer. I'll get a blanket."

He went to the closet behind his bed, leaving Vika to disrobe, if she would. He wanted to step away from her for a few moments to give her some space. He'd tossed her around like a ragdoll—Pain had. He wouldn't blame her if she turned and ran from here and never returned. He hated he couldn't control the demon from within, though he had been able to hold on to his magic. If the demon had gotten its mind over that, nothing would have been safe.

And had he almost pushed Vika down the stairs? He slammed his forehead against the closet door frame, cursing himself. Because it was his fault. He was the one who had purposefully journeyed to Daemonia and had brought back the means to torment Vika.

Grabbing a folded blanket from the shelf, he turned to find a wet witch standing right behind him, her sodden clothes in hand and her lips shivering. She wore a bra and held her clothes before her bare loins, and looked like a drowned kitten.

He couldn't dream to look at her in a sexual manner. Instead, he wrapped the blanket around her shoulders and hugged her against him. "I'm so sorry."

She didn't say anything. He felt her cold lips touch against his collarbone.

"Slip your underthings off and I'll have them dried in a bit. I'll make hot tea. Can you forgive me, Vika?"

"Wasn't your fault."

She managed a weak smile, but he sensed she'd been pushed to some edge and had fallen. Wrapping the blanket about her, she then performed a bra removal without exposing herself to him.

"I'll toss them in the dryer." He dangled the sheer white bra. "Does this need special care?"

She shook her head. "Dryer's fine."

"Go sit down." He kissed her wet head. "I'll be right back."

She turned and shuffled to the couch, where instead

of sitting, she folded herself into an upright ball on the gray velvet cushions.

Earlier when he'd clung to her on the threshold, she'd said she didn't want to do this anymore. Neither did he. Not if it caused the one perfect thing in his life pain.

Swallowing down a vicious curse, CJ inwardly screamed at his demonic passengers. But he couldn't let on to them how desperately his heart ached to see Vika in such a state. Already they were aware she was special to him. The pain demon had known. Any chance they got, they would use that against him. The deadliest cuts struck to the heart.

The washer and dryer were located off the bathroom. He shuffled out of his jeans and tossed them in the dryer. Vika's delicate bra gave him pause, but she'd said it would be okay, so he tossed that in, as well. Claiming a folded pair of black jeans, worn and torn at the seams, he pulled them on, toweled off his wet hair and grabbed a clean towel for Vika.

He gently patted her hair with the towel, she sitting there with her eyes closed and shivering lips. When she opened her eyes, she touched his forearm where Pain had dragged the jagged metal down his skin. It had hurt like a mother. And every moan, every shout had only bolstered the demon into writhing ecstasy.

"It's healed," she whispered in a tiny voice.

He kissed her forehead. "Yes." He forced himself to go make tea. A stupid ritual, but the hot liquid should warm her up.

*You could wrap her in your arms and simply hold her. That would warm her.*

But he had no right to touch her like that now. He'd destroyed the trust they'd built over the past few days.

He put the teapot on the stove and sighed, glancing over his shoulder to the shivering witch. "Welcome to my nightmare."

The azure chandelier above the comfy gray sofa cast blue shimmers against the surrounding clear crystals. The effect was strangely calming, and staring at it brought Vika into her body and to a place of stillness. Shivers dissipated as she focused on the colored light beams as if they were lifelines.

Wanting more than anything to walk away and be done with the dark witch and his manic infestation of demons, instead she'd moved as if by rote when CJ had directed her to disrobe. Defeated and out of sorts, she'd simply complied, as if the soul bringer were requesting she do the same. Shivers had encompassed her body, but now she was warming thanks to the soft thermal blanket wrapped tightly about her limbs. She'd stay because leaving this protective cocoon felt impossible right now.

That thing—Pain or CJ—had almost tossed her down the stairs. It was difficult to look at him without cringing, yet logically she knew the man had nothing to do with it. CJ had hurt himself at the direction of Pain. She cringed forward to remember his bloody wounds stirred to streaks by the rain, and how Pain had laughed and then moaned as if harming CJ's body were an erotic turn-on.

Would he—it—have laughed at her had she tumbled down the stairs, surely breaking bones?

*Don't think about it. That didn't happen. You were able to get into the light.*

CJ sat on the couch next to her and handed her a cup of black tea. The glass cup fit into her palms, and the warmth quickly traveled up her arms, seeking her core.

"Sorry," he said quietly. "I'm just…so sorry."

She sipped the cinnamon brew and it slid down her throat, bringing her back to life, to the surface, where she bobbed for air yet wasn't sure if she could find a steady rock to land.

"Stop apologizing," she said. "We know it wasn't you. I just needed a few minutes to collect my thoughts."

He nodded, his head bowed and his hands clasped between his legs before him. He smelled like rain. His bare, broad shoulders were rounded, defeated, revealing more spellwork tattoos. Were none designed to protect him from demonic possession? It was sad to see him like this, but at the same time, Vika couldn't quite rally to head his cheer-up crew.

Tonight they'd been beaten by the demon.

Yet despite her revulsion, she wanted to be here, sitting quietly beside him, because home felt too far away right now. And she was too tired to leave. They needed to be together, to come to terms with the unspoken alliance they had entered into with a few kisses, touches and promised trust.

Outside the rain continued to clatter the windows, yet the lightning had ceased. Vika hoped they were safe from another power outage. If the lights went out again, she was doomed.

"Are you hurt?" he asked, his voice cracking on the final word.

"Scuffed the skin on my palm, but otherwise, I'm just shaken."

And bruised, her consciousness whispered. *Your heart has been bruised.*

That made little sense to her. Her heart could be bruised only if she felt something about the man beyond the desire to clean him up.

*You do.*

CJ took her hand and examined the palm, carefully touching around the tenderness. It hurt, but she didn't pull away. Placing his palm flat against hers, the one covered with black tattoos, he closed his eyes and whispered, "Flesh, bone, blood, vita."

Heat scoured her palm, but not painfully. Rather, it was as if she'd placed her hand in a bowl of warm water. With a tightening of her skin, CJ then kissed her palm and relented.

The abrasion had healed. Vika had been witness to witches who could heal before, but never so quickly. If this was his magic depleted, then she would marvel to see him at full potential. Yet it had been his perceived power that had compelled her to explore the dark witch. Indeed, a witch's greatest power originated in the minds of others.

"Thank you." A few more sips of tea slowed her frantic heartbeats. "Those healing tattoos are amazing. Your cuts are healed, as well. Is it just the one tattoo on your arm?"

"Here." He touched his biceps where the circular healing sigil had been tattooed in black. "I've also one on my hip and my right foot."

She sat upright and moved closer to Certainly's body, not quite touching. To look over the artwork on his skin distracted from other devastating experiences. "You've so many tattoos. You said from the ink witch?"

"Yes, Sayne. One of few ink witches remaining in the world."

Tapping the back of his tattooed hand, she then traced the design carefully. "Are they all spells?"

"All, save one." He held up his right arm to display the wrist. Vika studied the delicate design of a rose with barbed wire twisted throughout its petals. "Thoroughly and Merrily—my twin brother and our older sister—have the same. It's in remembrance of our mother. Witch hunters got her like they got your grandmother."

A hot tear wobbled in Vika's eye. "I'm sorry. The tattoo is beautiful." Though she didn't ask why the barbed wire. She could guess, knowing how the ignorant tortured witches, and it was unsettling. "Someday, I'd like to learn about all your tattoos. Especially the ones on your hand."

She traced the innate lines on his palm that had been there since birth, and then the black spellwork. The center featured a sak yant design in an eye shape with scribbles she guessed could be Arabic, but could be some demonic tongue for all she knew.

"What does this one do?" She traced the eye.

"Entrance and closure. Opens me to receive, and as well, when combined with other spells on my body, can give me access to another witch's spells. But I can also use it to repel magics."

"And these lines around your thumb?"

"Focus. I can trap a person's focus with a snap of my finger. Or deepen my concentration beyond a meditative state."

"That sounds dangerous. Like you could go into a catatonic state."

"Almost. I use it now on the nights when I lie awake under the lights."

They held gazes for so long, Vika thought she heard her heart cry out. It was a small cry, one she found unfamiliar. A needy, yet understanding vocalization pulsing through her veins. She turned on the couch to face him and slid a palm along his cool cheek.

*Bruised internally, but so ready to heal.*

CJ's hair was wet still, and his skin so cool. His gaze did not sway as she followed her fingers along the stubble edging his jaw, and before his ear and along the hairline, framing his masculine structure. The demon mark remained, a modena of violence marring his neck. She touched his lips and found them as cool as hers felt. The rain had been relentless, scouring their bodies as mercilessly as Pain had tortured this dark one.

"We survived," she whispered. "One, along with the other, *cushlamocree*."

Kissing him was the only thing she wanted to do. Ever. Settling softly against his mouth, hushing her breath against his, breathing in his careful sigh. Legs coiled up to her chest beneath the blanket, she leaned against his chest and spread her fingers over his jaw.

His utter sadness at having hurt her and pushed her around wavered out from him in tangible vibrations. He regretted deeply. She kissed away the regret, hoping to polish his confidence. Quietly, she told him the trust between them had been tried, and it had survived, albeit tattered.

"My sister Eternitie believes nothing is coincidence," she said. "That the people who pass in and out of our lives, no matter how fleeting, do so for a reason. So maybe you're here to mess up my life."

"It needed mussing. But not like this, Vika." He touched her shoulder, and she winced. "It's bruised here. Hell, I'm so sorry."

"Apology accepted." She kissed him and held there, unwilling to break the contact, the blissful connection of their lives breathing in and out from one another.

Outside, a streak of lightning flashed, but no thunder followed. The storm had retreated. As had the chaos occupying this dark witch's soul.

Vika let the blanket fall off one shoulder, and she nuzzled her body as close as she could against his, her breasts cushioning against his hard chest.

"I saw the demon in your eyes," she whispered. "Do you think I could capture it with a soul gaze?"

When two witches held each other's stare, it was called a soul gaze. They could read the other's soul, all the goodness and evil painted across it.

"You don't want to look into anything I've residing within my soul, Vika. Great Hecate, haven't you seen enough?"

Closing her eyes, she nodded and whispered against his mouth, "Touch me." She clasped her hand within his and pressed his knuckles against her breast. "Make me yours."

"I... Vika?"

"It's just us now. And a gazillion chandeliers. Take me beneath the glamorous light that keeps us safe. I want to feel you inside me, CJ. Chase away the dark and fill me with the light I know you possess."

His fingers curled over her breast, sliding down the blanket, and he gave her one last questioning look—which she answered with a nod—and then bent to kiss the swell beneath his hand. She tilted back a shoulder, lifting her breast, and stretched a leg out across his lap. With a shift of her hip, she slid onto his lap.

Drawing a finger down his chest, she traced the triple scythes curved under his right nipple. They formed a sort of tribal claw mark. "Isn't this a were-wolf symbol?"

"It is, but it's inked with silver."

"You don't like werewolves? I find them quite gentle." She kissed the silvery scythe below his chest and then brushed her lips over the tiny nipple.

CJ inhaled and spread his hands over her breasts, his fingers playing softly over her hard nipples. Compelled toward him, she arched her back, giving him all of her to hold.

"And this one?" She glided her fingertips down his

rigid abs to the three parallel lines slashed through with shorter horizontal lines.

"A grounding spell. My skin is marred with ink while yours is unstained. Pure." He leaned forward and claimed her nipple between his lips, softly, then dashed his tongue around it.

Vika tilted back her head, her wet hair a thick mass down her spine. Reaching down, she stroked the hardness straining against his jeans. He hadn't buttoned but had zipped, and with a finger she teased the tuft of hair exposed in the V-shaped opening.

CJ's forehead nudged her at the base of her neck and he hissed. "Grandmother is watching."

"Should I take it off?"

"No, never. It's a part of you. I'll be careful."

"Your wards against other magics are off?"

"Took care of that when I tossed your clothes in the dryer. I am ever open to you, Vika. Oh, yeah, right there."

Massaging his erection through the fabric, she wanted to get to it, to release him so she could feel him inside her. But she took her time, enjoying every lick, every kiss to her breast, every squeeze of his hands, and the subtle glisten of magic humming between the two of them.

It was the dark hand covered in tattoos that scattered a shimmer over her skin as it glided her flesh. She wondered if he was aware of it, and then figured he must be. On the other hand, if he'd been more focused on magic than women...

"It's like fire," she gasped as his fingers glided down

her mons and teased at her folds. "Any of those tattoos designed for the sensual arts?"

"Ah?" He tapped her thigh with his fingers, which electrified the intensity of his touch. "I hadn't thought about that."

"Seriously? CJ, when our skin touches it hums with our combined magic. But this hand covered in spell-work? It's the same touch, but quadrupled in intensity."

"I had no idea. How about this?"

He glided between her legs and inside her, and it was as if an instrument heated and hardened and designed to get her off. Two fingers, not a sex toy. Vika worked her hips and glided up and down upon him, wanting to own every sensation, to steal his magic for her own pleasure. "Oh, yes, touch me like that."

"You're so hot," he murmured against her breast, his tongue slipping across her nipple. "I can feel our combined magic, too. Makes every part of me burn. Show me how you like it, Vika."

"I'd like it with your pants off and you inside me. Quickly, I want to come with you deep inside me."

He shuffled out of his pants and Vika straddled him. His face was a riot of color from the overhead crystals, his eyes closed as he glided inside her, his hands gripping her hips firmly. Seared by his heat, Vika slapped her hands to the back of the couch, feeling him deep within her, so thick, filling her, radiating within as their magics joined forces and the hum of their connection reached a heady vibration.

He had but to shift his hips and thrust inside her once, twice, then the climax overwhelmed and he bucked her up and down upon his body as the dark witch swore to Hecate and then blessed her in the same breath.

"Pax, sax, sarax," she whispered. An Elizabethan chant to prolong orgasm.

CJ thrust back his head, growling in delicious pleasure as she sensed the orgasm renewed, surrounding him in its stunning grip. She surrendered and got wrapped in the threads of giddiness. They seemed to float, wrapped together, soaring over the floor, entwined in rapture.

Skin against skin, Vika breathed in CJ's being, his breaths, his rapid heartbeats. She felt him, *knew* him— and then she felt the infestation. It roiled in wicked delight, snatching at her with claws that couldn't reach yet were so close.

Pulling away from him, she leaned over his blissful smile. Breathing heavily, she shook her head. What a way to come down. Chased by demons. He couldn't be aware of what she had felt. She didn't want him to know.

"Amazing," he murmured, and blew her a kiss.

Vika nodded and had to struggle with her sudden fear to lean forward and rest her head against his shoulder. They were safe under the light. She hoped.

# Chapter 11

CJ woke, not because it was morning and the light nudged him awake—his circadian rhythm had given up the ghost months earlier—but because his body generally woke after a few hours' rest. The daylight paled in comparison with the cacophony of prismatic light, which always made him blink in disgust. He'd never get accustomed to the unnatural light.

His lifeline. Would he need it always?

They'd moved to the bed from the couch to continue their lovemaking. Turning onto his side, he looked over the sinuous, long lines of Vika's body and marveled she could sleep under the light. Uncovered, lying on her back, from his side view her curves and lines were as if a sculpture done in porcelain. Each glide and rise of bone so subtle. At her small breasts the nipples were soft and like a tuft of crushed roses. Garnet hair spilled over the white sheets and his arm, and he stroked a few strands against his mouth, wondering if silk could ever feel so rich. The brilliant strands running over the black spellwork on his hand seemed to want to hide the darkness.

That she had forgiven his transgression against her with grace and heated desire spoke volumes for her character. She had seen beyond the demon and into *him*. He—Certainly Jones—was in there somewhere. He just needed to rise above, without having to build a chandelier umbrella to carry about after sunset.

It wasn't fair to her. She shouldn't have to endure his demons merely for a part of him. He might ever be able to give her only a part. Never the whole Certainly Jones. Not so long as Pain and War and others resided within.

Sighing, he turned to his other side, putting his back to her. Pulled in two directions, his heart wanted to wrap a big bow about Viktorie St. Charles and embroider his name on the ribbon. He would braid the ribbon into a spell and knot it on both ends so it would bind them forever. Yet his tormented soul wanted to hurt her, to see how far he could push the red witch and learn how much that would please him.

A good man would dress her and push her out the doorway, and then change his address and set up wards against her.

He'd never claimed goodness. The things he did were oftentimes selfish and egotistic. He wouldn't deny that.

But he could see that denial had gotten him into this mess.

As it stood, if they remained together and opened their hearts to one another, that was doing nothing to remove his demons. Would the sex reversal spell he'd found torn from the grimoire in the archives work? The possibility to try it was more real now that they'd made love, but the idea of broaching the subject while lying in bed didn't feel right to him. As well, he could not fathom allowing Vika to have sex with one of his demons, because the opportunity would present itself only when he was not in control of his body.

It was either try that or find more souls for Vika to shoot through him with her air magic.

Kisses tickled down his spine, and he closed his eyes to the delicious wonder of her tender regard. Truly, he'd been missing out on a lot over the decades not to have indulged in a relationship. He didn't deserve her, but he wasn't going to kick this luxury from his bed or his life. Only she could save him. He wasn't too proud to admit he'd accept her help. If she would give it.

"I was thinking," he said, as her kisses moved along his hip and up his torso. "Could I come along when you get another cleanup call?"

The kisses stopped and she moved in to spoon against him, wrapping her arm around and across his chest. "Yes. We'll give that a try."

He kissed her fingers. "I don't deserve you."

"No, you don't. But for some reason, I am smitten by you, dark one." She tumbled to her back and stroked her fingers as close to his cock as she could reach. "Wake me up with this marvelous wand of yours, witch."

"As you command." He turned and with but a few kisses fit himself inside her, and the twosome slowly welcomed the day. "It's too good here," he whispered. "Inside you. Don't want it to end."

"Why must it end?" Her body seemed to squeeze about his cock and Certainly clung to her hips, pulling her closer. "Don't think beyond the moment, lover. You like this?"

He nodded, let out a tight moan.

"Then open yourself to me, and only me. Let's cast a spell between us with this movement, this delicious tug and push of you inside me. Oh, CJ…"

Her breath hushed against his cheek. Her body stiffened against his, and her fingernails dug into his skin. He held her as orgasm swept through her like magic, and when it spilled out from her pores and into him, he cried out in joy.

Be damned, wicked demons. He would hold this light in his arms as long as he was able.

CJ walked Vika out to her car. It was well after noon, and the sun beamed white high in the sky. It warmed the bridge of her nose and her cheeks. Almost felt as tingly good as her hand did, the one clasped by CJ's spellwork hand. She'd grown accustomed to the gentle hum when their skin touched, which was stronger when this particular hand touched her. It made her feel alive and vibrant.

And it also made her feel as if she belonged to him.

That her magic responded to his so positively, and not dangerously, was a good thing. Stopping at her car door and clicking it unlocked, she turned and swung her lover's hand. "Our mix of dark and light must offer the universe a balance it appreciates."

"I was thinking something similar. We meld together well. No sparks, no reactive, vicious magic. It can sometimes be a problem for witches of opposites practices, or so I've heard."

Vika touched the nail at her neck. "Apparently, grandmother approves."

He kissed her and slid his hands down her hips, coaxing her against his body, the hardness of him making her moan and pull him tight against her. "That guy never rests, does he?"

He pumped his erection against her a few times. "Not around you, no. Is that a bad thing?"

"Bad?" She thought of how shocked her sister would be to learn she had finally made love with her bad-boy witch. "I'm not sure bad is so awful anymore. I kind of like your sexy badness, dark one." Running her fingers through his hair, she drew out the length and pressed it to her cheek. "I don't want to leave. Not you. Not this." She nudged her hip against his erection.

"Return to me directly after the cleaning job, please?" He toed her shoe; he'd padded out barefoot.

"I will." She slid inside behind the wheel, and CJ leaned in to kiss her. She couldn't get enough of his commanding kisses. When his hair spilled over her face and neck, she felt as if he were marking her with a sweep of a midnight veil.

"Libby is waiting," she reluctantly said, and he relented the passionate kiss.

"The shop fixed the ole hearse up nicely. I'll pay you for the damages because it was my fault— What's this?" He rubbed his thumb on the dashboard and showed her the rusty-brown color in the whorls. "Looks like—hell, is this blood?"

"I…don't know. You were in the driver's seat when we crashed. And afterward you did have dried blood on your forehead."

"Shit. I forgot all about that." He furiously rubbed at the blood, licked his fingers, and then rubbed some more. "Do you have some cleaning spray in the back?"

"I do right here in the glove compartment." She retrieved the small spray bottle and cleaning cloth and handed it to him. "CJ, what's got you so frantic over a drop of blood?"

"You know any witch can track you with your blood."

"Yes, it's associated with the soul, it binds oaths and gives witches power over one another."

"Exactly. I never leave mine where it can be found and used."

"I get that. But seriously, it's a minute speck. What reason do you have to think someone is tracking you? Certainly?"

He gave the dashboard one last swipe and handed her the cleaning stuff. Not going to answer her question. And she sensed the answer must be a doozy.

"A secret?" she tried. She hadn't known him long enough to delve into the complexity of a centuries-old dark witch. Though she'd thought they'd given one another their trust. "Fine. You have yours—I have mine. I should get going."

"Don't shut me out, Vika. I just can't talk about it right now. I don't even know if it's anything to worry about. Will you cut me some slack?" He stroked his thumb along her cheek, his hope-filled gaze daring her to leave him in a huff.

She couldn't. She wasn't the kind of girl who stomped away over matters left undiscussed. "You going to tell me about it sooner, rather than later?"

He nodded. "See you after the job, Witch of My Dreams?"

"You'd better have dinner ready." She blew him a kiss and pulled away, checking the rearview mirror as she did to find the tall silhouette of her dark witch coaxing her to turn around and kneel before him, to worship him, perhaps even…love.

At every turn he was confounded! The powdered blood on the map had led him to a neighborhood tucked behind the Luxembourg Gardens, and he sensed one of the vehicles had Certainly Jones's blood on it or in it, because it made sense if he'd been in an accident. Yet once again, the blood dispersed, this time, blowing completely off the map, as if wiped clean.

Ian Grim looked up from the map. "He's got to live around here somewhere."

He summoned a raven to his shoulder and fed it the blood he'd processed for the spell. "Give me your eyes," he said, drawing his senses outward to connect with the bird's.

* * *

CJ felt the tracking spell as it tore away from the threshold of his loft. When had it affixed to the threshold? Possibly last night when Pain had been in control.

Not good.

Running to his spell table, he grabbed salt and devil's bane and began to mix as he chanted a ward.

Grim was gaining on him.

He glanced to the kitchen, where the small bone whistle sat on the counter, warded from view by any others.

"I won't let you get it, Grim. You don't get to play with mortal lives anymore."

## Chapter 12

"This call is peculiar," Vika said to CJ, who sat with legs straddling the stick shift in the middle of the hearse's seat. Libby sat to his right, and hadn't stopped grinning since they'd all crammed into the front—and only—seat. "It's at Père Lachaise. Never a good thing. Could involve ghouls or imps, probably demons."

"Demons," he muttered, clasping his hands into a ball between his legs. "Great. I'll stay out of you ladies' way and hope for the best."

"So what's your soul like, CJ?" Libby asked gaily. She smelled like sugar, which he liked, and her body nestled against his was all curves and softness, a direct contrast to Vika's slender sleekness.

"Libby."

"I mean, is it intact?" Libby continued, ignoring her sister's admonishment. "Do the demons control it all the time? Do you know if you left Daemonia with a soul?"

Vika flashed the evil eye at her sister, but the rear-view mirror was angled to catch CJ's confused look. She rubbed a hand along his thigh, reassuringly.

"It's in there," he said. "But that's about all I know. An incorporeal demon wouldn't be able to hitch a ride if I hadn't a soul."

"That's interesting. I wonder what it'll be like after the demons are gone."

"You're thinking my soul will be left in tattered condition?"

"Probably. I don't mean to be rude, but you know…"

"It's one of the drawbacks of practicing the dark magic," he offered. "My soul has never been clean, at least not your sister's definition of clean."

Vika cast him a wonky look, but he merely shrugged at her. The idea that they had attracted one another—dark to light—was something he wasn't going to argue.

Libby asked, "Why do you practice dark magic?"

Vika and CJ said at the same time, "Someone has to." They exchanged grins in the mirror, and CJ added, "It balances the universe. Good and bad. Evil and bright. Without the dark there would only be good."

"I don't see much wrong with that."

"You would, if it were to occur. Trust me, the world needs the other side of the coin for balance. So, Libertie, you are Vika's younger sister?"

"Yes, by two years. Our other sister, Eternitie, is the oldest. She's off tromping through the wilds of Africa."

"I have a sister, too. Merrily is older than my twin

and I by ten years. I have no idea where she is right now. Haven't seen her for decades."

"That's awful."

"It may seem like that, but I know wherever she is, she's fine. She's an adventurer and often gets caught up in her travels. I think she's studying shamanistic traditions."

"Sounds like Eternitie," Vika said. "She's an adventurer as well, and likes to learn new things. But she does check in with us every month or so. I'd go mad if I went as long as you did without hearing from her."

"Eternitie kicks shamanistic ass," Libby agreed. "What kinds of magic do you practice, CJ?"

"At the moment, very little. Though some magics I still possess in full strength. I'm a skilled allotriophagist."

"An allo-what?"

"He can make others vomit strange things like pins, stones, worms," Vika said.

"Toads are my favorite," CJ added.

"Eww. So not hitching a ride on your vibes, dark witch," Libby said. "Tell me about those tattoos on your hand. They're so black, and they look evil."

CJ turned his hand over and again caught Vika's look in the mirror. This hand hadn't served evil earlier this morning in bed with her. "The designs are fine-tuned spells put there by an ink witch. This one here is bespelled for transprojectionary dislocation."

"Ohmygoddess, you can move things through the air? That's so cool. Can I look closer?"

Vika slid her hand through CJ's tattooed hand as

she turned the hearse and pulled it through the gates to the cemetery. "No time. We're here. You don't mind graveyards, do you, CJ?"

"Some excellent ingredients for spellcraft can be found on such grounds. I think I'll have a look around while you two are busy cleaning."

Pére Lachaise boasted over a million occupants, seventy thousand tombs and ten miles of labyrinthine paths. The Parisian necropolis also sat on unconsecrated grounds. Excellent shopping for a dark witch.

Certainly used his pocketknife to scrape the thick layer of yellow mold from the letter *E* on a tombstone around the corner from where the St. Charles sisters were cleaning up a pile of vampire ash. After he'd asked for something to store his finds in, Libby had given him a few plastic zip bags. So far he'd collected the mold and some grave dust, and he now headed toward the dead cat behind the next tombstone. It had been reduced to bone by the efficient rats that scurried around even now, unwary of human or paranormal presence.

He sat on the edge of the raised stone tomb, pinching his fingers along the zip bag to seal it. He closed the pocketknife. Observing the sisters revealed an exercise in efficiency and professionalism. They both had their roles, and each worked with zeal. The determination on Vika's face was impressive. She did take cleaning personally.

"Can't believe she hasn't picked up my place yet," he said, sort of as a spoken wish, but then, "Nah. That would be forward of me." He liked his disorder as it was, because within that array he knew exactly where everything was.

That she even tolerated him being around her was immense. He'd seen the bruise on her shoulder last night while they'd made love. The pain demon had shoved her around, and he was surprised, and thankful, she didn't have broken bones.

"You allowed it to happen," he muttered, feeling he should be able to control the demons from within.

Must be more than half a dozen remaining. It wasn't as if he could do a roll call, but he suspected he'd experienced all that occupied his soul. There was or had been: Carrion (whom Vika had obliterated that first accidental meeting), Menace, War, Lust, Protection (whom he wished would appear more often), Chaos, Pain, Grief, and, well, he hoped that was it.

Why hadn't a desire or gratitude demon hitched a ride? Any man could appreciate either of those two. Although he should be thankful he'd attracted the one benevolent demon, he'd yet to notice that any of the protection sigils worked against the other demons, save to make them flinch.

Sighing, he waggled his tattooed fingers, smirking at Libby's curiosity and Vika's sudden discomfort when her sister had asked to examine them more closely. Vika had swooned at the use of his magical touch. He hadn't been aware of that particular magic since he'd only recently completed the glove tattoo. Nice bonus. He suspected Vika wouldn't mind if he practiced on her until he'd achieved mastery.

"Ready, CJ?" Vika called.

"Ready for what?"

His heart stuttered. She must have found another wandering soul. Plastic bags in hand, CJ dashed down an aisle between tombstones and rushed over to the hearse.

"Stand right there!"

He stopped abruptly at Vika's held-up hand.

She nodded at him, as if anticipating something big. He couldn't see the corpse light, but he noticed her eyes followed something in the air before her. Sweeping out her hand, Vika chanted an air spell.

The brightness blasted him in the chest and toppled him backward to land on the aboveground stone coffin of Jacques Letendre, Beloved Father. Arms splaying back and chest lifting as the soul traveled through him, Certainly gasped in the fetid air. Brilliance burst through his extremities and tugged at his muscles, as if attempting to peel them from his bones. He clenched his fingers, his entire body stiffening. The entrance ward on his palm burned, and then his muscles relaxed. As the soul moved through him, he cried out joyously to experience the warmth and utter gentleness. It all happened within five seconds.

Libby rushed to the tombstone and preened over his prone figure. A red curl slipped out from her Tyvek cap and dangled over her purple-dusted eyelid. "Hell. That was some kind of kinky! Did it work?"

CJ slapped a hand on his chest. "Goodbye, Menace."

Vika leaned over him. "I got the bastard who tried to total the hearse?" She pumped a fist. "Yes!"

He pulled her down onto him and kissed her, she in

her hazmat suit and white Tyvek hat, and he with his bags of grave dirt near his head. The two made out there on the coffin while Libby packed up the back of the hearse.

"Thank you. Again," he said, tugging the white cleaning cap from her head to let the garnet waves spill over his chest. "Was that the only soul?"

"No, I've collected half a dozen at least. They are already attached to my soul. Can't use them. But I felt one approaching apprehensively, so knew I could use it. Now, let me see if I can find it."

She climbed off him and wandered about behind the tombstone, and gave a triumphant whoop.

"That's my girl," he said, sitting up and brushing the grave dust from his sleeves. "My Intrepid Gatherer of Corpse Lights. Were they all vampires?"

"Yes." Libby hitched her hip onto the tombstone and sat beside CJ. She tugged out the earbuds and they dangled at her chest, tiny strains of rock music echoing out. "Weird, huh? We've had a rush of multiple vamp deaths. Generally Vika and I are never called in for such a job. Who's taking out all the vampires? And they're going for the hearts first."

"The hearts. How do you know that?"

"The heart is the last to ash if it's been previously removed from the body. We found one tossed under those dead weeds over there. Completely drained of blood, and not ashy. You want to see?"

"Uh, no, I get the picture. So it's not a slayer?"

"I doubt it. Why would a slayer take the time to rip

out the heart? Unless he's a psycho. And I do have a fond place in my heart for The Order of the Stake."

"Is that so?"

"Dated a knight from the Order last year." She gave him a sidelong look through her lashes. "Sexy Scandinavian man, but I think he also fell into the psycho category, too."

Soul bringers and mortal vampire slayers? This chick had some strange passions. But she also had the patented St. Charleses' oh-so-sexy lash-glance. "Are you reporting this finding to the Council?"

"Of course. But what are your suspicions?" She leaned closer to him and fluttered her lashes. Her eyes were as green as Vika's. "Think it's a witch looking for a source?"

"I have trouble with that suggestion."

"Me, too."

"A witch only needs one vampire heart, once a century," he said. "How many have you come upon lately?"

"Half a dozen at the very least. Could be a coven."

Certainly hadn't an idea what it could be, but this information gave him pause. He'd been out of the loop since his return from Daemonia. Generally he had a good idea which witch was up to what witchery, and why. And if the Council got wind of dirty dealings, that wind usually drifted below to the archives.

Maybe TJ had heard something? If it was so strange as to cause the sisters pause, he thought someone should look into it, or ensure it was being taken care of by the Council.

"Would you ladies mind dropping me at my brother's house on the way home?"

"You're not coming home with me?" Vika asked, sliding her hand into his, and all smiles now that she'd caught the soul. She glanced skyward. "Right, it's getting late."

"I have a curfew," he said to Libby, then frowned. It was the truth. He wasn't in control of his life.

He needed to change that.

Vika kissed him and the threesome left the cemetery with bags of vampire ash, cat bones and grave dust.

Vika exhaled as the last corpse light left her body and attached itself to the soul bringer. Reichardt went into his usual closed-eye trance that clued he was finished with her, so she bent to pull up her dress as Libby walked into the kitchen.

"Sorry." Libby backed out, and then popped her head through again. "Done?"

"I am."

Libby snuck over to the cookie jar and tugged out a plastic baggie that harbored within half a dozen chocolate chip cookies.

Salamander purred about Vika's ankles. She was sure the cat still sensed their former connection when he'd been human, which is why she hadn't the heart to bring him to the pound. She'd never been a big cat lover; still wasn't. He approved of her more when CJ was not around. They'd dropped him off at his brother's place.

When the soul bringer opened his eyes, Libby handed him the plastic bag. "More cookies?"

He took the bag with both hands and held it before him to study. With a nod of acknowledgment, the stoic man disappeared.

"That nod is so sexy," Libby said, tilting out a hip and catching a palm on it. "I'll break him down, sooner or later. I put a little magic in that batch."

"What kind of magic? Not a love spell. Libby, please tell me you did not."

"I would never! What witch would risk a love spell and always know the guy's feelings were brought on by magic and not his heart? I want to gently influence his subconscious. Make him remember my name. So when he eats a cookie, he'll think of me."

Vika tilted her head. "Subtle. I like it."

"I thought you would. You heading over to CJ's?"

"I…may. I've been thinking a lot about the sex spell."

"Don't tell me. Have you and he…?"

Vika hummed casually as she dusted the counter for nonexistent specks.

"Vika?"

"You said not to tell you."

"Agh!"

Smiling, Vika nodded. "Last night. And this morning."

"Nice. I was surprised when you invited him to Pére Lachaise, but then to see you two making out on the tombstone—whew! So, is he a good lover?"

"That man has many surprises hidden beneath his

dark exterior. Not the least of which is contained within his tattooed hand."

Libby's eyes grew wide with wonder.

"And that's all I'm saying. But as for the sex spell, I want to try to seduce one of his demons."

"Seriously? You think you can seduce a war demon, or ugh—Pain?"

"No, I'm hoping to snag a desire demon or something a little easier for starters."

"What if there isn't a desire demon inside him? You should bring me along in case it gets dangerous."

"And what could you do for me if it does?"

"My air magic is better than yours."

"True. But I don't want you there for the seduction. I have to do this on my own. Maybe. I'm not sure he'd approve of the method. It requires both witches to put forth their blood and then we have sex, and well, the host should be open and then we can cast out the demon during sexual congress—with the demon—which I know he would not approve of. I'm thinking I'm not going to tell him."

"Isn't that bloodsexmagic? The kind vampires once used to steal our magic?"

"It's a different form, but yes."

"You've never conjured demons before, nor have you cast them out. Vika, I'm not sure about this."

"You were the one to suggest it!"

"I know, but…" Libby worried her lower lip.

"I can do this." She clutched the nail at her neck. "With Grandmother's help. Yes, I think I will do it that way. I'll let CJ believe we're going to do it his way, but then at the right moment, I'll have to kill the lights to bring forth the demon and seduce it."

Libby winced.

"If it works he's one step closer to a clean soul."

"And you need to make it clean," Libby muttered as Vika walked out of the kitchen.

Yes, she did need to make him clean. Yet in the process, was she dirtying herself with lies and mistruths? And what if she could manage sex with a demon? It would be with CJ's body, not as if she'd be doing the nasty with a real corporeal demon.

Or so, that is what she kept telling herself.

# Chapter 13

"So what's in the bag?" Certainly asked as he poured a goblet of crème de violette for Vika and sat on the couch beside her.

She patted the tapestry bag she'd set on the floor. "Supplies."

"For what? You planning on doing a little cleaning? I know this place is a mess—"

"Spellcraft supplies," she clarified. "For…" She tilted her head and studied him, and he sensed a teasing challenge in her mien. "I want to suggest something to you, and I hope you'll take it with the same hope and goodwill it is presented."

"All right." He swallowed the rest of his chartreuse and sensed he might need a refill, but instead of pouring, he held the whole bottle of pale green liquor at the ready. "I am open to whatever you suggest."

"There's a spell Libby and I found in my grand-mother's book of shadows. A sex spell."

"Is that so?"

"It's for expelling demons. Two witches have sex and recite incantations, and it opens the one for demon exorcism. Kind of similar to how it's done using a familiar, but…not."

He smirked and rubbed his jaw. He hadn't seen that one coming, and yet… He pulled out the folded paper from his pocket he'd been carrying around for days and handed it to her.

"What's this?"

"I found this torn from one of the grimoires after we made out in the archives. Haven't wanted to bring it up until—" he nudged her cheek with his forehead, where she smelled like lemons, and kissed her aside her mouth, where he scented violets "—we got closer."

She read over it. "It's a sex spell. Great minds, eh?"

"I'll say. You want to conjure some wicked magic?"

"I've heard sex spells are as wicked as they get. I've never done anything like this, CJ."

"They are dangerous. When one is in the throes of sexual orgasm, it's difficult to concentrate fully and all sorts of things can go wrong. But if utilized properly, the spell can be effective."

"Have you any tattoos for such spellwork?"

"Did you notice any last night?"

She stroked her fingers over his jeans, and his cock responded with a heavy swelling. "I didn't see any in this vicinity."

"Mainly because I'm not letting anyone with a sharp instrument near my jewels. But no, no sex spells."

"Pax, sax, sarax," she murmured.

"Yes, the chant to prolong orgasm."

"It worked," she said on a breath.

"Oh, yeah. I'm not sure how this can work though." He tapped the paper. "It can draw the demon out of me, but there's no promise of expulsion from this realm once that's done. I don't want a stray demon wandering about Paris looking for another host."

"If it's incorporeal it'll get sucked to the place of all demons, as the others did when I expelled them from you."

"Right. In theory. But what if it wanted to have sex with you?"

"I don't think, well— I'm sure that won't happen."

He felt sure it would. And he didn't want Vika to have to deal with that, nor could he conceive of allowing such a thing. "No, I don't think I can do this."

"But, CJ, it's the next best thing to me accidentally stumbling onto another corpse light while you're around."

"That happy accident has occurred twice now. Not so accidental, if you ask me. And what if, once released, the demon entered you?"

"What do you mean? How would it enter—?"

"If it can latch onto a new host, it will. If a simple corpse light can attach to your soul, I don't want to think of what a demon could do to you. Yeah, I don't think this is a good idea."

He stood, but Vika grabbed his wrist, and he reluctantly sat down.

"We can do this, Certainly. I want to do it for you." She touched him above his temple, where she must have felt his pulse. It felt like her own brand of skin magic, humming softly, a reminder of their combined powers. "If we think it's not going well, we can abandon ship. No losses, just some great sex." She touched her grandmother's nail. "And I've this as protection. Please? I want to try this for you."

"I don't understand. After nearly tossing you down the stairs the other day, forcing you on a manic car chase, and generally being an asshole when occupied by my gang of demons, how can you still want to be kind to me?"

"I don't understand how you can still ask such a question."

"I know we've grown closer. Hell, making love with you is amazing. I feel connected to you, Vika. But I don't want you to trip over the exciting stuff and land in the messy stuff. Said messy stuff being me. I know you think I'm in your life to muss you up, but—"

"Don't you trust I'm smart enough to handle this relationship?"

"Is this a relationship?" he said softly. "Because if it is, how did I get so lucky?"

She smoothed her palm along his cheek. "Look into my eyes, lover."

He did so and found he could stare endlessly into Vika's eyes. To fall into that inviting forest and know freedom. Peace.

But he would not. Glancing aside, he said, "We should never soul gaze. Not until the demons are gone."

"Then let's make it happen." She kissed him, her mouth open and soft, tearing away his reluctance kiss by kiss. Wrapping his arms about her, he pulled her onto his lap. His hands strayed to her breasts, her thighs, her mons beneath the short crocheted skirt.

"Mmm, we've a good start," she suggested.

And he wasn't going to lose this erection anytime soon. Nodding, he relented.

"Thank you. I brought along some things listed in the spell, but I don't have the rue."

"I have hellebore and rue. And red candles. You need red for sex magic."

"And blood," she said softly. "You'll need to consecrate your athame."

"And I'll require something a little stronger than chartreuse. Probably whiskey." He drew her face toward him and centered on her gaze. "You sure about this?"

She nodded, her eyes alight with possibility. "Race you to the spell table."

Glasses on to read the spell, Certainly had taken off his shirt and pointed out the tattoo above his right hip to Vika. It wasn't for sex spells but for endurance and strength.

"And, it can deflect a bullet," he said proudly, tapping the tiny compilation of stacked symbols queued in three narrow lines down his side, where the muscles flexed and drew her attention away from the dark lines.

"You ever test that claim?" she asked.

"In the nineteen-sixties I took a bullet to the leg." He took a swig from the whiskey bottle sitting on the spell table. "It skimmed off me and hit an oak tree instead. Thanks to this."

Vika nodded, not sure if she could buy into that or, more likely, the possibility the shooter's aim had been off in the first place. Stroking the sexy, hard cut of muscle that defined his torso just above his hip, she said, "Should I ask what reason you gave another person to want to shoot you?"

"Probably you shouldn't. It was a volatile time."

"Uh-huh."

The ingredients necessary were all to hand as Vika stood beside Certainly preparing them in the mortar. He offered her the whiskey and she took a careful sip. She wasn't much for hard liquor, but despite her determination, she was feeling tense about accomplishing her goal. If all went well, she would have to trick her lover. "Mmm, what's that?"

"Tunisian vanilla for the sensual mood we need to create." He rubbed the inside of the bean pod against the bowl of the mortar then stroked his finger behind her ear. "I love this scent."

"You perfuming me, lover?"

"Words, smoke and the sensory all combine for a stronger spell," he murmured against her neck as she tended the ingredients, and his attention wandered. "This dress is so short. It's not your usual Morticia wear."

"You don't like my long dresses?"

"Love them. You wear them so tight, makes it easy to visualize what's beneath. Mmm, and what is beneath makes me so hard." He nipped playfully at her earlobe, and she squirmed up against his rock-hard chest. "But this is purple. Bright and bold. It's not you."

"It's Libby's. I thought I'd try something…different for the spell." His fingers trailed down her spine and to her derriere. "Figured it would be appropriate for bloodsexmagic. You like it?"

"Vivacious Vixen," he cooed at her ear, nuzzling to scent the vanilla he'd stroked there, while his hand slipped beyond the, indeed, short hem of her dress. "No panties."

She wiggled her hips. "Not a thread. Where's the rue?"

Without stopping the gliding strokes his fingers dashed over her thighs, CJ reached high to the overhead shelf for the rue and handed it to her.

"If you think I can concentrate on spellwork, red witch, now knowing you are pantyless, you had better think again." Moving around behind her, CJ kissed her hair. His finger swept forward, between her legs, and lashed her wet folds. "Of course, that's the point of this all, isn't it?"

"Oh, yeah."

"Then I'm sure you won't mind me getting started now. What's next?" he asked on a breathy tone.

"That's everything. We need to smudge the circle with this and— Oh. Oh, that's…mmm-hmm…"

"Bend," he whispered.

Vika obeyed his command, spreading her arms to

the sides along the wood worktable and bringing her head forward over the mortar fragrant with vanilla and herbs. She tilted her hips, seeking his expert control. "Oh, mercy, Certainly."

He unzipped his jeans and hugged up against her derriere, sliding a hand around in front to tickle her sensual folds. She pressed a hand over his hip. "No, we can't. We have to conserve the sexual energy for the spell."

"Right." He stroked her faster, wetting his fingers deep within her. "Just getting us ready. You're so wet, I don't know if I can wait. We ready? Damn, this short skirt!"

He tugged her upright and kissed her passionately. Vika felt all the man's frustrations unloose in that kiss. It was rough and needy, and unstoppable. He wanted her now. His body shuddered with restrained control. She took secret delight in owning the power over him.

"I think we're ready." He set his glasses on the table and snagged the whiskey bottle. "Grab the mortar."

He'd poured a wide salt circle earlier, in the north corner of the living area, which sat before the floor-to-ceiling windows. The circle was big enough for a couch to fit inside. Or two people.

Or one very angry demon.

"Don't break the circle," Vika said, cautioning him as they stepped inside. She set the mortar by the tote bag she'd brought along and ensured the remote for the chandeliers was tucked in the couch cushion where she'd left it. Within arm's reach. "Light the candles."

CJ had placed six red candles around the circle, and now with a snap of his finger, he ignited them in succession. Simple parlor trick, not fire magic, unfortunately. "You coming down from that hot, slippery passion, sweetie?"

She hugged him from behind, grabbing his crotch and giving it a good squeeze. "Not even."

Blowing whiskey-tainted breath toward the final candle, he sent a stream of flame spraying out from the wick. "Let's do this, oh, Torturous One."

They stepped inside the circle, and CJ unzipped his pants.

"Take them off," she said, stepping before him and trailing a finger she'd dipped into the vanilla emulsion along the waistband. A shift of his hips slid the loose jeans down. His marvelous, thick shaft sprang up, ready for her touch. Looking over his body, decorated with tattoos, a literal map of spellcraft, Vika then took hold of his hard-on and led him to the center of the circle. "Take off my dress."

"At your command." He did so, while she maintained a firm grasp of him. She wanted to keep her subject close, and also the control she felt in holding him would aid in the spell's efficacy and her confidence.

"If this works," he said, "and we come together, the demon should be expelled into the circle. We both jump out. Then you have to send it to Daemonia."

Yes. That was the part she knew wouldn't work. Why? Because she'd never ousted a demon from this realm before, and she wasn't confident she could without years of study. Her spell required something else, a more intimate connection that would seduce the demon and thus allow her control over it.

CJ reached outside the circle and took a pull from the whiskey bottle. Vika touched his wet lips and tasted it on her fingers. He, in turn, dipped his fingers into the mortar of scented potion and then trailed his finger over her skin, riding the rise of her breast and moving up along her neck. He dashed his forefinger over her lips, opening her mouth and slicking his finger in along her tongue. She licked him, beginning the process of surrender to the sensual, the magical and opening themselves to one another.

Hell, whom was she kidding? That process had started the moment he'd first kissed her, and she hadn't come down from the wanting, sexual high since.

"You're my girl," he whispered against her mouth. "Bright red light that shines upon my darkness. Never felt so right than with you, Viktorie. So right."

What they shared did feel right, even when it was so wrong.

Beneath the eerily bright storm of suspended chandelier crystals, they knelt before each other and clasped hands. The Latin words they chanted had been scribed through the centuries. There were only a few, but that was all they needed. It was the intonation and the rhythm that defined the atmosphere and opened it to their combined magic.

Arms raised and fingers entwined, they bowed their foreheads to one another. Certainly kissed her and whispered, *"It sil heve."* It will happen.

Dark and fervent, CJ groped her body roughly, mov-

ing his palms all over her skin. The electric hum of
the tattoos on his hand ignited her nerve endings. The
rhythm of their chant beat through her veins, setting
a musical tone to their breaths, their desire, their intentions.

On their knees before one another, she stroked his
erection against her belly. Their bodies grew slick with
perspiration and desire. Vika's chants slowed as her
mind dallied with riding the pleasure and concentration upon the task. She could master this spell and
her lover at the same time. Stroking, squeezing and
pulling his hardness produced an agonizingly wanting moan from CJ.

He bent to suckle her breasts, the tug-lick-nip of his
mouth to her skin coaxing her senses wide to receive.
The heat of the surrounding candle flames danced
through her pores. Attar of roses and rue scented their
gasps, and Tunisian vanilla glided in the wake of seeking fingers and mouths.

So close, she could feel her lover shuddering toward the edge, racing faster than she because, while
her body sung in harmony to CJ's melody, she had
split her focus.

She must not risk failure.

And when his neck tightened and his biceps grew
hard, he gasped and slammed his hips against hers.
Vika reached for the remote, and as CJ cried out in
orgasm, she switched the chandeliers off.

# *Chapter 14*

Vika stepped out of the circle and waited as CJ, bent over and huffing from the ecstasy of their communion, slowly lifted his head—and growled at her. His lascivious gaze was red and without light.

"Come to me, witch," he said on a tone that rattled the air as if a death knell.

"Who are you?"

"I am…" He slapped a hand on the floor as he crawled forward, but, wary of the salt, he stopped, hissed and sat on his haunches, displaying a proud erection. "Want."

Nice. She'd snagged one that could be controlled, hopefully, with sex.

The demon in control of CJ rubbed a palm down his abdomen, yet hissed when his hand crossed over one of the tattoos for which Vika had no idea of its power.

"Come." He gestured with his tattooed hand, and Vika's skin tingled with anticipation. He could make her skin hum with but a touch of those fingers. But she must remember she was dealing with a demon, not her whiskey-and-vanilla-scented lover.

She walked around the circle, knowing the pale moonlight glanced off her sweat-glistened skin. "I want you to look at me first. To feel desire. You say you are Want?"

"I am Want. I need. I crave."

"What of me? You're so greedy. Have you no care to pleasing me?"

"I will fulfill all your needs, red witch. It is Want's desire to see you writhe in ecstasy. Return to the circle and I will show you desires you cannot imagine. The feeble dark witch I occupy knows nothing about pleasing a woman."

She would stand to argue that point, but…not with a demon.

The only writhing she wanted to see was CJ's body as it released the demon. But she had to keep the demon in the mood and sexually jacked up in order to catch it unawares. "Let me watch you satisfy yourself."

CJ grimaced and chuckled lowly. Vika had to remind herself it may have her lover's face and body, but it was demon through to the core, or in fact, the very soul.

The demon stroked his erection, wet with his release, his wicked gaze not leaving hers. She held his stare as she backed to the couch and sat, spreading her legs and fluttering her fingers over her folds but not touching.

She had to control the demon carefully. And really, she was not feeling any pleasure at this moment, yet she had to make it look good.

"Yes, touch yourself, red witch." He stroked faster.

"I thought you were the one who intended to satisfy me?" She cupped her breasts and squeezed the nipples, moaning at the soft pain heightened by the previous make-out session with her lover that had rendered her achy.

"You won't let me out. I have to do things this way. Alone, so alone. There. Yes. Squeeze harder, witch. I want to see you squirm upon the couch."

"I need you inside me," she gasped, feeling the instinctual pull for the satisfaction CJ's touch promised.

*Not CJ. Don't forget!* She glanced down to ensure the tapestry bag was at hand's reach.

Springing up, Vika approached the circle and leaned over her frantically stroking demon. "Do you wish to be inside me, Want?"

He nodded furiously.

She dragged a foot over the salt circle, opening it, and then quickly stepped back to sit on the couch, slipping the knife from the tote as she did so and tucking it between the cushions.

The demon sprang upon her, bold, erect and fierce. He shoved her shoulders back and spread her legs. Not so rough, he actually maintained a touch of gentility, which gave her pause. Could CJ be aware inside? He would hate her for this trick.

"Love the dark," he growled. "Will give you my special darkness."

With no reluctance he entered her, and she thought it felt hotter, harder, fiercer than ever. Vika dragged her fingernails across his back as he began to thrust over and over.

*It is CJ. My lover. No other.*

Yet the growls were demonic, not of this realm. Otherworldly.

Biting her lip, Vika clung to the man, determination fixing her to the goal.

CJ paused above her, his jaw tight, and then cried out, the goal of orgasm achieved.

Vika dragged the knife across her palm then slashed it over the demon's chest. Now she did not consider this was CJ's flesh. The demon did not notice as it thrust inside her, bleeding the last waves of orgasm into its body. She slapped her palm to the open cut and recited the expulsion spell, and followed with a forceful, "Begone!"

The demon tilted his head down over her and growled, "Bitch."

Shoulders racked backward, CJ's body flew off hers and landed on its back, sprawled across the salt circle. He moaned in pain and gripped his chest, coiling forward to clutch the bloody wound.

Gripping the cushions, Vika breathed out heavily, her heartbeats thundering. She leaned forward, panting, waiting. Had it worked? Was her lover lying on the floor, or had she unloosed a dangerous demon to this realm? The salt circle was broken. It could escape—

Remembering her plan, she quickly flicked the lights on. Thousands of blinding lights, red, green, amber and violet, danced across her bare stomach. Crystals tinkled. A candle hissed out in a curl of smoke.

CJ moaned as if burned by the brilliance and tucked his head toward his chest.

After long moments of tense waiting, she dared to approach the prone witch. His chest heaved. His fingers grasped the floor. Certainly swung his gaze at her. "What happened? Did it work? Why are you—?" He touched his penis, finding the sticky remnants of his pleasure. "Did we?" And then he slapped a palm over his bleeding chest. "Vika?"

"I had to do it that way. We could have never contained the demon otherwise. I didn't think I could exorcise the demon within unless I let it out and controlled it."

He rubbed his bloody fingers together. "You let it out? Who? Which one?"

"Want."

"Fuck." He beat his chest and growled at her, "You had sex with a demon."

"I had sex with you, CJ."

"But I don't remember it all. I don't think… Why can't I? You fucked the demon? You lured it out. We had agreed not to take it this route. You never told me—" He spied the remote in her hand. "Vika, did you plan this?"

She nodded, sucking in the edge of her lip. Guilt quickly replaced the elation she had felt to find her lover responsive and, seemingly, of his mind. "It's gone though, right? It worked?"

He nodded in agreement, but slowly, unsure and

definitely not on the same page as her. Touching the cut on his chest, Vika saw it had already healed. Scar tissue gleamed beneath the line of smeared crimson.

"I wasn't in control," he said. "It was the demon with whom you had sex. You could have been hurt. Or worse."

Yes, worse. Yet she hadn't allowed herself to go there while in the midst of the wicked seduction. It would have weakened her. Rendered her unsuccessful. "But I wasn't hurt."

He brushed the salt off his thigh with an absent gesture. Looking at her, he waved an accusing finger. "You should have told me your plan. I would have never allowed you to do this."

"Exactly." She sat up straight, not about to cower at his tantrum. "That's why I couldn't tell you. You should be thankful. Another demon is gone from you. Doesn't that please you in the least?"

"To know you risked your life? No, I am not pleased." He swept up to kneel before her and clasped her wrists, gently, pleadingly. "You could have been hurt. What if it hadn't been Want but something like War?"

"I would have never let War out of the circle. I'm not an idiot." She struggled to pull from his grasp, but he held firmly.

"Vika." He pressed his forehead to her knuckles then looked at her. "I would walk the world with all the demons inside me to keep them away from you. To keep you clean. I don't want you touched by their evil. Please, you have to understand that."

She did understand that. And she wasn't feeling guilty for the heck of it. The sacrifice had to be made. The plan had worked. But she could not count it as a success. "Sorry."

"This can't happen again. I can't allow it."

She stroked the hair along his cheek. "I did it because I care about you."

Shaking his head, he bowed it before her. "If you knew the things I had done, you wouldn't care so much about me."

Twining her fingers through his long hair, she wanted to brush it aside her cheek, take it into her mouth, but she daren't. "We've all done things we regret."

Like right now. Regret was a bitter taste upon her tongue, and she wanted to purge it. It felt murky and evil, as if she had dragged her tongue across CJ's infested soul. By the goddess, was she taking on his darkness?

"I don't regret going to Daemonia," he said. "Nor do I regret the things I did to get there. It was necessary evil."

She couldn't imagine a reason to venture into the place of all demons, to risk his life. And for what? This must be the secret he'd been unwilling to divulge to her earlier. "Tell me?"

"I can't. I won't. Put your clothes on."

He stood and wandered off to the closet behind the bed, leaving his final words an abrupt command that bruised her without touching her skin.

Vika pulled the purple dress over her head and

tugged it down. This had gone over not at all as she had planned. She'd expected his gratitude, not anger. Apparently the man's morals were much less murky than she had thought.

Truly, had she taken a turn toward the dark? And meanwhile, was Certainly traveling toward the light?

*I can't. I won't.*

What he had done must have been truly evil if he could not reveal his motives behind the quest to Daemonia.

He lingered near the bed, dressing slowly, and she got the distinct impression he didn't want to talk. Suddenly chilled, Vika stuffed her things in the tote bag and slipped on her shoes. The mess of salt and the guttered red candles called to her urge for order, but more than that, she felt she was not welcome.

"I need to go," she said, and as she walked toward the door, tears came to her eyes because he didn't ask her to stay.

## Chapter 15

When the door closed with an abrupt click, CJ sighed. He shouldn't have let her walk out like that. But he hadn't known what to say without raising his voice and going on a rant. Vika's actions hadn't jibed with who he thought she was. She'd lied to him.

Not exactly a lie. Worried she wouldn't be able to handle the interior exorcism, she hadn't divulged her complete plans for the spell.

"Not like you're much better, eh?" He tugged up his jeans then wandered over to the salt circle to assess the mess. "She did exorcise another demon."

The want demon. He knew War, Pain and Protection, along with a few others, were still inside, tittering at him. Laughing, because the weakest demons had gone and now the most powerful could use the space to garner strength.

Sitting on the couch and blowing out a breath, he picked up the remote that he'd programmed to switch all the chandeliers on or off with one press of a button. She'd known exactly what to do and when. The perfect means to exorcism—coax the demon to the fore and out of the protective circle—but so dangerous. Had War or Pain reared their heads, Vika would have been helpless against them.

*Against you. It is you who harbors the monsters. You are responsible for her safety.*

Shoving a hand over his hair, he tilted his head and growled at the constellation of prismatic light, which had become the ugliest thing in his life. He hated the colors, the riot of flashes, the constant minute tinkling. All he wanted was peace. Quiet.

Darkness. An utterly empty and demonless darkness.

And he wanted it with the beautiful red witch in his life.

"Want," he muttered, and smirked. "Even when you are gone, I still want."

He'd wanted many things in his lifetime. Some of those things he had taken, stolen, used nefarious means to obtain, but none had he ever wanted so that he felt the need in his very bones. In his soul. Yes, that writhing nest of twisted demons and darkness occupying his soul. It wanted Viktorie St. Charles.

Was it the demons who desired her, so they could toy with her, play with her, torture her?

No. He felt real desire. In fact, CJ believed he loved her.

And how dare he—him, the witch who had traveled

to Daemonia to steal only to keep something away from another witch—even think he could stand beside Vika as an equal and deserve her love in return?

Libby popped her head through the bedroom doorway and gaped at Vika, who lay across her bed, arms stretched high over her head and fingers toying with the cream lace edging the pillow sham.

"What?" Vika asked.

"Your shoes are on the floor."

"So?" Vika winced at the bright streetlight beaming through the window.

Upon arriving home, she had wanted to sweater herself within the sheets and sleep away the night. She'd gotten this far, but she had expected Libby to pop a curious nose into her room sooner rather than later.

"They're in the middle of the floor, toppled, as if tossed there…" Libby paused dramatically, and then said, "Haphazardly."

"What are you getting at, Libby?"

"What's wrong with you?" Her sister climbed onto the bed and leaned over Vika's face, her hair spilling over a shoulder. Pink polka dots danced about her white retro dress cinched with a smart plastic pink buckle. "You have a filing system in the closet. Shoes must be immediately put away so as not to cause trippage. You taught me that yourself. And you're wearing my dress. What in the goddess's shampoo?"

"You said I could," she muttered defensively.

"I did, but I didn't think you were taking this one. The short one. Vika, you never wear short stuff. You say it's unladylike. That the tease is much better the less they see. Oh, mercy, I think the dark witch has put a spell on you."

She pressed the back of her hand to Vika's forehead, as they often teasingly did. It certainly wasn't a way to determine bewitchment.

Vika smiled and coiled toward her sister. "It's true. He has bewitched me, bold and bright."

"You know it for sure?"

She nodded. "I lied to CJ because I've fallen under his spell. Tricked him with the bloodsexmagic spell."

"Oh, hell. You never lie. And you smell like whiskey and vanilla. Merciful goddess, what kind of trouble are you in, Vika? We'll have to reverse his dark bewitchery. We can do that. I just have to—"

"You'll do nothing." Vika clasped her sister's hand and squeezed. "I'm in love, Libby. Despite his probably never wanting to speak to me again after what I did to him hours earlier, I love Certainly Jones."

"Love? Huh. What did you do? The sex magic? How did it go?"

"I exorcised another demon by seducing it and letting it have sex with me."

Libby's mouth dropped open. "You had sex with a demon?"

"It was Certainly's body, but…"

"Oh, my goddess." Libby plopped onto her back, and they lay staring up at the ceiling, shoulders hugging. "My sister is screwing demons."

"One demon. And it wasn't in demonic form. It was CJ. For the most part."

"But a demon controlled his body. Oh, mercy me."

"Libby, don't get all worked up over it. I'm safe, and I was never in danger. It had to be done. For him. Because I love him."

"Well, it's a kick, isn't it? Love?"

"Oh, yeah."

"There's probably something I should tell you."

Vika waited, sensing what her sister would reveal.

"I'm in love with the soul bringer."

"I know that."

"Yeah, I'm kind of an open grimoire, aren't I? But I had a thought the other day about Reichardt. You know he's been alive for millennia, and he's emotionless. And I suspect all he does is ferry souls all day, every day. Day and night."

"That is what soul bringers do."

"Right, but, I don't think he's ever gone on a date."

"Most likely he's never had the time."

"Yes, but what I'm getting at is…" Libby rolled to her side and Vika did, too. Her sister's eyes were a lighter shade of green than hers, and freckles danced upon her nose. "Vika, I think Reichardt is a virgin. He has to be."

"Your mind goes to weird places, freckled one."

"I know, right? I'm in love with a two-thousand-year-old virgin. Can it get any worse?"

"I think that is the pinnacle of worse. But look at it this way. He could be so teachable."

"You think?"

No, she did not think, but she didn't want to make it any worse than it already was for her sister. The soul bringer wasn't a man in the sense of the word. He wasn't dating material. "You taught him to like cookies."

"I did!" Rolling to her back again, Libby hugged herself. Her sister's optimistic view of the world never failed to infect Vika's sullen moods and lift them. Just a bit this time.

"So you're in love with a virgin," Vika tossed out there.

"And you're in love with a demon-infested dark witch whose idea of clean is giving the sheets a shake once a week."

"His sheets are clean. Bamboo, actually. So soft and snuggly, especially when he lays with his back against mine. Mmm, the man is hot. Anyway, we did it on the couch last night."

"Yeah, you and his demon."

She closed her eyes, and an inward cringe was her reward. She never should have gone the sneaky route. CJ had not been able to look her in the eye, and his body language had spoken loudly he'd wanted her to stay away from him. She deserved his hate. Well, not his hate. Perhaps mild disgust, distrust surely, but never hate.

How to win him back?

Did she want to win him? After the many times his demons had tormented her, she should have been allowed that moment of defeating one of them, no matter the method to success.

Yes, she wanted her dark, wicked witch. Because in

his embrace, she felt right, as if his arms were the only place other than her home she should be.

Yet what had he done? What CJ couldn't tell her, she wanted to know. She couldn't avoid thinking about that detail he didn't want her to have. It was dark and evil, she suspected.

*Don't think about it.* Yeah, right. Now the thought would never leave her mind.

If she could get a few more cleanup jobs she could grab a bunch of souls and—well, she didn't know how to utilize the souls once they'd stuck to hers. CJ had to actually be there, ready to take a soul before it entered hers.

This was a complicated mess. And for sure, he'd never let her attempt the bloodsexmagic on him again. Not that she wanted to. She had had sex with a demon. What was she becoming?

She tilted a look to her sister and found the same bewildered look reflected back at her.

"I know," Libby said on a sigh. "What are we going to do?"

The vacuum cleaner rumble set the clouds of crystals to a mad sort of rain dance as CJ moved about the loft, pushing it into long-forgotten corners and collecting his abandoned clothing along the way. He wasn't sure what had gotten into him, but the place had needed a good going-over.

By afternoon, he'd dusted every surface, organized his spell table and even alphabetized the spell cards and the herbarium. He'd found a missing snakeskin boot and tugged it on to admire it alongside its match. A feather duster had reached only the bottoms of the chandeliers, so he'd performed an air spell to dust the crystals from ceiling beams down to the smallest crystal. When finished, the loft beamed brilliantly.

Too brightly for his taste, but surely this would only aggravate his demons all the more.

Fixing himself a frozen cheese pizza in the microwave, he mused that he'd let his diet slack since his return. Normally, he made everything fresh. He was hungry and hadn't gone shopping for days. Should probably head out for groceries before the sun set. But his thoughts, now the cleaning had been done, took a sharp turn toward her.

He hadn't called Vika. Hadn't dared to go over to her round white house and clatter on the shiny brass knocker. He knew he must be the one to make the first move. And he knew what that move involved.

The truth. The whole truth and all its devious details.

He glanced to the item lying in plain view on his kitchen counter. Plain only to him. The cloaking spell surrounding it was the most powerful magic to his arsenal, and no one, not even the demons within him, could see it sitting there. Vika had stood right beside it more than a few times and hadn't sensed its presence.

He held his hand over the bone whistle but retracted from picking it up. The truth was going to wrench out his heart and drop it on the floor before Vika's pretty little feet in a macabre splatter. Witches required a beating heart once a century to maintain their immortality, which must come from a vampire. *The source,* as the unfortunate vamp was called by witches. Vika would take one look at his dark and disgusting heart and wouldn't want to sweep it into her bin. She'd run from it, metaphorical as the whole scenario was.

And that kept CJ at home through the evening, safe beneath the prismatic light, sorting through his herbs and tossing out the old stuff in order to avoid the vicious truth.

Ian Grim stared up at the dusty chandelier laden with black crystals. Why did it compel him so? He'd been sitting here beneath the massive structure for hours, his mind unable to grasp anything but the bedamned light fixture.

It meant something. He just didn't know what that something was. So much so, he'd been compelled into this ancient mansion, which now served as a museum, and had snuck beyond security into this private bedchamber.

"Certainly Jones," he muttered. "I will not let you get the better of me this time. I am so close. So close!"

He reached and was able to tap the lowest-hanging crystal. It caught the sunlight and flashed in his eye.

"You are not untouchable. If I have to go through your brother, Thoroughly, I will."

Pouring out a measure of safflower petal onto a crisp sheet of parchment, Vika referred to her spellbook for the correct measurement.

She had agreed with Libby for once and hadn't

called CJ this morning. Sometimes the man had to step up and make things right. And wasn't absence supposed to make the heart grow fonder?

"Not if his heart is angry with what I've done." She sighed, and the exhalation drifted the airy bits of safflower across the white paper and into a random scatter.

Studying the scattered bits, she utilized a form of tasseomancy, tea leaf reading, which was Libby's forte. Skilled enough, Vika muddled over the flower petals' design. And what she saw clenched the muscles about her heart and stole her breath.

"Libby!"

Her sister scrambled into the room, a spatula laden with raw cookie dough in hand. "What? Did you burn yourself? I told you waterfiremagic was tricky stuff."

"It's not that. What do you read in this?"

Libby carefully approached the counter and looked over the strewn safflower petals. She clasped a fist to her chest. A gob of cookie dough spilled down her befringed apron. "Oh, my goddess. A warlock? What does that mean? Do you think it's CJ?"

"I don't know. He would have had to commit a grave crime against the Light to be deemed warlock. Oh, Libby, he's been keeping something from me. Something dark. He says he can't tell me about it." The sisters hugged. "What is CJ involved in?"

# Chapter 16

CJ rang the doorbell. It tinkled as if a faery making her appearance in some silver-screen cartoon. Appropriate for this white round house in which lived two gorgeous red-haired witches. Checking the bouquet of yellow roses in hand, he inhaled the crisp fruity scent. They were miniroses, which gave him a smile. He'd never seen the like, and the froth of gay, tiny petals seemed the much-needed prelude for what he had to do today.

After all the rain they'd gotten the past few days, the sun hung high in the sky and the air was humid. No thunderclouds in the forthcoming days, according to his senses or the weatherman on the television who used fancy gadgets to forecast what CJ could do with a little attention to his elbows.

The door opened and Libby's effusive smile slipped from her face. "Oh. You."

Feeling the derelict, CJ sucked in a breath. He hadn't expected this visit to be easy. "Is your sister home?"

Libby stepped aside to allow him to enter.

"Sit there." She pointed to the white leather couch then stood before him, hands akimbo, looking him over.

The cat jumped onto his lap and curled its tail beneath CJ's chin. He didn't think shoving it off would make him look good in the sister's disapproving eyes.

"Ex-boyfriend, eh? How did he get like this?"

"A warlock did it to him," Libby said with no humor at all. "You know anything about warlocks, dark witch?"

"I, er…" What was she getting at? "No?"

"Uh-huh."

Fingers playing with the coiled nail at her throat, she made show of giving him the mongoose eye, and CJ felt the stab at his kidney as if she'd really done it. So the witch wielded psychological magic. Good for her.

"Yes, good for me. And no, I can't read minds, but your face is a pitiful chalkboard of all your sins. Vika is out in the garden. You sit tight, and I'll go find her."

CJ stood. "If she's in the garden, I can go out."

"Not with those pitiful bits of unnaturally dyed flowers, you're not."

He looked over the bouquet. Dyed? "I thought your sister would like them."

Libby rolled her eyes. "Yellow for apology. Oh, you

poor misdirected, lovesick fool." She inclined her head forward. "Are you lovesick?"

He nodded, offering a wincing smile. "I am."

Libby's heavy sigh combined mistrust with empathy. "Best to leave you to your own devices then. Through the kitchen and out the double doors. Don't touch the windows in the doors. I just cleaned them. If I see your fingerprints on the glass, I will hit you with some painful magic right below the belt."

"All righty, then."

"Wait."

He stood frozen, not daring to move.

Libby sidled closer, her eyes glowering over him appraisingly. "Did you bewitch my sister?"

"Purposefully? No, I would never employ such tactics."

"Yeah, I'm not so sure about that. I can't figure a reason my sister would fall for a guy like you."

"She's fallen for me?"

"Dude, my sister does not sleep with just any man. Especially not someone like..." Another sigh. "You. She's got to feel something for him, you know?"

"I think I do know that. I didn't bewitch her, Libby. Promise."

The tension was thick enough to swim through, and CJ made haste through the kitchen and away from the Window Gestapo, being careful to touch only the silver door handle and not the glass, which gleamed like the crystals suspended from his chandelier collection.

He stepped out into a lush garden that put his pitiful dyed roses to shame. Flipping the bouquet around behind his back, he stepped down the limestone steps in his recently paired boots and took the path beneath a wrought-iron pergola frilled with violet passion flowers. The yellow stamens stuck out their tongues at him as he passed beneath. Foolish witch and his stupid flowers, they whispered on the wind.

He passed by pennisetum, hydrangea, mugwort and various mints. The fragrance intoxicated. He could sit on the stone bench, eyes closed, and name each flower by smell. As part of his magical education, he'd studied botany. A wise witch knew all plants and flora to utilize in his spells.

To his right a red glass witch ball hung suspended above white heliotrope. Hoping to catch some insect souls?

Spreading his free hand over the tops of the snowy queen's lace growing waist-high along the path, he angled on the cobblestones and spied Vika's long black skirts. Garnet hair pulled neatly in a long braid gleamed under the sunlight. Always in need of a muss.

Except yesterday. She'd come dressed to seduce. Why hadn't he picked up on that right away?

Didn't matter now. Whatever her intentions had been, she had in mind only to help him. He was thankful for that. And he'd gotten over his pouty anger over her not telling him the whole truth before they'd engaged in the spell.

Vika stood, a clasp of silvery seathorn in hand, and smiled softly at him.

That unexpected smile warmed his heart. It had been a day since he'd seen her. It felt like forever.

"Viktorie," he said, failing at every kind of sweet and meaningful hello he could summon. He kept the miniroses tucked behind his back. "You're a bright flower among the rest."

She tilted her head and crossed her arms over her chest. Not about to make this easy, despite the lingering smile. But the seathorn nettles could sting his skin with a simple brush. He imagined she could do the same if he spoke incorrectly.

"I've come to apologize. It was awful of me to say those things to you after you had exorcised another demon at the risk to your life. I appreciate what you did for me. I'm sorry."

Her smile grew as she accepted the apology with a nod. "I'm sorry for being deceptive. That wasn't me yesterday. And yet, it was."

"You had to do it on the sly. I wouldn't have allowed it if I had known."

"Still, I should have discussed it with you. From now on, no more hiding truths. I promise and vow upon my grandmother's memory." She touched the nail at her throat.

"Me, too. Concealing truth is as bad as a lie."

"If that is so, then what do you have behind your back?"

"Nothing." He shrugged. "Ah, hell." He held forth the pitiful offering. "I picked them up in the supermarket on the way here. They are weeds compared with your gorgeous garden. Just thought they'd look pretty in your hair."

She accepted the flowers and brought them to her

nose. Eyes closed and mouth slightly open, she drew in their fragrance, as artificial as it may be. Drawing her nail down the stems, she snapped off the head of one yellow rose and handed it to him.

CJ pressed the stem into the silken depths of her hair. "Another," he said. She handed him another rose, and he placed it next to the other until all had been crowded into the tightly combed braid. He took out one and crushed it between his forefingers, then rubbed the oil behind her ear and dared to trace it between her breasts. "I anoint you Diva of the Dahlias, and Grand High Priestess of My Heart."

"I accept your offering, dark one, and promise I will not again use deception to chase out your demons." Then she cracked a smile and kissed him. "I missed you."

"I thought you'd hate me."

"I wasn't pleased with your reaction, but I can put myself in your position and understand. But one less demon is better than not."

"For sure. I'm not finished apologizing yet. I need to give you my truth. It can't be right between us until I do that."

"What truth?"

"Let's sit." He gestured to the bench beneath the stone grotto near a koi pond that wept thick vines frilled with gold and tangerine honeysuckle.

She joined him on the bench and slid her hand into his, which was a good sign. Their combined magics hummed through his veins as if a natural reaction. But now the tough part. The necessary evil.

"Must be dark indeed if you're so worried about it," she offered. "I don't think there's much more you can say or show me that can be worse than harboring an infestation of demons."

Yeah? This truth was going to blow that out of the water.

CJ took Vika's hands in his, so elegant and graceful. She could master all magics with these delicate fingers. Just as he opened his mouth, they heard a scream from inside the house.

"Libby?" Vika dashed down the garden path, her long skirts held near her thighs.

"Saved by the scream," CJ muttered, and followed her inside.

He'd been close to confession, and now that he'd been granted reprieve, the relief felt immense. Maybe he hadn't been so ready to reveal his selfish deed after all.

They found Libby kneeling on the gleaming black-and-white-tiled kitchen floor, bent over a sprawled man in dark clothing.

"The soul bringer?" CJ wandered around the man's long body. "Is he dead?"

"I don't think so," Libby said frantically. "He suddenly appeared!"

"He's not breathing," Vika noted.

"He never breathes. He doesn't need to. He's angelic by origin. Oh, Vika, I was pouring myself a glass of orange juice, and—bam! What do you think happened?"

"Crash landing?" Vika tried. "He isn't due to scrub me for days."

"Shake him awake," CJ directed.

All of a sudden, a flurry of brightness wafted up from the soul bringer's chest. The corpse lights danced as if dandelion kites on the breeze.

"Souls," CJ said in wonder.

"Yes." Vika stood over the soul bringer. "I don't know why they're coming out of him, but I've got to catch them. Save them for him."

She held out her arms and lifted her chest to receive the fluttery souls. A few wobbled toward her.

"Vika?" CJ tried. He shouldn't, but—there were so many. And how many times would they be granted such opportunity?

"Oh, yes! Xum!" She swept her hand toward him and blasted him with air magic, catching a corpse light in the path.

The force of impact slammed CJ against the wall. He cried out as the brightness moved through him and he felt a demon exit his soul. Chaos, surely. "Another?" she said, and again sent a soul through him.

"Vika, I'm not sure," Libby started. "Reichardt could be in pain. He won't come to!"

Vika blasted CJ with two more souls. Protection and another demon were sucked to Daemonia. He grasped for hold against the wall but slipped down, landing on the floor, and his head wobbled forward. "No more," he muttered. "Enough." Heaving, he panted at the exertion the exorcism had required.

"Now, to make sure I don't lose any of them." Vika moved about the kitchen, pursuing the phosphorescent lights, both the ones straight from Reichardt and those she'd moved through CJ.

Libby pulled up one of Reichardt's eyelids. "He's in there. I don't think he's dead. This is so weird."

"I think I have them all," Vika declared.

CJ observed, because he could not move, so taxed were his muscles. Vika's skirts swept over his boot-tips, and a trail of tiny yellow roses scattered in her wake as she went to kneel by her sister.

"Let's get the poor guy off the floor. Carry him into the living room and lay him on the couch. CJ?"

"I'll be right there." He pushed to stand but fell forward onto his palms. The muscles in his arms trembled as if he'd been lifting weights for hours. Damn, that had taken a lot out of him. "Give me a minute."

"We can do this. Libby, take his feet. I've got his shoulders." Together they recited, "Atollo" for *lift,* and the prone man's body was made lighter.

The sisters carried the soul bringer through the swinging kitchen doors, while CJ pulled himself up by the counter. A smile overtook him. He'd lost another three demons. Unfortunately, one had been Protection. Despite whatever had happened to the soul bringer, it had been remarkable timing. Still didn't excuse him from telling Vika his secret.

"When I'm more able," he whispered. Whew! Felt as though he'd run a marathon. Staggering through the swinging doors, he wandered into the living room, where the women had arranged the motionless soul bringer on the couch.

Libby was frantic. "Maybe he hit his head? He could be in a coma!"

"He's not bleeding."

"Do soul bringer's bleed?"

They both looked to CJ, but all he could do was shrug. "I don't know. Don't angels have blue blood? But he's not really angel now, he's more…I don't know." He steadied himself against the wall from a wave of dizziness. "Whew! That exorcism took a lot out of me. I need to lie down. Vika, can we talk later?"

"Of course, you were going to tell me something. You feel all right?"

"Weak but elated." He kissed her. "Thank you for having the mind to think of me just now. Three more gone."

"Glad to do it. Yes, you go home and rest. I'm going to help Libby figure out what's up with Reichardt. Can I come over later?"

"I'll be waiting for you."

"I hope not. Get some rest, because I'll have plans for you when I get there."

"That's my wicked witch."

On the way home, CJ got a text from his brother, Thoroughly. When he arrived at home, TJ stood by his door, arms crossed and hair pulled away from his face with a leather strap that queued down his back. His twin and he were identical, though TJ was more stylish and tended toward extroversion. But adventure was all CJ's mien.

"You don't look so good, brother," TJ said as they entered the loft.

"Just had a bunch of demons blasted out of me. Takes a lot out of a guy."

"You found someone to exorcise the demons?" TJ slapped him on the back. "Good going!"

Beelining for the kitchen, CJ poured himself a glass of water from the tap and drank the whole thing before asking his brother why he was there.

"I had a visit from Ian Grim."

CJ set the glass down hard. "Why would that bastard go to you?"

"Apparently, he doesn't know your new address. You've warded the hell out of this place. A Russian spy satellite couldn't find it."

CJ glanced to the bone whistle lying on the counter, shielded from his brother's eyes. Spy satellites, indeed. And thinking of Russians... He'd hated leaving Vika so quickly, and with the problem of the soul bringer, but she and her sister could manage it.

"So you decided to come over here and show Grim the way?"

"I'm not stupid," TJ said. "I cloaked my steps. But you, brother, have some explaining to do. Seems Grim is upset over something you took from Daemonia. Something he wants."

Pacing beneath the glitter of chandeliers, CJ winced. He hadn't opportunity to tell Vika, so the universe was forcing it out of him now, one way or another. He splayed out his hands. "I couldn't let Grim get it. You know we've been rivals for ages."

"So this is some sort of power play? What did you take, CJ? And is it going to threaten the world as we know it?"

CJ shrugged. "A small portion of it, I'm sure. But I'd never use the thing. I wanted it out of Grim's hands. You know."

"To show up Grim. Hell, Certainly Amadeus Jones, you can never seem to get beyond the selfish streak forged like tarnished brass through your blood. What is it?"

With a sigh, CJ shoved his hands in his pockets and confessed, "The call to the Nacht März."

Thoroughly's expression dropped to a cold gape of awe, and the witch invoked a deity he did not subscribe to. "God help us."

## Chapter 17

Vika handed Libby a cup of chamomile tea, which was steeped with fennel the way she preferred it. Her sister sipped yet held her vigil positioned on the couch arm, above Reichardt's thick crop of midnight hair. She stroked her fingers down his cheek and over his goateed chin.

Nothing wrong with unrequited love, Vika figured. As long as Libby didn't abandon all hope for other men. Real men whose hearts beat and were not made of glass. Men who could return her love with open arms and kisses.

She sighed, and Libby followed suit with a bigger sigh.

"He's going to be okay," Libby said, though her tone belied such belief. "Do we still have the compendium of the paranormal breeds?"

"Possibly. You want me to find it? Yes, I will. It'll give you something to do while you're sitting shiva over the guy."

"Vika, he's not dead, and we're not Jewish."

"His heart isn't beating."

"It's glass. It can't beat."

"Uh-huh." Vika rose and wandered into the spell room. She located the book, which was thin but folio-size so it was an awkward carry, and laid it on the coffee table for Libby. "I was going to head over to CJ's, but if you need me here?"

"No, there's nothing you can do. I've got him covered. I mean, you know."

"I know." She kissed her sister's forehead. "See you later. And if he wakes, give me a call. I'd like to know how he's feeling when he comes to, and the reason he's here."

Vika took the stairs in CJ's building up. Her heart dropped when she tried the light switch and it didn't flicker on. It was afternoon—outside the sun shone—but the stairway was shadowed with no windows or other light sources.

"Doesn't mean anything," she said. "He's up in his loft. Safe under the light."

And then she heard the wretched sobbing echoing like a death mourn from deep within a freshly dug grave. Tugging up her long skirt, she hastened up two flights of stairs, along the way avoiding the broken glass from the shattered lightbulbs. She stumbled onto

CJ's prone form. He clasped her arms and pulled her down, clinging.

Falling into his embrace, she nuzzled her head against his hair, preparing to face whatever it was within him that had control of her lover. He hadn't lashed out at her and wasn't growling, so this one might not be such a trial.

"You are her," he said with a sniffle. "The one his wretched heart needs so desperately. But it is not to be. This one can never have happiness. Such mirth is only for dreamers and the bold."

"Oh, my dark one. Who are you?" she whispered.

"Grief," the demonic voice wailed out, burying his face against Vika's shoulder.

How to deal with grief? On the scale of emotions, Vika could relate to many, save this one. She'd never lost anyone close, nor had she experienced true tragedy. Her grandmother's nail hummed against her skin, reminding of her family's grief.

Perhaps she did know it.

"He's so dark, isn't he?" CJ muttered. "Darkness is better. Though, nothing is better, is it? It's all tragedy and misery. Where we belong. Not out there in the light. It's stifling there. Too bright. We've lost the light. We don't deserve it."

Certainly's body heaved, and he sighed a sigh for the worlds. Grieving his loss of the light, even while the demon thrived in the darkness.

"He's pined for the closeness you hold before him as if a tease. When he returned to this realm with us, he abandoned his hermit ways and began to seek more.

Something beyond his own selfish interests. Foolish witch. More will only result in sacrifice, and ultimately loss."

She wouldn't listen to what the demon said. It was forged from a deep emotion she couldn't imagine affecting Certainly. Yet the mention of loss frightened her. A sense of foreboding nodded its head.

The safflower petal reading had suggested a warlock had entered her life. Could it be Certainly? She hadn't opportunity to ask him, and still he had wanted to tell her something. She could not have a relationship with a witch who had broken the witch's rede. No matter how much she felt she knew CJ, if that were his confession, the game would be changed.

Best not to raise the subject until Grief was gone. Right now she had to get him into the light. The electricity wasn't out. The lobby had been lit. Someone—likely some demon—had knocked out all the bulbs. Four more flights to go.

"Walk with me," she said, surprised when CJ slid his arm into hers and did so. "Tell me your sorrows."

"I have so many."

They took the stairs, a funeral march to Vika's heart.

"I have seen it all. Death. Violence. Rage. Annihilation."

"I imagine so."

"You cannot imagine Daemonia, red witch."

"No, and I never wish to." The final staircase remained.

CJ paused. "If you wish to avoid grief you will walk away from us."

She kissed CJ and led him upward. "Never. He means too much to me. I love him."

"You shouldn't. You're a foolish witch."

"I happen to think I'm lucky." His front door was open, thank the goddess.

But before she could lead him over the threshold, CJ clutched her arm and shoved her against the wall. Taking her in, he swept his red eyes over her face, down her body. She didn't struggle because he was not rough, merely needy. She would give him what she could.

"I am made of him," CJ said. "I cannot exist without Certainly Jones."

An exhale spilled out Vika's sudden dread. "You mean you couldn't have hitched a ride in CJ without having already existed within him?"

"Exactly."

"But what has he to grieve?"

"Life. His family. Lost his parents long ago. Very violent that. They'd taken what he now possesses. Foolish witches."

"I didn't know," she said on a hush. "What does he possess?"

"Oh, no, witch, you won't get that from me. I cannot exist if he tells you his truth and shares his grief."

"Then you are good for him. You give his grief voice."

At that statement, CJ tilted his head in wonder. And Vika used the moment to catch him unawares and tug him across the threshold. She closed the door behind them and flicked on the lights. A blast of prismatic light swept the room, and CJ yelped as the demon re-

treated to the darkness of his soul. Stumbling against
the wall, he slid down, his legs sprawling across the
hardwood floor.

"That was misery," he muttered, gripping his hair
and pulling. "Hell." His body shaking, he wrapped his
arms across his chest, drawing up his legs. "I'm not
sure I can fight them much longer. It's draining me."

Vika's heart went out to him. Never had she seen
him so vulnerable. And yet Grief had voiced his heart-
ache. She drew him into her arms and kissed his head.
"It will be better, *cushlamocree*."

"That word. You said it to me once before. What
does it mean?"

"I think it's Irish. My mother used it when we sisters were sad or frightened. It calmed us."

He nodded. "I could feel my soul crumbling every
moment the demon held reign. My parents...they were
tortured by a mistake they made. I can't explain it completely. Yet you led me toward the light. Thank you."

"You thank me far too much, witch. Just doing what
had to be done. I can't begin to understand what you're
going through, but if I can soften the pain, I will."

"You do."

"Let's get up and make you some tea."

"Just give me a moment to enact a spell." He reached
to his left biceps and tapped one of the tattooed boxes,
muttering the Latin spell for—Vika recognized it—
peace and relaxation. Sort of like an aspirin spell. With
a sigh, he propped his elbows on his bent knees. "Better."

"How many left inside you?"

"As far as I can determine? War, Grief and Pain."

"Now that's a festive bunch."

He laughed and took her offered hand and stood. "How's your sister and the comatose soul bringer?"

"Holding vigil. I figured I could slip out for a bit. You had something you were going to tell me?"

"I do. And now that Grief has brought it up, I can no longer avoid the confession. Let's brew some peppermint tea for an open mind and truth."

The soul bringer suddenly sat upright. Libby scrambled up from the floor, where she'd been perusing the compendium. "Reichardt? Are you okay?"

"O…kay?" He nodded, looking around, taking in the living room surroundings, from the gleaming crystal chandelier to the white leather sofa and glass coffee table adorned with fresh daisies from the garden. "I landed *here?*"

"Yes, in our kitchen, actually. You freaked me out because you fell from out of nowhere. What happened?"

"Where is Viktorie St. Charles?"

"She's with CJ. Why? What's wrong? I don't understand what happened, Reichardt."

She wanted to pull him into a hug and smother him with kisses. He was back! But, much as her fingers slid closer to his hand, Libby knew better than to press the man with effusive displays of affection.

Reichardt rubbed his brow. His jaw muscle pulsed in a sexy way that caught her eye. "I was expelled from Above by His Most Highest."

"What? *The* Guy?"

"Yes." He cast his gaze about the room and to his lap, turning his hands over, as if he were still orienting himself. "Here?"

"You're still wondering why you landed here? Maybe you went the one place you most wanted to be?" she said with hope.

He nodded. It wasn't exactly an agreement. "During the expulsion I was only thinking to land someplace safe. Interesting."

"So why were you expelled?"

His kaleidoscope eyes fixed to hers, and Libby gasped as if fixed in the sight of a pistol. "Apparently, I've been ferrying tainted souls Above. I had no idea they were tainted. But now I understand. It is Viktorie's fault."

"What? No, she—" Libby closed her mouth.

Her sister had been using the souls to chase demons from CJ. And then she'd catch them and give them to Reichardt. Souls tainted by demon exorcism. Oh, great goddess, she could not let Reichardt find Vika.

"You want a cookie?"

Vika sipped the peppermint tea and then resumed the shoulder massage she'd insisted on giving CJ. He didn't protest overmuch, and it had been an excuse for him to remove his shirt. Not that she needed an excuse. But also, she wanted to relax him so they could talk. It had seemed he'd something dire to tell her out in the garden earlier. And Grief had intrigued her with hints of the secret. She wanted to make it easy for him now.

Sliding her hands down his back where the largest sak yant tattoo held court, she was surprised to find so much tension knotted in his muscles. And then she was not. While normally a witch was ultra-aware of his or her body, she assumed harboring demons would put any person's muscles—and soul—into a twist.

"I wish I could have exorcised Grief for you," she said.

He slid a hand over hers. "It'll happen. Come here." He pulled her onto his lap and kissed her. "I was fully present with Grief. I let it speak for me."

"You…? Certainly?" She touched his cheek, so warm and stubbly. "Do you want to talk about your parents?"

"There's not much to tell that you probably can't guess. Witch hunters got them early in the twentieth century. My brother and sister and I watched in horror as their bodies burned at the stake."

"Goddess," she whispered, pressing her cheek aside his bare shoulder and wrapping her arm across his chest.

"But not before they committed a grave crime against the Light by summoning something…evil."

She touched his thigh, reassuring him.

"I have strived for peace ever since." He settled against the couch. "Vika, before I went to Daemonia my life was a constant, unchanging force. I enjoyed my work at the archives and spent most hours of the day there, researching and studying magics I hadn't yet mastered. I've always been focused on improving my arsenal of the craft. To the detriment of a social life. My best friend, Lucian Bellisario, calls me Brother."

"Because the two of you are so close?"

"No. It's because I've led a monkish life. Especially regarding my social and sex life. I'd much rather hole up in the archives than hold a conversation or engage a woman in, well…" He sighed. A flick of his tattooed fingers made him smile. "I'm not a complete monk. But I've never had a relationship that lasted beyond a week. Nothing that could begin to broach an emotional connection. Nothing that touched my heart."

How sad. She couldn't imagine not engaging with others, even if only as friends. That truly was something to grieve. "Because of your parents?"

He sighed. "Perhaps. I've been afraid to establish a connection for fear it would be taken away from me. But since I've returned from Daemonia with a soul full of monsters, I've had a sort of mind adjustment. I don't want to be a monk. I want to enjoy life. I want to have a relationship. To know love. To know what it's like to have someone who cares for me and misses me when I'm gone."

"Everyone should experience that."

"But I've always set it aside."

"No more?"

He shook his head. "No more. And since I've opened myself to this new way of thinking, look what has come to me."

She nestled against his chest and kissed him at the base of his throat beside the vampire spell. "I care about you, Certainly. And I do miss you when you are away from me."

"I feel the same. It's an amazing feeling, yet it hurts to know I can care about someone so much, and to also know if anything ever happened to you I would be torn apart." He hugged her tightly. "There's no easy way to have closeness, is there? If I put myself out there, allowing for love and companionship, it is at the risk to my heart."

She smiled. "That is how it works. Welcome to the real world, Certainly Jones. I hope you stay. And I don't ever want to hear you've plans to return to the place of all demons."

"I promise you I will not."

He slid his hand down her back, stroking her softly, and Vika felt a buzz in her loins. "Whoa!"

"What was that? Did I do that?" He studied his tattooed hand. "I didn't enact any spells."

"Not that I'd mind." Vika slid her hand in her pocket. "It's my phone. Just got a text." She checked the phone's tiny screen. "Vika, B careful. Reichardt on warpath 4 U. Can only feed him so many cookies. He's coming!"

"What the hell?"

Knowing her sister would never kid about something so serious, Vika stood and grabbed CJ's hand, pulling him to his feet. "The soul bringer is coming for me. We need to ward this place. Fast!"

"All right." He grabbed her hand and turned her around, so they stood back-to-back. "You know the angelic warding spell?"

"The zymeloz?"

"Yes. Let's do this!"

* * *

Libby pushed the plate of cookies toward Reichardt while she texted the warning message to her sister.

"Why are mortals so attached to those electronic devices?" he asked, munching a cookie.

"It's a handy thing. I can send a message to a friend, and it's faster than calling."

"It seems impersonal."

She lifted a brow. Had the soul bringer suggested *she* was doing something impersonal?

"It allows me to keep in touch with my sister without actually bugging her."

"You say she is at the dark witch's house?"

"Did I say that? I don't think I said that. Have another cookie."

Taking a bite, Reichardt growled. "I owe the witch a good flaying for the damage she did to my souls. I think I will do that." He finished the cookie. "Flay her open to bleed out the souls clinging to her sticky soul."

"No!" Libby gripped his hand. "You can't do that. She's my sister. You are not allowed to hurt her."

"I need no permission to mete justice when it is due. Perhaps I will break her in half and squeeze out the souls. It is less messy than flaying. Thank you for the cookies, Libertie."

And he disappeared. Gone. Without so much as a goodbye, or an "I'm sorry, I must now go torture your sister."

Libby frantically texted Vika.

They stood in the center of CJ's loft, beneath the dazzle of light. Spell enacted, each scanned the periphery, their senses alert and hearts pounding. Vika had no idea what the soul bringer could want her for, but it couldn't be good.

Suddenly the entire loft shook. The chandelier crystals tinkled and light beams flashed over their skin in a riot of prismatic color.

"He's here," she said, looking toward the roof.

"I can't believe he found me through my wards," CJ said. "No matter. He'll never get past the zymeloz. As well the protection demon has put up sigils against angels. Don't drop my hand!"

Back-to-back, they held vigil as the soul bringer pounded against the roof, the windows and the walls, yet could not gain entrance.

Libby almost dropped her sparkly purple iPhone when the man appeared directly before her. "Reichardt! That was fast. You didn't find Vika?"

"Give me that texting device." He grabbed the phone from her. "Show me how this works. I will send a message to your sister."

"Uh." Well, a text was much better than being flayed alive. "Okay. What do you want me to say?"

"You show me how to do it," he said, and his forceful command sluiced through her like molten fire, and she wanted to do anything to make him happy.

"Use the letters to write your message."

His fingers were thick, but he got the hang of it quickly.

She read aloud what he typed in. "Come to me or

I will kill your— Oh, goddess!" Libby dashed for the garden door.

Reichardt materialized before the gleaming double doors, stopping her as she slammed up against his mighty build.

"Oh." Her hands landed high on his chest, and she could feel his firm pectorals through the black shirt. He wasn't warm, but neither was he cold. And wow, his muscles were so hard and...touchable. "I've always wanted you to hold me."

"I will hold you until your sister surrenders herself to my bidding."

"Not very nice of you, but I'm cool with the holding part."

She was Vika's only hope now. And she had a plan. Of sorts.

"What I'm going to do will freak you, soul bringer, but then again, you have no concept of being freaked, am I right?"

"What do you mutter about?"

"Hold on, Reichardt. This is my kind of magic."

And she kissed the stoic soul bringer. His mouth was as firm and compelling as his pectorals. Closing her eyes, Libby gave him every ounce of unrequited desire she had. He did not react. She did not relent.

And then...

The soul bringer's palms slid up her back and pulled her—gently—closer.

Five minutes felt like an hour as the soul bringer had battered at CJ's walls. And then silence fell and Vika could hear her heartbeats over her ragged breathing. And the ring of her cell phone.

She read the text message—from the soul bringer.

"I have to go home." She started toward the door and Certainly followed. "He's got Libby. He'll kill her if I don't return."

"Wait." He stopped her at the door. "Did he say why he wanted you to go there?"

"No, but—"

"But if he's threatening your sister, I don't think that's going to play well to your hand. Think about it, Vika. What would make the soul bringer so angry he would come after you?"

"He never gets angry. He doesn't do emotion."

"Exactly. Yet he would have torn my place apart to get to you. It's something about the souls, has to be."

"But he's gotten all the souls stuck to me. Even the ones I've used to exorcise your demons. He has them all."

"Save the ones you gathered while he was knocked unconscious."

"He can have them. He doesn't need to threaten me for that. But if he's threatening Libby, I'll rip out his glass heart and smash it against a big rock."

"Then I'm going with you. You'll need me. You know those bastards are infallible and basically indestructible. Our magic combined may have some effect against a soul bringer."

"He better not hurt Libby." She handed him her keys. "You drive. I need to summon some powerful magic."

# Chapter 18

Vika ran up to the front door, but Certainly chased after her, insinuating himself between her body and the door, and stopping her before she could grab the doorknob. For as much as he knew she needed to get inside and help her sister, he wasn't about to let her walk into a death trap.

She'd warded herself in the car against retaliatory magic and angels, but he suspected there wasn't much magic that would work against a soul bringer. He had never bothered with a spell tattoo because he'd known it would be useless. The soul bringer was angelic in origin and demonic by nature, yet he was something else entirely, and neither Above nor Beneath would lay claim to his ilk. And he was, in a word, indestructible.

But they'd been able to hold him off at his loft; that meant they could shield themselves against him.

"Look at me," he said, bracketing Vika's face and forcing her to calm herself. "Take a breath."

She nodded, slipping her fingers down the front of his shirt. He felt her nerves jitter against his skin. He grasped her firmer, forcing her to look at him. If he could hold her gaze for a few moments, he could redirect her worry.

"Hold my hand," he said. "It'll combine our powers and enforce the ward." She did so. "Your grandmother's nail, too."

Nodding, she clasped the nail at her throat. CJ felt the powerful hum of magic and took it into his system, bolstering his own weak magic. The demons within churned at the intrusion.

"Whatever you do," he said, "you have to remain calm. Don't get emotional. That's what he's got over you. Whatever he appears to be doing, think about it twice, three times, before reacting. If he's holding your sister, do not approach him, because he will—"

No, he wouldn't say "snap her neck" much as he suspected such a result.

Vika got the message. "I'm calm. As calm as I can be. I'll talk to him rationally. I can do that. But promise you'll keep an eye out for Libby? If you see a chance to get her away from him—"

"I'll go for it. Promise." He pressed her shaking hand against his heart. "I love you, Vika."

She exhaled and her gaze went watery. He'd never said it to her. Bad timing for it probably, but he needed her to know he was on her side.

With a nod, she said, "Let's do this."

They walked through the quiet living room, taking in everything. Nothing was out of order, save the opened compendium of paranormal breeds lying on the floor before the couch.

Certainly paused beneath the chandelier. It wasn't lit, and the evening fast approached. He closed his eyes and drew in calm from the crystals. Touching his left hand to the barbed rose on his right wrist, he remembered family. *Anything for family.*

"In the kitchen," Vika whispered, and gestured he take the lead.

CJ walked through the swinging doors first. The couple over by the garden doors broke away from each other—they had been in an embrace—though Reichardt gripped Libby's wrist, keeping her from fleeing his side.

Startled unexpectedly by what he'd seen, CJ got a decidedly loose vibe from the soul bringer. Had they been kissing? Yet the looseness was followed by a dark anger when Vika joined him.

He tilted his head to whisper to Vika, "I think that's lipstick on the soul bringer's mouth."

"Vika!" Libby said. "I was hoping you wouldn't come so quickly."

"I'll bet," CJ muttered, and didn't hide his smirk.

The soul bringer appeared to find his stoic mien and stepped forward, holding Libby firmly. Yet Libby didn't appear in dire straits. In fact, she brushed the hair from her face and fought a slippery smile.

Reichardt announced, "I will demand recompense for the tainted souls you served me, witch."

"Recompense?" Vika's hand squeezed CJ's hand. "Tainted? Are you okay, Libby?"

"Best I've been."

"You're not in trouble?" Vika asked cautiously. "The texts?"

"Oh, yes, I am in trouble. Reichardt wants to kill me if you don't do what he says. But—" Libby flashed her sister a look that said more than CJ could understand, though he suspected she wasn't terribly upset being held by the soul bringer.

"You used the souls before allowing me to scrub them from you," Reichardt explained. "They are tainted by the dark witch's collection of demons."

"Oh." Vika flashed a look to CJ. "I hadn't considered that."

He hadn't considered it, either, but it made sense. Of course the soul would take on residue from the infestation within him.

"Above would not accept the souls," Reichardt stated. "Which leaves my record blemished and inaccurate. I must be remunerated appropriately."

"It's not her fault," CJ posited. "I was the one who tainted the souls."

Reichardt crossed his arms in thought, which made him drop Libby's wrist. But Libby remained by his side, actually clinging to the brute soul bringer. There was not room for a quick dash to get her away from him. And CJ had to wonder if Libby would allow him to rip her away from the guy's side. Was she really so blind to the danger?

"I demand a reprieve," Vika said.

"On what grounds?" the soul bringer asked.

"On the grounds you should be thankful I've been letting you scrub me all these years. I could collect the things and go on with it. It is only by my permission you are able to gather the souls from me and keep your record unblemished, and you know it."

Reichardt tilted his head. In wonder? CJ was surprised at the soul bringer's seeming entrance to emotion. Everything about the man was…off. The lipstick was not his color, but he suspected Libby had been doing her darnedest to change his religion.

But could a kiss actually reach inside the stoic soul bringer's chest and soften his glass heart?

The man reached out toward Vika, and CJ moved in front of her, protectively. With a flick of his fingers, Reichardt sent something toward them. It hit CJ in the chest like a spear, and he felt it move slowly through the entrance tattoo above his nipple, as if a tangible blade cutting his skin and serrating his muscle. When Vika's body jerked against his, he knew she'd been pierced, as well. The soul bringer moved his fingers up, and CJ's and Vika's feet left the ground, suspending them above the gleaming kitchen floor.

"Don't do that!" Libby pleaded. She made to rush for them, but Reichardt grabbed her by the hair.

"You are alive only at my will," Reichardt said to CJ and Vika.

Their personal wards were not working, but CJ sensed they weren't in danger. The soul bringer might offer a deal if they talked nicely to him. And he felt little pain. As well…he felt the slither of something dark exit his soul. Another demon?

Libby struggled against the soul bringer's hold, but he held a firm grip on her hair.

"He's going to hurt her," CJ heard Vika whisper.

"No, he won't." He hoped. Just because the lipstick had been smeared didn't mean the man had suddenly developed compassion.

"I've souls!" Vika yelled. "The ones that came out of you when you landed here. Take them!"

"I will. But that is not the payment I seek."

CJ had to act. But without control over his body right now, there was only one means to get the soul bringer's attention.

"I will pay Viktorie St. Charles's debt to you," CJ tried. "Ask of me what you will to satisfy your request for remuneration."

With a nod, the soul bringer lowered his hand, bringing CJ and Vika to their feet. He pulled back his hand, tearing the invisible spear from their chests. CJ caught his palm against his chest, and blood oozed over his fingers. And something exited his soul. Hell, the soul bringer had allowed another demon leave.

He wasn't sure how to feel about that when Vika fell against him, liquid heat spilling down his back. The soul bringer had hurt his woman. The bastard would pay.

"You hold many souls in the balance, dark witch," Reichardt said. "Your trip to Daemonia was fruitful, yes?"

"Uh." He didn't want this to come out now. It was something he needed to tell Vika about in privacy.

"Should the Nacht März be rallied," Reichardt continued, "you will snuff out the lives of countless mortals. So like your parents, eh?"

"I have no intention of doing any such thing," he said firmly. How the soul bringer knew his secret he could not question.

"But you must," Reichardt returned. "So many souls would appease my masters of Above and Beneath. If you wish to pay Viktorie St. Charles's debt, then you will call forth the Night March."

CJ's shoulders dropped at the not impossible but terrible request. He felt Vika clutch at him from behind. Libby cast him a pleading, wondering gape.

Upon his escape from Daemonia, he had carried a wicked darkness to this world. He had never intention of releasing it. His means had been to keep it from the hands of one warlock who would.

And now he must commit the one act of evil he could not fathom to save Vika's and Libby's lives.

# Chapter 19

"You have forty-eight hours to enact the Nacht März," Reichardt announced to CJ. He shoved Libby toward them, and Vika lunged to catch her sister in her arms. "I will either return to reap the souls from the march, or those from the St. Charles sisters. It is your choice, dark witch."

The soul bringer dematerialized.

Vika hugged her sister to her, but she could sense Libby's desire to turn and grasp for the disappearing soul bringer. Even after he'd held her in dire straits, she was still puppy-eyed over him.

"What's the Night March?" Libby asked CJ.

"Yes." Smoothing a hand over her sister's head, Vika lifted her chin and eyed her lover cautiously. "Doesn't sound like a picnic."

"It's what I've been wanting to tell you since earlier in the garden." CJ rubbed a hand along his thigh then gestured toward the living room. "Can we have some privacy?"

Vika hugged Libby to her, unwilling to let go of the one safe presence she felt in this room.

CJ glanced out the patio doors. Night had fallen, and she sensed his surprise. While the kitchen was lit with halogen bulbs, she wasn't sure they had the ability prismatic light did to keep back his demons.

"In the living room," he said, walking by her and Libby, "under the chandelier."

"You going to be okay?" she asked her sister.

"I'm more than okay—"

"Libby." She wasn't about to let her gloss over this one with the sunshine-and-roses-I'm-in-love charade. "Reichardt threatened you. And he would have gone through with that threat if CJ hadn't offered something more appealing in trade."

What that was, she wanted to know. And then she didn't. Couldn't be good, whatever it was. And it had something to do with his parents?

"I don't know about that." Libby trailed a finger over her lip. The lavender lipstick she always wore was faded.

"You kissed him?" Vika guessed. She'd not believed CJ earlier when he'd suggested the same.

Libby nodded, accompanied by a huge grin.

"A kiss? But how? Really? But it couldn't have meant anything to him. He's—"

The soul bringer could not have a grasp on the finer

concepts of attraction and connection, even straight-forward communication.

"I know it did mean something to him. Vika, as I was kissing him, he put his hands around my back and pulled me closer. And when I pulled away from the kiss? He leaned in and kissed me."

"Really? Well." She wasn't sure how to process this information. It flew in the face of her knowledge, although she had to admit she was no expert on the topic. Truly, the sky had fallen. "Maybe the soul bringer can be brought to change."

Looking ready to burst with joy, Libby nodded enthusiastically.

"But, sweetie, he's serious about his threat to me and you."

"I know." Wincing away the enthusiasm, Libby stilled her excited tittering. "That's the awful part about all this. I know he means it. But CJ will save us."

"I'm not so sure. This Night March doesn't sound like something we want to offer in exchange for one witch's soul."

Or two witches' souls, if her hopes for Reichardt's heart actually softening for her sister didn't pan out.

"Oh, goddess, you're hurt?" Libby touched Vika's chest where blood stained her dress.

"Some kind of intangible spear went through me, and I assume, Certainly. It hurt, but now it doesn't. I'll be fine."

"I'm sorry, Vika."

She squeezed her sister's hand. "I'm going to talk to CJ and learn more about what he's agreed to. You…

try not to fall too hard, please, Libby? Take a few moments and step back from this immense attraction I know you feel for Reichardt and be rational about it."

"I can try that. But you weren't on the receiving end of that kiss. Oh, my goddess!"

Yes, and she should be there for her sister when she wanted to squeal about a kiss, as they had been for each other previously. First kisses were always the best, the most magical, and if unexpected, then even better. How it had occurred, she couldn't imagine.

"I'm going to the garden to pick a sunflower." Libby kissed her and scampered out.

Recalling the symbolism for the flower, Vika murmured, "Sunflowers for foolish infatuation. Oh, Libby."

No one ever said first loves were easy. Vika believed a person could have many first loves in their lifetime. Sometimes the relationship ended with one of the twosome being turned into a cat.

Other times?

"There be demons," Vika said on a sigh, and pushed the doors open leading into the living room.

Certainly stood beneath the chandelier, arms out to receive her, and she walked up and took that offer. It felt great falling into his arms after the incident in the kitchen. It wasn't every day her life was threatened, as well as her sister's. Despite her job and the awful things she witnessed almost daily, she'd never worried for her life or injury, because until now she'd never put herself in danger.

CJ's kiss reached down into her soul and swept warmth across it she never wanted to lose—including her soul. If it fell into Reichardt's hands, she wasn't sure what she'd do. People could survive without their soul, but they would grow dark and tainted. Open to evil.

Did evil trace this man's veins?

*Don't think about it. Fall into his arms. Take this moment.*

Inwardly, she chastised herself for any words that may have turned Libby against seeking love with Reichardt. Love was too lush and wondrous not to take it when it came to you.

"I love you, too," she said. "I didn't answer earlier when you said it because my mind was on my sister. But I feel it. It's real."

"I didn't say it to get you to reply in kind, but now that you have, you can't imagine how that makes me feel."

"I have an idea."

His confession he'd avoided relationships because he'd been so busy studying magic reminded her anyone could become obsessed with anything. Like cleaning. And soul bringers.

"You healing?" he said with a tap to her wound.

"Yes, it doesn't hurt at all. That was something weird. How about you?"

"The healing wards have done their work. How's Libby?"

"She's going to be fine. As weird as it is, I think I want her to find what it is she seeks with Reichardt."

"I've never known a soul bringer to show interest in others. But that was lipstick on his mouth."

"She said he actually kissed her back."

"Wow."

"I know, right? And I don't think it was a heat of the moment, wanting it to be true when it really wasn't, either. He really kissed her."

"Stranger things have never happened. And trust me, I've seen all kinds of strange."

"I bet you have."

"Get this for strange…" He pressed her palm over his chest. "When Reichardt held us suspended in the kitchen, I think the spear he shot through us exorcized another demon."

"Really? You felt it leave?"

He nodded. "Grief, I suspect."

"That leaves what?"

"Two remaining."

"You're so close, CJ." And to stare into his gaze too long might reveal those strange things to her. Vika tilted her head to break the look. "So talk to me, dark one. Tell me about this Nacht März, and is it as terrible as it sounds?"

"If you think calling all demons who walk this earth to order to slaughter all mortals in their path terrible, then yes. But don't worry, I would never think to send forth the call."

"That is what you brought here from the place of all demons? A means to call them out?"

"I did. It is the call to the Nacht März."

Just the two words, said with a gruff German tone, sent a chill up Vika's spine. "Why would you do that?"

"It is the reason I went to Daemonia in the first place. I wanted to obtain something another witch wanted desperately. It was purely selfish on my part. Well, mostly. I mentioned earlier my parents did something horrible. They once enacted the Night March. I don't know their reasons, but father was always dabbling about the edges between dark magic and malefic magic. They were branded warlocks, and not soon after is when the witch hunters got them."

"Certainly, I'm so sorry. But…why would you want the same device if…?"

"The last thing I ever wanted to touch in this known universe was that bedamned call to the Nacht März. But recently I discovered another witch had his sights set on it. I knew if I didn't get to it first, the other witch would, and that he would actually use it."

"What other witch?"

"Have you heard of Ian Grim?"

Vika's heart thudded hard against her rib cage. Her knees felt loose and wavery. "The warlock?" It was a name most witches knew and were careful to avoid. She hadn't met him, and she was glad for it.

Certainly nodded. "We've been rivals for decades. Dancing about one another in a macho display of one-upmanship. If he masters a level of dark magic, then I have to exceed him. If I accomplish lithoboly, then he responds in kind. I don't know how it all got started, but it's been a strange fuel to my quest for magical knowledge over the decades."

"I don't know how you can associate with that man. Grim practices malefic magic. He's committed countless crimes against the Light and mortals. He is designated a warlock for a reason."

A warlock was a witch, male or female, who had committed grave transgressions against the Light. A pariah cast out from the fold.

"Oh, goddess, the warlock." She touched her mouth, remembering the scattered safflower petals.

"I don't associate with him as if a friend or colleague. We are each other's nemesis. I've always gone out of my way to show him up and prove I'm the better witch."

"The cock of the walk?"

"Truth? Yes, it's like that. I'm a guy, Vika. It's what we do."

When he tried to kiss her she inclined her head away. CJ had journeyed to Daemonia merely to obtain something he could use against another witch? And something that had such profound evil memories related to his parents. So not cool with her. This had been what the petals had indicated. Ian Grim was involved in her life in a manner she couldn't quite figure yet.

"What does this item do beyond summoning demons? What is it, exactly?"

"It's a whistle made from the bone of Lucifer's left wing. When blown, it summons all demons who walk the earth, and their only command is to destroy life. Thus, the night march of demons."

"Sounds apocalyptic."

"On a small scale, yes."

He was so callous about it. That he'd brought the thing to this realm was not bold macho posturing but pure idiocy.

"It must have been returned after your parents had used it."

"Yes."

"Well then, would you put it back if I asked you to?"

"But then it would be available for Grim to take." He puffed up his chest. "I can't risk that. As well, I did make a promise to you never to return to Daemonia. And besides, if I returned the whistle now, I wouldn't be able to save your life by fulfilling Reichardt's request."

"You would consider using it to save my life? That is reprehensible, CJ."

"I will never use it! I am not like my father." His jaw tight, his eyes shut just as tightly. "I just…need some time to figure out a plan. Your life is in danger. I don't want to lose you, Vika. I love you. I— Fuck, this is a fine mess."

"Never would have happened had you not taken the damned thing out of Daemonia. Damn it!" she cursed her use of the proper name.

But really, if she hadn't heaped bad luck upon herself by engaging with CJ, then she could hardly expect karmic retaliation by the mere mention of the name of so foul a place.

She paced away from him, hands to her hips, her black skirt sweeping the floor. Touching him right now was the last thing she wanted to do. Stupid man. She understood males' machismo and their need to one-up each other. Rivalries between witches were not uncommon. But to bring something that could destroy mankind into this realm, even if he never had intention to use it? She couldn't understand why his parents' sins hadn't kept him far away from the place.

On the other hand, keeping the dread thing out of the warlock's hands was a valiant accomplishment.

"Is it warded? How does Grim not know you have it?"

"I'm sure he felt it the moment I returned to the mortal realm with the Nacht März in hand. But I do have it cloaked. You've walked right by it every time you are in my home."

She gaped at him.

"And I cloak my footsteps constantly," he continued. "Grim can have no idea where I live."

"You've the thing at your home? You hid it from me?"

He nodded. "Not a safer place to keep it than right in the middle of it all. I've hidden it from everyone with wards. Even the demons inside me cannot access it, thank all the gods and goddesses for that one."

"I should think the demons would see through your wards."

"Me, too, but so far, it's worked."

Vika sighed and shrugged her fingers through her hair. The braid had loosened, and a few remaining yellow roses tumbled down her dress. The day had been long and trying. She'd had to deal with Grief, and Reichardt's threats, and now this revelation?

"What of the witch's rede?" she asked. "And ye harm none. Seems what you've done is grounds for ostracism to warlock status." She turned to CJ. "Or would that serve to your advantage? Showing Grim you can do the warlock thing as well as he?"

"No. It's not like that at all. I've not used the thing, nor would I ever. Vika, please, if you've learned anything about me is I have a moral compass."

She lifted her chin. She did know that about him, but it was becoming more difficult to believe it.

"Despite the dark magic I practice, I pride myself in following the rede. I go out of my way to ensure the safety of mortals. Always. I'm sorry." He winced then let out a soft chuckle. "It seems I've been apologizing to you a lot lately. No getting beyond it. But will you let me think about this? There must be a means to work this out. I won't let the soul bringer near you or your sister."

"What if you've no choice? What if it comes down to hour number forty-eight and you haven't solved the problem? I don't know, CJ."

"You don't trust I can handle this."

"I didn't say that, I just..." She didn't trust he could handle this. And she did. But truly, he couldn't bring the thing to Daemonia only to again risk Grim getting his hands on it. "Maybe we could get Reichardt to scrub you of the demons? If we insist you can't work the Night March spell properly while occupied by them?"

"Why do you always think of me, Vika?"

"Because I want you whole. To be free of the demons."

"I love you for that. But I think I want to keep the remaining two. I might be able to use them. How, I'm not yet sure. If I can bring up the war demon..."

She swung a condemning look at CJ.

"Would you talk to War?" he posited. "The demon might be our only hope. It's the strongest one inside me. I imagine he wouldn't mind waging a war against a few thousand demons."

"That's…" A strangely good idea. And not. That would mean actually calling the demons to walk the earth. So risky. Anything could go wrong. "That would mean I'd have to talk to War while he's in control of your body. I don't know if I can do that. You were so angry with me when I spoke to Want."

"This would be different. And I sure as hell am not asking you to have sex with War. It was just a thought. I think it should be a last resort."

"What about asking Grim for help?"

CJ stiffened defensively.

"Just a suggestion," she said, and glanced upstairs where Libby had retreated to her bedroom. No doubt about it, whatever they planned, it would be a slippery situation. "Let's think on this then. I need more tea. I've had a long day. Come on, I'll brew you a cup."

Her lover pointed upward. The chandelier was his lifeline.

"Right. And I'm not ready to talk to War or even Pain. I'll bring it out to you."

With a stiff scrub brush, Vika swirled the organic green cleanser around inside the porcelain toilet bowl. It was past midnight, but she couldn't sleep. Cleaning usually relaxed her, but she foresaw heading to the downstairs bathroom next because after polishing the mirror, scouring the tub and wiping down the vanity, she still hadn't found peace.

A sigh behind her indicated Libby stood in the open doorway. "I just scrubbed that one yesterday."

She had, and it hadn't needed a repeat scrubbing so soon, but it was a means of avoidance.

"So," her sister said on a sleepy tone, "you'd rather scrub toilets than be with your boyfriend downstairs?"

CJ had pulled the easy chair directly beneath the chandelier and had bunkered down for the night. Using the excuse she was tired after tea, Vika had left him with little more than a kiss on the cheek.

"It's complicated," she said, setting the brush in the tub to rinse. "And I'm mad at him. Sort of." She blew out a surrendering sigh. "Why can't I be angry with him? I want to be. Shouldn't I be? It's like, if I go down and hug him, I'm agreeing to all the dangerous, reckless, foolish things he's ever done."

"No, if you hug him that means you're human, and you need the connection as much as he does." Libby yawned and tugged up the fluffy terry cloth lapel of her robe. "Also, while everyone around you is telling you how wrong he is for you, you actually see into his soul and know he is the only one for you."

"Are you talking about me and CJ or you and Reichardt?"

She let out a soft chuckle. "Both. Go sit with him. It creeps me out to know he's down there alone, probably staring wide-eyed up at the chandelier. How can he sleep? Does he sleep?"

"He does, for short periods. You're right. I can't

leave him alone. You get some rest. We'll need to stay strong for whatever the next few days bring." She hugged her sister and then wandered down to the living room, where the light hurt her eyes.

"Can't sleep?" he muttered. "Or feeling sorry for the pitiful witch who can't go home without risking a battle with his own demons?"

"A bit of both." Vika picked up the compendium from the floor and then settled onto the easy chair next to CJ. "Mind if I join you, oh, pitiful one?"

"Vika, I'm—"

"No more apologies. It is what it is. You've done things. I'm still not sure how I feel about that. But for now, I know I can't stay away from you, and I wanted to be close. I'm tired, so I may fall asleep in your arms."

"Please do. But what's with the book?"

"Demons," she said on a yawn. "I want to know what we're dealing with."

"Smart witch you are." He opened the book on his lap, while Vika nestled closer to give the book some room. Tilting her head against his shoulder, she watched his face as he paged through the book.

The incorporeal demon was listed, and CJ read the page, explaining that the demons from Daemonia were the upper crust, so to speak, the royalty of demons. While the lesser demons most often tread the mortal realm and were shunned by those from Daemonia.

Closing her eyes, she allowed his deep yet quiet recitation to lull her. He smelled good. Like a favorite sweater taken out from a cedar drawer and snuggled against one's face. Hers.

She'd said she loved him.

Love? Possibly. Yet shame on her for falling for a man she had known was trouble from the beginning, and for allowing her heart to lead her when normally— Hell. What was so wrong with following her heart?

Besides getting attacked by demons and being threatened with the removal of her soul?

Sighing, she spread her fingers down his chest and felt the hum of his protection wards against her palm. "Take down your wards," she whispered.

With a few whispered words from CJ, the hum ceased, and Vika pulled up her leg to snuggle in closer to her lover. "Can we have what we think we want from each other?"

"Yes. No. I don't know, Vika." He closed the book and slid it down aside the chair and returned her hug. "I want you. My heart craves your beauty and light. But I'm not so stupid to think that selfish desire isn't hurting you."

"Why must it be selfish to love someone? I struggle with that, too. Like if I relax and let myself love you, the world will not approve, that it'll sneer at me and say I'm asking far too much. I don't want to feel that way. I take my reluctance as a portent."

"Your saffron petals tell you anything about us?"

"No, only that a warlock is present in my life."

"Grim." He sighed. "Because of me."

"Do you think he'll come after me to get to you? *Is* he after you?"

"I suspect so. I sensed a push against my wards right after the accident, and then the following day. If Grim obtained some of my blood, he would be able to track me down but, ultimately, wouldn't have been able to breech my wards."

"The blood on the dashboard."

He nodded. "But he has nothing of yours and shouldn't be aware of our connection, so the petal reading baffles me. Are you sure you're not aware of any other warlocks in your or Libby's life?"

"Trust me, I do not consort with the like."

"Didn't think so. It could be a vague reference to my parents, though they're totally out of the picture. And now that Grief is gone, I'm feeling oddly at peace with their sins."

"I'm glad you got that. You shouldn't have to suffer for the things your parents did. But still, there be demons."

"Indeed." He stroked her neck, playing with her hair. "What the book said about the ranking of demons. It could serve to our advantage if we have to enact the Night March."

"I don't want to think about it, but I know it's important that we do. I trust you, Certainly Jones."

Vika yawned and fell asleep, her ear pressed to his chest, the soft rhythm of his heartbeats lulling her to Nod.

# Chapter 20

CJ had left at sunrise with a kiss and mention he was heading to his brother's house.

Libby tended the garden out back, humming the theme from some overhyped love song Vika had heard far too many times on the radio. Her sister was in love, and such emotion manifested in an amazing aura that literally tilted the flower heads toward her as she walked by them. Touching a white rose made the blossom grow thicker, the core of it tinting deep red, and Libby smiled at the result.

Vika, on hands and knees, with rubber gloves and kneepads on, swept the scrub brush over the tile kitchen floor. It was as though she were trying to rub out the soul bringer's existence as she forced the brush over the places where he had stood holding her sister in a death grip.

"Maybe I'm jealous," she muttered, and sat back, dropping the brush in the bucket of vinegar and lemon water.

Not a single thing to be jealous over. Besides, she had her own man. As dark and troubled as he was.

She had dived headfirst into this adventure with Certainly, thinking more of the high she'd get from cleaning him up than the real possibility she might actually fall for the guy. And now that she had, life had become remarkable and miserable. She wanted the romance and passion and closeness, but she did not want the demons, dark magic and threats from the soul bringer. Nor did she want to see the world over-run with demons courtesy some macabre Night March.

Would it be wrong to bail from the relationship in hopes to save her sister and herself from Reichardt's wrath?

"I can't do that." She wrapped her gloved hands about her upper arms and leaned against the door frame, Libby's spectacular communion with the flowers in sight. "I do love him."

She admired CJ's intelligence and all the magics he had learned over the years. He was a calm and thoughtful man, despite his obvious inner struggles. He thought of others before himself more often than not, though any man was allowed a few selfish hang-ups, such as a decades-long testosterone-fueled battle against a warlock.

Physically he moved with such ease through the world. Grounded wherever he stood, strong with muscles yet even more powerful with wisdom and magic.

But what she loved most about Certainly Jones was his ability to survive, even when the worst struck.

Love involved more than the romance, passion and closeness. It involved sticking it out through thick and thin, seeing beyond the bad to the light on the other side. Even if that light was obnoxious and glittered madly. She'd never look at a chandelier the same again.

Salamander meowed, but he did not move from the living room doorway, where she had begun scrubbing and the floor was still wet. Wise cat. He'd never been so thoughtful of her hard work while in human form. Some men were born animals, she decided with a smirk.

"My relationships have never been outstanding," she noted, woefully at a loss over what, if anything, she could ever do to make Sal's life better. As far as she knew, he was simply a cat now and did not have memories of his mortal life. She hoped.

"But the nun's life is not for me. Better to have excitement and danger than boring and mellow, yes?"

Salamander looked away, unconcerned with her emotional struggles. An animal through and through.

CJ's suggestion she convince the war demon to slaughter all the demons raised upon inciting the Nacht März was a clever idea. And she had no doubt the demon was capable. But did she have the courage to stand up to War? Could she influence the demon to do her bidding? She'd withstood Menace, Pain, Lust and even Grief. A little war shouldn't be so difficult.

With a heavy sigh, she sunk against the door frame. The sky was bright, and she imagined CJ must be out enjoying the light. She hoped he was but knew he was probably stooped over his worktable, concocting spells, searching for some means to solve this problem.

"He needs to relax. He's the world on his shoulders, or rather, in his soul. He needs someone to…"

Support him. He needed her.

Vika sat up. Why wasn't she there at his side? When the man most needed her strength, she had opted to stay home and clean?

Tugging off the rubber gloves, she stood and left the bucket and gloves where they lay. Narrowly avoiding a trip from Salamander, Vika headed out the front door. She couldn't let him go through this himself. Love was stronger than that.


CJ tucked his cell phone in a pocket and looked out across the fifth quarter of Paris from the rooftop. The Luxembourg gardens put up a frothy green canopy not far off. TJ had no ideas for how to solve his problem, though he was going to think on it. He shouldn't ask his brother's help. He had begun a family and should not be asked to risk his life now.

A raven soared overhead and landed on an electrical line, cocking its head to take in CJ. "You think I should listen to the red witch?" he asked, shoving his hands in his jeans pockets.

Vika had suggested he bring Grim in on the matter. Ridiculous. And yet, keeping one's enemy close was never stupid.

"Hell." He closed his eyes, tilting back his head.

Sunlight bled across his skin, but he still felt cold. Worthless.

Unworthy of her trust, which she seemed to give so freely. And each time she did, he bruised that trust, or shot it all to hell. What was he doing wrong? Why could he not step up to the challenge of Viktorie St. Charles and successfully accomplish the task?

"Vika," he muttered, sending her name out through the ether. "I want to be deserving of your love."

CJ stepped down from the roof stairs and into the sixth-floor hallway just as Vika reached his door. "Vika."

"I couldn't stay away."

"I was hoping you'd sense my thoughts. I drew you to me."

"I won't argue that."

A smear of grease dashed his jaw and he was shirtless. The muscles on that witch were commendable. Witchcraft did work more than the mind. Add the surprising allure of the tattoos, and she was a lovesick fool. Now Vika knew why she had stayed away. Because near him she lost all sense and simply wanted to kiss him, hold him, touch him. Become a part of him.

"What's got you so smiley?" he asked.

"Just admiring the sexy view."

He preened a hand down his abs, seeming to take her comment with surprise.

"Think I should get a tattoo?" she asked teasingly.

"Maybe my name on your gorgeous derriere?"

"Would that make you happy?"

"It would surprise the hell out of me to find a mark on your perfect skin. And one with my name? So wrong."

"Or maybe so right. I could sit on you whenever I chose."

He chuckled.

"You fix the generator?"

"Tip-top shape now. Sometimes I amaze myself with my mechanical ability. TJ is usually the one who fixes things. So, I thought you said you needed to keep an eye on Libby. Did you bring her along?"

She tugged him to her, and he slid his hands over her hips. "Libby is under a powerful spell that can't be uncast."

"Love," CJ whispered, savoring the tone of it.

"Yes, love. It's a condition I'm familiar with of late."

"I like the condition."

"And I didn't want you sitting alone muddling over the dire consequences the world has forced upon you."

"I don't want to worry you with this stuff, Vika."

"Yes, well, a part of being in a relationship is knowing when to let the other person worry."

He leaned in and whispered her ear, "Relationship?"

"We have both dropped the *L*-word. I think that implies a relationship. Can you deal with that, dark one?"

"I think I can, Sybarite of My Soul. Let's go inside. I have to wash this grease off."

"Probably you should shower," she said, following him inside and strolling under the spectacular glitter of the prismatic light.

"You think I smell?"

"No." She drew a finger along his cheek, avoiding the grease. "But if you need help, you know…reaching the hard places." She slid her hand down, over his erection.

"I think I do. Temptress."

Relationship. The word felt like elixir to his brain as CJ soaped up under the warm shower stream. Actually, he wasn't doing the soaping. Vika's fingers glided over his skin, caressing his muscles and slicking his arms and thighs. Vetiver, earthy and astringent, drifted into his senses and dizzied his thoughts. Now was no time for concentration. Now—

He let out a deep, satisfied moan as Vika's mouth slipped over the swollen head of his erection. And he'd avoided relationships for what insane reason?

He slid his fingers down her slick hair and gripped the top of the shower bar with his other hand. She was a master at bringing him to climax. When he could no longer hold back the tremendous wave surging toward explosion, CJ cried out.

His wicked mistress slid up his body. "That's my own form of watersexmagic," she said.

"You can practice it on me anytime you like, Mistress of the Magical Tongue." He kissed her wet mouth. "Now it's my turn."

He waggled his tattooed fingers at her, and she kissed the tips of each one then placed his hand over her slick, hard nipple. He had but to tap them lightly, focusing on heightening the sensual energy beneath his touch and driving it into her skin.

Vika moaned loudly and bit into his shoulder. The pleasurable pain signaled he was gaining experience with skin magic. Sliding his fingers down her slick belly, he teased her sensual peak until she came gently in his embrace, a sigh honoring his skills.

After the shower, they dried off then wandered, naked, to the couch to snuggle in each other's arms wrapped beneath a blanket.

"Thanks for being here for me," CJ said as Vika snuggled against his bare chest and twirled a finger through the dark hairs queued down his belly to his, once again, erect penis. "It means a lot. I realize I had no clue what I was missing over the years. This *being together,* holding you and feeling your skin against mine—I don't know how I survived so long without it."

"I know you said you've been monkish, but you've had lovers over the years?"

"Sure, but nothing serious. I don't know that I've ever sat on the couch with a woman and just held her, smelled her hair, felt her heart beat against my chest. This is awesome. Better than any magic I could conjure."

"How many magics have you mastered?"

"Haven't counted. I can do lithoboly, levitation, transprojectionary dislocation, catoptromancy, allotriophagy—"

"The allotriophagy disturbs me."

"Yes, but you would be surprised how useful it is to cause someone to vomit up nails or beetles."

"Don't ever use it on me."

He kissed her nose. "The only magic I want to wield against you is the warm, fuzzy kind I'm feeling right here." He slid her hand over his heart. "I can't believe I'm talking like this. Such words shouldn't be natural to a guy who has avoided connection with another person for so long. You've put a spell on me, I know it."

"I don't believe in love spells. Such false love could never be true."

"I agree. Mmm, I love you."

She stroked his erection. No pressure, just soft, sweeping strokes. He could waver back and forth between the ridiculous pleasure of it and their quiet conversation.

"So about your idea of me speaking to War," she said without stopping her ministrations. "I'll do it if you think it will work."

"Really? It could work. And I trust you're strong enough to handle the situation. Thing is, do I want to put you at risk?"

"I don't think we have any other option, do you?"

"Other than handing over your souls to Reichardt? I don't want that for you, Vika. Trust me, coming from a man whose soul is as dirty and dark as they get, I don't want that for you."

"Yes, but at least you have a soul. Would it take long for me to...change, should I lose my soul?"

He hugged her and nuzzled his face into her wet hair.

She clasped him firmly. "We're not going to consider it because we'll try plan A at first sign of daylight."

"Talk to War?"

He sighed. "Yes."

With a nod, she resumed her strokes, and within moments brought him to a rousing orgasm.

## Chapter 21

Vika walked around the salt circle. The smell of brimstone prickled at her determination, but she maintained composure. Trapped within the circle was her lover. CJ's body craned forward, his shoulders cutting through a beam of sunlight that marred the dark ritual. With an unnatural jerk, he straightened, thrusting back his shoulders and lifting his chin. He seemed to take on muscle, bulk and command. Vika knew it was an illusion of demonic possession.

"Who are you?" she asked firmly.

"War," growled out in sepulchral tones from her lover's mouth. "Let me out, witch."

She waggled a finger at the demon. "I want to talk to you first."

"I don't deal. I walk or no talk."

"Then I guess we'll stand and stare at one another, shall we?"

The demon lashed toward her with clawed fingers, which scraped the invisible wall warded about CJ's body. It would hold strong unless the salt line was smeared to break the circle. After her experience with Want, she would not again do that.

Crossing her arms over her chest, Vika picked at a nonexistent fleck of lint on her dress sleeve, made a point of exaggerating her yawn, and tilted her head wonderingly at the man she loved, but whom at this moment she feared. Mustn't show that fear.

It was more worry than fear, actually. If she could exorcise this demon right now she would, but they needed it more than she wanted to get rid of it.

"The dark witch is wise to keep you for his woman," the demon growled. "You are strong. Tight. We can feel you when he is inside you. So hot. Your moans stir us all."

Despite how uncomfortable that information made her, she did not flinch, not even when the demon revealed his teeth, which seemed to have grown longer and pointed. Could an incorporeal demon affect her vision of its host? Possibly.

And that was a good thing. She'd never be able to face the demon were he the easygoing, gorgeous man with whom she had fallen in love.

Long minutes passed with her pacing and War glowering at her from inside the circle. Black candles flickered beneath the unlit chandeliers. So bright, too, the sun. The demon was patient. She was more so.

Overhead, the crystals tinkled softly, as if wind were sifting through them, but there were no open windows. The clatter rose, and she realized the demon was doing it. It possessed great power—beyond CJ's magic. But not enough to harm her while it was contained. She hoped.

"You want your freedom?" she asked. "You must strike a bargain between me and Certainly Jones."

The demon lifted his chest and looked down Certainly's long, narrow nose at her.

"I've a war for you," she proposed. "Tomorrow night."

"The Nacht März the dark witch controls?" The demon scoffed. "That is not a war but merely a massacre of innocent, unprepared mortals. It offers no challenge, no sides standing against one another, no return fire."

True, but she had to work with what had been provided.

"No mortals will be harmed if you do the job we request of you."

"Which is?"

"Annihilate any and all demons called forth to the march."

Certainly tilted his head, mouth open in an uncomfortable grimace.

"Does not the satisfaction reaped through destruction and murder fulfill you? You are a knight of Daemonia," she said, appealing to the demon's elite breed and CJ's suggestion he would consider himself greater than the demons treading this mortal realm. "Would you not care to annihilate so many demons who walk this realm, some claiming lineage from Daemonia, when we know they are but lowly maggots?"

That sparked red light in the demon's dark gaze. Gone were CJ's jade eyes; they were now actually black. He nodded, his breath growing raspy with desire. CJ's fists clenched tightly. "You want me to slay them all? I can do that."

"I know you can. I would not have come to you with such a challenge did I not believe you could. You and... perhaps Pain?"

The demon's lip flinched. He rubbed a fist down CJ's bare torso, dragging the silver-laden werewolf spell to a distorted curve. She risked losing War by implying he needed help. But the more demons involved—even if contained in but the one witch—the better.

"It would be an interesting match. We are pleased Grief is gone. Whiny insolent. What prize are we promised for leading the vanguard?"

"Your return to Daemonia."

War slapped his palms against the invisible barrier and bellowed, "I want the dark witch's soul."

"No deal."

Vika turned and walked toward the kitchen. Only place to be away from the demon's sight was in the bathroom. That would appear weak, like a female running to cry in the girls' room. This was the only way to maintain the facade of power.

"Stop!"

She paused near the kitchen counter, tilting a hip

against it but keeping her back to the demon. An inhale drew in courage.

"This imprisonment inside the dark witch has been worse than the mortal hell and Beneath combined. I have no freedom, save the darkness, and yet must battle the others for a few moments of control. I am made of the dark witch, and yet, it is a foul dwelling. In Daemonia, at the least, I will have my freedom."

Excellent.

"The deal is you will slay the Night March and then vacate the dark witch's soul," Vika said, approaching the salt circle. "No amendments, no changes. And Pain must agree. I request to speak to that demon, as well."

"War grants spoils," the demon said darkly. "My spoil is a kiss from the red witch."

Vika's breath caught at the base of her throat. Seducing the want demon had been easy enough, but to allow this one to kiss her? She could sense CJ's protests in the flinch of the demon's hand. He would not wish her to agree. But had she any other choice? It would be as if kissing her lover. Only not.

"Agreed. Allow Pain to speak to me."

With a cackling snicker, War bowed his head, and in the next breath, the demon slammed his body against the barrier. CJ fell backward, stumbling, and then made a run to the side. The demon slammed CJ's body from side to side and back, and then smacked his face over and over until the flesh reddened.

"Pain, I presume," Vika said over the childish antics. She must not wince or show sign of horror at the sight of her lover being mauled from within. "You heard my request. Will you work with War to vanquish the Night March?"

"Can I twist their heads from their bodies and chew their limbs to the bone?" the creature cackled. He dragged CJ's fingernails down his chest, leaving red abrasions that drew up a macabre grin on his face.

"If it pleases you to do so."

But imagining it happening while the demon occupied CJ hurt her heart. What was he sacrificing by allowing these demons to control him during the march? His sanity? His life? She hadn't considered it.

*Stop thinking, and do this!*

"You may do whatever is necessary to stop the march from harming mortals. Not one mortal must be sacrificed, do you understand?"

The demon pressed its face hard against the barrier, distorting his nose and mouth as it asked, "Me kiss the red witch, too?"

Vika rolled her eyes and shook her head. "Very well. If you can manage a simple kiss without hurting me."

"Where is the joy in that?"

"Then the dark witch refuses to allow your touch."

"Wait! I can touch softly. But I do need to taste blood. It'll be quick, I promise."

Vika winced, tilting her head away so the demon could not see her reaction. "I want your promise you'll agree to the terms of the pact. You'll work with War to annihilate the Night March then submit to exorcism back to Daemonia."

"Agreed. Me don't like this realm. Mortals are too soft. Need the challenge of my own kind. And me no able to access this dark witch's magic from inside. Want my own magic back!"

"Very well. We have a deal." Vika pressed her palm to the barrier, and Pain gnashed his teeth at it. "Until tomorrow night, gentlemen."

She flicked the switch on the remote. The chandeliers blasted on to full glow. Pain squealed and flung CJ's body against the barrier. The dark witch fell through it and landed across the salt line, sprawled and groaning.

Vika knelt next to him and stroked her fingers over his bleeding cheek. "Success."

"I heard," he said on a breathless gasp. "And you promised yourself as spoils."

"Just a kiss. And I know you will chaperone that."

Certainly chuffed out a weak laugh. "As best I can, lover."

"So, until tomorrow night?"

He nodded. "*Eine Klene* Nacht März?"

"Oh, that's bad. You were not meant to make jokes."

"Sorry, couldn't resist. I, uh… There's someone I need to go see today."

"Stay here with me. Please?"

He kissed her, lingering at her mouth, tendering her softly in the wake of the vile interaction with the demons. "It won't take long. It's an idea for backup. Plan B, if you will."

"But you're going to keep me in the dark about it."

He nodded. "You'll be waiting for my return?"

"I'm not going anywhere."

He pressed his forehead to hers. "That's all I ever

wanted to know. The feeling of someone waiting for me, wanting me to return to their arms."

"It's a hard thing to endure, the waiting. But I know you have to prepare. Will you at least tell me who you need to see today?"

He stroked her lips then bowed his head, unable to look at her. "Ian Grim."

## *Chapter 22*

*I am made of the dark witch.*

CJ could not stop replaying that statement War had made while contained within the salt circle. Grief had said much the same.

Did he carry these demons inside only because he possessed some element of them already? Of course he grieved, and didn't every man possess a hint of menace? Lust, why yes. And even carrion he could justify, for though he practiced vegetarianism, his mouth still watered when passing cooked meat.

He wondered if Vika had caught on to that statement, and what she thought it meant.

But War? No.

Really?

*You have been warring against Grim for decades.*

Perhaps. And now, for the first time, he was considering asking the warlock for help.

He twisted around a corner deep in the seventh quarter that led toward Les Innocents and knelt on the cobbles, tugging a small vial from his pocket. Inside were a few strands of Ian Grim's hair, collected decades ago when he'd had opportunity. Crushing one with the hilt of his athame and spitting upon it, he then recited the location spell. And waited.

Grim also had DNA from him, probably hair, and for sure the blood taken from the scene of the accident. They generally did not cloak themselves, because they liked the play of never knowing when the other would come looking for them. But CJ wasn't cheating by cloaking since his return from Daemonia. This was a new twist to their decades-old game. And never before had he involved someone he cared about. New rules had been created. Besides, all was fair when dealing with a warlock.

A raven crowed and coasted down the narrow alley, swooping over CJ's head. The sign he'd been waiting for. Tucking the vial in a pocket, he took off after the bird.

They skirted the park and wound down an industrial neighborhood that edged the fifteenth quarter. The air was heavy with gasoline fumes and the rush of traffic from the distant ring road. He tracked the raven to an abandoned building covered in graffiti, where he heard a man's laughter echo out from the glassless windows.

Dropping his cloak would alert Grim immediately, unless the man was too focused on whatever was going on behind the closed door. Worth the risk. CJ whispered the cloak release, and he felt it shed from his body as if a sudden gush of rain falling over his shoulders and dropping at his feet in a splash, without the wet.

Inside, the laughter suddenly ceased—to be replaced with a female scream.

CJ kicked the rusted metal door open.

The female's body fell backward, away from the man who stood over her. Her dripping heart pulsed in his hand. She groped for her chest, but as she did so, her body ashed, and before flesh and bone hit the floor, it had shaped into an ashy female form and dispersed in a plume about Ian Grim's feet.

The warlock, who held the heart to his mouth but apparently hadn't drank or bitten into the heavy muscle, grinned at CJ and tossed the prize aside. It landed on the floor in a splatter of sticky ash and blood.

"Certainly Jones. It's about fucking time."

"How many vampire hearts do you consume in a century?" CJ asked, knowing he'd worded that one wrong. He should have been more precise, narrowing it down to a year, or even a month.

"As many as I can manage. A man has to stay vital to keep his partner alive."

Yes, Grim's strange woman who, rumors told, had once been beheaded during the French Revolution, only to be resurrected—her head sown upon a different body—and was now kept alive with blood transfusions.

Grim glanced to the ashy mess. "Damn it, now

you've gone and spoiled my count. I may have to start over if I'm ever to get to Daemonia. How the fuck did you manage it?"

"I didn't eat their hearts." CJ wandered into the room, noticing two more piles of ash along the wall. A senseless waste. But who was he to judge? He'd made sacrifices to get to Daemonia.

He hadn't seen Grim in ages, and the man was always different. Tall, yet short for his blocky build, he wore his blond hair in a military cut, which drew CJ's observation to the man's disturbing eyes. Green, yet gray. They changed like a cat's eyes. Or a Fallen angel's eyes.

Yet a constant was Grim's self-important smirk.

"So you got it." Grim paced before him, making an arc on the floor with his path, as both men were never keen to get too close to the other, wary of any possible magical retaliation. His fingers waggled near his thighs, as if a gunslinger judging when best to draw. "The Nacht März."

"Is that what you think?"

"Wow, you're trying an evasive tactic with me? I know you better than your own twin brother, Jones. I can feel your lies on my skin like faulty spellcraft missing its mark."

Grim was confident of his skills, and smart. He could read CJ, as CJ could read the warlock's nervousness in his pacing.

"As a matter of fact, I do have it. I'm enacting the march tomorrow evening."

Grim's expression was a treat. Rarely could he surprise the man. And then his surprise turned to fury. "That should be my call! I was the one to discover its existence."

"Only because of my father."

"Indeed. Following in Daddy's footsteps, eh? You'll be warlock soon enough."

"Never."

CJ dodged the incoming blast of air magic. A simple cast that further detailed Grim's lack of confidence at this moment. He was grasping for whatever was to hand, not thinking.

"You wanted the damned thing? My snatch," CJ said. Keeping his left hand open and ready to repulse retaliatory magic, he stood calmly. "It's always been first come, first served with us, yes? You did take the Sidon's Eye right out of my hands."

"Your lover's fickle hands, you mean."

CJ sighed. The winter of 1936. Sidon's Eye would have granted the holder great power to see beyond this mortal veil and into the Edge, a place much more interesting and far less explored than Daemonia. Unfortunately, Certainly's lover's greed had been more vast than his curiosity over the object. That had been the last time he'd trusted a woman, or had the time for one.

"I'd like to invite you to witness the March," CJ said, putting up his palm to block, this time, an arrow of vampire ash stirred up from the floor and aimed for his eyes. The ash dispersed about his palm and went around his head on both sides. "That is, if you stop acting the child and accept the fact I won this round."

"How did you do it? In order to gain entrance to

Daemonia, a man must consume a vampire heart a day, increasing in succession daily for a month." Grim glanced aside to the bloody heart, still pulsing on the floor. "I've not the stomach for it. And I'm only on day twelve."

CJ shook his head. Not about to divulge how he'd achieved that one. His father's grimoire had revealed a dangerous secret entrance. "Tomorrow at midnight in the C tunnel beyond Val de Seine. Come alone. You can claim the Night March after I've summoned it."

"And why would you give me that control? You're up to something."

"I most likely am."

And Certainly drew up the cloak once again, turned and walked out of the building, confident Grim could not see or sense his departure. He chuckled when the warlock let out a frustrated shout and kicked at the ash pile. He'd won this round.

Regrettably, he could take no pride in such an accomplishment because it had dragged the woman he loved into the center, and it now threatened her very soul.

Libby held the flashlight while Vika fastened the prism before the bulb. She'd removed the glass and, after trying string and cord, found wire worked best, along with a bit of solder.

"You think this is necessary?" Libby asked. "A backup plan? Don't you trust CJ?"

"Of course I trust him."

"But we found the ward." Libby nodded to the open

grimoire on the spell table. The ward could be placed on an individual, unknowing, and would protect the person from malefic magic.

"The ward is against Grim. I don't know why he went to talk to the warlock, but for whatever reason, I want to have that tool to my arsenal should it become necessary to use. This—" she studied the completed flashlight "—is to keep me safe."

Libby's eyes teared. "This is too big for you, Vika."

It was, but she didn't want to admit it. If CJ could handle it, she could. She touched her sister's cheek, catching the teardrop and feeling its sadness enter her pores.

"Remember what you told me about love," Libby said. "Don't get lost in it."

She was already lost. And she liked being there.

"We both ignored that sage wisdom," she said. "Have you any regrets?"

Libby shook her head and couldn't stop her swooning grin.

From the sixth-floor window, Vika tracked CJ's race home from the café at the end of the street. The sun had slipped behind the Louvre, and the sky was yet pale, but darkness clung to the recesses between buildings as if plaque in a demon's teeth.

As he crossed the street below the building, she grabbed the remote and clicked the saving chandelier light back on, granting necessary solace.

"Two left," she muttered as if the light fixtures cared. "And then my dark one needs to do some remodeling. Much as each of them are all gorgeous, this mass gathering of prismatic light is hideous."

She did like the one with the black crystals and silver arabesques that soared six feet high. That one would look lovely over the gray couch.

What was she doing? If and when CJ no longer had need for the prismatic light, he may well want to keep the chandeliers.

Libby had foreseen she was hooking up with CJ to clean him. Her greatest cleaning project ever. But something had changed. While she still wanted his soul clean of demons, she didn't need for him to change, to become less messy or to stop practicing dark magic. She liked him exactly as he was.

"Seems I don't have a type after all," she said with a smile. "Or maybe I've changed that type."

Either way, she was satisfied with letting go the urge to change him. It slipped from her without so much as a goodbye, and she turned to greet her lover as he walked through the door and landed in her arms.

"Everything go as you had hoped?" she asked, nuzzling into his cedar and chartreuse embrace.

"I won't know until tomorrow night. I needed to know where Grim was while I had the Nacht März uncloaked. What better way than to invite him to the party?"

"You're not serious? You told the warlock where we'll be?"

He nodded then kissed her before she could object to his foolish actions. Falling into the depths of his claiming kiss, Vika abandoned protest. Seemed to be the way to manage this beautiful dark man.

"You straightened up around here," he said.

"Made the bed and did a few dishes. It's a compulsion, CJ. You have to accept that about me."

"Okay, but I'll have you know my compulsion is to mess up the bed again." He lifted her into his arms and carried her over to the bed, tossing her to land on the clutter of pillows. Shirt stripped off before she could speak, he crawled across the bed toward her. "Let's make sexmagic tonight."

"To increase your magic for tomorrow?"

"No. Just for us." He waggled the fingers of his tattooed hand. "Don't you want me to master this magic?"

Vika settled against the pillows and tugged up her skirt, revealing her bare feet. "Let the mastery begin."

Vika drew her fingers over her lover's bared chest, tracing a few of the tattoos and marveling at their intricacy. The werewolf scythe gleamed silver with each flex of his muscles. "Didn't that hurt to get the silver embedded in there?"

He slipped the dress from her shoulder and kissed her there. "Tattoos always hurt. But whiskey helps numb the pain."

"I see." She tapped a tiny design slightly left-center of his chest. "This looks like…is this a tiny battery?"

"It's my kick-starter," he said proudly.

"What?"

"Command central, if you will. You know how our bodies are ruled by the earth and electricity?"

"Of course. *I sing the body electric,*" she quoted Walt Whitman.

"Since I dabble in so many dangerous magics, Sayne suggested I have a kick-start in case, well, my heart ever needs it."

"A little tattooed battery is going to give your un-beating heart enough juice to revive you?"

"With the correct connecting tat." He displayed his left hand, and his pinkie fingertip was tattooed with what looked like electrical coding one might see on a building schematic. "I touch this to the battery, and bam!"

"That is…" Vika cringed. "It creeps me out, actually. To even think your heart would stop beating makes me sad."

He spread his hand through her hair and drew her in for a kiss. "Don't worry about me. I don't like it when you frown. Let's try some electrical magic of our own, eh?"

"You mean like work it into sex?"

He nodded and tugged down her dress to puddle about her feet. In turn, he dropped his jeans, and just when she reached for his semihard erection, he grabbed her fingers and pulled her hand up between them. "Let's form the connection first, then the sex will be electric."

"All right. You show me the way." She had heard of witches sharing their innate electricities and knew how it worked, but she had never the opportunity to attempt it.

Both held their palms flat before one another, as if

pressing against a mime's wall placed between them. Their palms were but half an inch from one another, their bodies as close, yet they did not touch. The body generated amazing heat, and it could be brewed to an alchemical mix by combining with another—without even touching.

Immediately, Vika felt the heat warm her palm. She looked into her lover's jade eyes, and he winked. "Draw it over one another," he directed, then recited the word to contain their powers within their beings. "Contineo."

It felt like static electricity snapping against her palms as Vika moved them slowly before CJ's chest without touching skin. And he, in turn, moved his up her arms and neck, and when he neared her breasts, her nipples grew so hard and wanting, she felt the desire tweak at her core and she had to press her legs together to contain the pleasure. The paired electricity snapped and vibrated until it found a rhythmic hum that wavered as if the nerve system under her skin, and perhaps it was just that, was awakened by CJ's innate biology.

"That feels so good," he said, drawing his hands lower over her stomach, where her muscles eased and tightened in anticipation of how good it would feel—right there. "That doesn't hurt?"

"No, it's…so good," she said on a gasp as the vibrations hummed through her loins. "Makes me want to scream, in a good way. Oh, CJ, if I touch you will the connection break?"

"No, we're just charging up now."

"Then I need to touch you." She gripped his erection, and he hissed and swore. "As good as I think it sounded?" she wondered.

"Fuck yeah. My whole... It's as if... So crazy. I need to be inside you now."

She pushed him backward and he pulled her with him onto the bed. Every bit of her skin and muscle and bone hummed as if orgasm had taken up residence permanently. It couldn't last forever, and she didn't want it to, but right now she needed to stop thinking and fall into it all before it was lost.

Crawling over CJ's legs, she fit herself onto him and let out a guttural cry of delight as his cock filled her with such intensity, she felt weak in the head, in the best way possible. Above her the chandeliers tittered as if a minor earthquake, reacting to their combined magics.

"I hope those things are secured," she said.

"They are. Vika." He gripped her arms and held her still upon him, his jaw tight and eyes closed. "Right there." And he swept his tattooed hand across a small box above his right side.

Suddenly enveloped by a spectacular pulse of pleasure, Vika thrust out her arms and threw back her head. Overtaken by exquisite electricity, their bodies sparkled as if a thousand wandering souls had suddenly entered, yet the feeling was all CJ as he came inside her. She could feel him claim her with the power that he wasn't quite able to control, and then she felt his inner demons shudder and slink away. They wanted nothing to do with this wicked magic.

"Who needs a kick-start," CJ gasped, heaving and

coming down from the high, "when I've got you, Bright Spark of My Being."

"That was—" Vika fell forward, collapsing onto CJ's sweaty, hot chest "—phenomenal."

"Well said, witch. Well said."

## Chapter 23

CJ toggled the bone whistle inside his clasped fist. Vika held the prism flashlight directly on his face, which was annoying but necessary. Darkness reigned in the subterranean depths beneath Paris. An essential location to bring forth War and Pain—and other earth-bound demons. If they could slay the initial horde—which should emerge closest to the call—then they could not repopulate and spread worldwide.

That was CJ's theory, anyway.

This task was dangerous, and he risked mortal lives should they not succeed. Should War and Pain refuse to comply—which was likely.

When had demons ever held good on a promise? Never, that he'd known. And with the promise of a kiss from Vika being their reward? Her kisses were amaz-

ing but probably not enough to make a demon heel and
kowtow to their commands.

It was either this option or surrender Vika's and
Libby's souls to the soul bringer. He absolutely refused
to do so, and he prayed this planned bit of trickery
would not be seen as such by Reichardt.

In effect, he was calling the Nacht März to fruition,
as Reichardt had requested. But he wasn't going to
allow a single demon to destroy mortals. Mortal deaths
hadn't been an exact stipulation in Reichardt's command. He had said he would reap the souls, but to
specify how to go about that desired result? Certainly
was stretching the bargain's parameters, but he was
willing to stand up and fight for what he believed in
if it came to that.

Right now, he believed in love.

Yet he felt twisted between the finer emotion and a
more menacing desire to destroy.

He could feel War and Pain inside him. Waiting,
standing at the edge of his soul, giddy with anticipation and the desire to wreak havoc, punish and pum-
mel. To annihilate.

So long as only demons were annihilated, Certainly
could completely get behind their anticipatory waiting.
He'd gladly allow them to take over his body and soul.

Pulling Vika into his arms, he kissed her, taking
the moment to devour her softness, the lush heat of
her mouth married to his. The easy glide of her body
against his. The love that filled his being he could not
fathom, yet he knew it inhabited his very bones. She
had changed him somehow. For had he never met her

would he have someday taken out the bone whistle and considered its use?

Never. And yet, if any of his demons had achieved permanent control, he wasn't sure if his wards would have remained and he'd inadvertently allow them to find the Nacht März.

Vika clung to him, her kisses desperate. He responded with a growl and tugged her closer. War and Pain wanted this kiss also, pressing their command onto her with a bruising touch.

Not yet. CJ broke the kiss, but he did not pull away from the one sweet taste in his life.

He didn't care anymore what Ian Grim thought of him, or if he could show up the warlock one last time. With Vika in his life, none of that selfish grandstanding mattered.

"I love you," he whispered, and nuzzled his nose alongside her hair. She smelled of roses and vervain. He wanted to imprint the scent of her within his senses forever. Just in case…

No, he wouldn't think it.

"Touching."

CJ's heart sank. Over Vika's shoulder, he saw Ian Grim stood not ten feet away, hands in his pockets.

Pulling Vika around to stand behind him, CJ stepped up to Grim. In the distance, a Metro train rumbled and its pale headlight grew stronger.

"Are you going to summon the Nacht März?" Grim asked, pacing before him. He wore a striped shirt and black vest, and long, lean dark trousers slouched at the shoes. Looking trimmer and more stylish than usual.

"I don't believe you'll do it. You've not the cojones. And I can't imagine what you'd do with an army of demons to your command. You know the streets of Paris will laugh and point at such a procession. Nowadays mortals see a paranormal being and they think it's a costume or a lifestyle choice, such as those insipid vampire wannabes."

"You weren't due to arrive for another hour, Grim." He flung out an arm, striking the man across the face with a blast of magic. It cut deeply.

Grim touched the wound, dragging his finger along it, which sewed the flesh seamlessly, leaving behind only a dribble of blood.

"You've mastered vita?" CJ was not surprised. Nothing Grim did surprised him anymore. The warlock was strong.

And he needed to get Vika out of here. Now.

"Rather simple procedure," Grim commented, flicking the blood away from his fingers with an elegant twist of wrist. "I've eaten the hearts of so many vampires I practically heal before the wound is inflicted."

CJ felt a quake in his soul. But it wasn't the warlock's foul deed. Rather, the prism light Vika held lit him only from behind, and War was getting too close to the surface, clawing for control.

"It's in your hand. I can feel the power." Grim held out his hand, palm up, and flicked his fingers.

Certainly felt the bone whistle jitter in his grip. He clutched tightly. This was not going down as he wished, so he'd have to improvise. The ground rumbled as the subway train's wheels glided over the iron tracks.

He could not allow the warlock to put his hands to such a brutal means to mortal annihilation. Time for plan C.

Turning, he slapped the whistle into Vika's grasp. Startled, she dropped the flashlight. He lifted her and tossed her across the tracks, using a blast of air magic to ensure she landed on the other side. He saw her land in a stumble, catching her palm against the scuffed concrete floor.

He stepped back from the edge as the train whisked to a screeching stop before him.

The car, lit with fluorescent bulbs, was empty. War growled and cringed at the light.

Grim let out a tribal yell and gripped his outstretched fingers, tugging CJ closer. The warlock used powerful magic to move CJ's body against his will. The tiles on the floor cracked and crumbled beneath CJ's boots. The bright lights from the train managed to keep back War and Pain—momentarily.

He could feel War rising to the surface, his chest growing full with anger and sulfur.

Knowing he had but moments to use his magic, CJ spit into his hands, slapped them together, then arrowed his forefingers above his head. He drew down the water pipe running overhead and landed it directly onto the center of Grim's skull. The warlock stumbled, releasing his air magic from CJ's body.

The train sped off. War growled, curling CJ's fingers into claws.

Grim shouted a reverse lumos spell, breaking all

the lightbulbs in the area in a rain of fine glass, leaving them in darkness.

"That wasn't very smart," CJ said to the warlock, who clutched his head where blood oozed from the crack in his skull. "But then you always do react before thinking. You ready for this?"

"Wha—?" Grim muttered.

War lunged forth within CJ, assuming control with a slash of his fist and stomp of boot. In the same instant, Pain eyed the bleeding warlock and cackled gleefully.

Vika twisted to sit up and spied another headlight beam traveling down the tunnel. Across the tracks, Certainly and Ian Grim battled it out in the darkness. She wondered how well the warlock would manage against the demons, which had both come out as soon as Grim had broken the lights.

The hard bone whistle impressed into her palm. Fashioned from Lucifer's wing, it was cold and hot at the same time. CJ's plan had been foiled. It had not been used to summon the dark denizens of this realm.

Relief washed through her, goose-bumping her skin. She'd never wanted him to attempt summoning all demons from this realm, she could admit to herself.

Yet *she* could now summon the Nacht März—and save her and Libby's souls. All it took was to blow the whistle.

To do so, or not?

Standing, Vika staggered. She'd landed awkwardly, bruising the skin on the heel of her hand, but she knew CJ had done what he'd thought best by getting her—

and the whistle—out of the warlock's grasp. Across the rails, sparks of magic flew between the two rivals. The demons could not access CJ's magic, so she had to guess the magic was all Grim's doing.

She stumbled down the terminal, away from the battling witches. The best thing she could do was to get the Nacht März as far from Ian Grim as possible.

Red safety lights flickered intermittently along the floor edging the drop onto the rails, but the crimson glow wasn't enough to keep back War and Pain. They must be taking it out on Grim instead of CJ, because a gut-wrenching scream was not her lover's voice. Maybe?

"Not CJ," she whispered with hope, and wandered into utter darkness.

Immediately before her, Reichardt materialized. A sheen of blue surrounded him as if an aura. Dressed in his usual black, he became a part of the dark void as the aura faded, yet his hand held out in waiting was visible.

"Give it to me."

She thrust her fist behind her back, clutching the whistle tightly.

"The dark witch will not command the march now," Reichardt said over the growing rumble from an approaching train. "Let me have it, or forfeit your soul, witch."

Vika heaved out a sigh and stood straight. She drew her hand around and examined her fisted fingers. Inside she held a powerful weapon that could call the demons to the streets to destroy any and all mortals who got in their way. Reichardt wanted to collect those poor, innocent souls. An abominable act she could never participate in and still respect the witch's rede.

And she had only to offer her soul in exchange to prevent such a heinous catastrophe?

The train stopped behind her with a squeal. Headlights beamed on Reichardt's adamant glare. She sensed CJ and Grim had moved onto the train in the course of their struggles. The interior lights should chase away the demons, which she wasn't sure would serve to her lover's success.

Looking into Reichardt's dark eyes, she saw her future. One day the soul bringer would carry her soul away. To Beneath, for surely she had not gained entrance Above. And if it be sooner than she had wished for, then so be it.

She nodded once. It was the right choice. The only choice.

The train started to roll forward.

Vika tossed the bone whistle before the surging car. It bounced on the iron rail, and a brilliant red light shot out as the wheels pulverized the unholy instrument.

Inside the car, Grim's bloodied face pressed to the window courtesy of Pain or War, before the train quickly traveled away. She couldn't see CJ.

Didn't matter anymore.

Nothing mattered now.

Yes, it did. *You love him.*

Reichardt stepped up to her and pressed his palm against her breast. "You chose incorrectly, witch."

Vika felt an incredible pull, as if her insides were being sucked to her core, tearing away from muscle and bone in the most wrenching means possible. She screamed as the pain overwhelmed, flashing brightly in her vision and then draining out to blackness. She fell to her knees.

At Reichardt's hand glowed her soul. He held it high and opened his mouth, dropping the glimmering ball of her essence down his throat.

Vika collapsed.

Crooning out her favorite country tune, Libby shifted her hips then paused from scrubbing the sink to do an air guitar move, using the pink scrub brush as her instrument. "Rock and roll!" she shouted, and then focused back on the task before her.

She'd missed her calling, but only because she couldn't carry a tune for more than a few notes. Then her voice wobbled off octave and it all went kittywompus from there. Didn't matter. She sounded awesome in the shower.

Her senses suddenly prickling, Libby stood abruptly from scrubbing. One gloved hand wielded the scrub brush, the other a shaker of lemon salts. With her wrist, she nudged aside a long strand of hair and turned to find Reichardt standing immediately behind her.

"Oh! You always come when I least expect it." She tossed the brush over a shoulder, and it landed in the sink with a clank. Tugging out the earbuds, she smoothed her gloved palms over her hips. "What's up, lover boy? I have cook—"

He pressed his palm to her chest, and for a moment

she thought she'd finally gotten through to the soul bringer, had breeched his hardened glass heart.

Screw the cookies; she wanted another kiss.

And then the pain swept her system and she screamed out her sister's name before collapsing in a heap on the kitchen floor among a scatter of lemon salts.

## Chapter 24

The train emerged aboveground as the window smashed out and CJ and Grim flew through it. Propelled by magic and demonic strength, they landed against a telephone pole—Grim's spine taking the brunt of impact—and dropped to the pebbled gravel below. Somewhere in the train yard, yard lights glowed, yet darkness mastered the air here behind a high garage that housed derelict train cars.

Pain grasped Grim's skull and twisted, but the warlock was, to Pain's surprise, strong, and he reacted with magic that shot through his host's skin with an erotic sting on icy needles. It felt so fucking good, he writhed in ecstasy and let go of his charge.

"Oh, me do love a man who can work my fetishes," Pain cooed.

The incorporeal demon released its grasp of CJ's

soul, and the next time Ian Grim's fist connected with CJ's jaw, Pain hitched a ride on the warlock.

CJ choked and spat up blood, staggering as he managed to remain standing. For the first time since the demons had overtaken his body in the subway tunnel, he felt a moment of clarity, of feeble control. Pain was gone, but War was not, and it still held a grip on him.

"Suck this, Jones!" Grim's fist blasted his jaw with a strength CJ hadn't felt before. Pain's power had been behind it. And as the world began to blur, he felt War rise up and take control.

"We had a deal," War spouted, as he lifted Grim bodily and tossed him against the brick wall. "You've abandoned ship!"

Pain laughed wickedly as he inspected the bloody gashes along his arm, torn there by the rough bricks. "Me get the warlock. You can deal with the dark witch. There's not going to be a Night March. The witch tricked us both!"

CJ felt War's anger squeeze about his bones. The demon roared and ripped a steel fence post from the ground. It charged Grim, who stood waiting for the punishment, Pain's crooked grin twisting his bloody mouth. CJ could not fight War's strength, yet he could feel it waning. They stood in a slash of yard light. How could the demons withstand the light?

"By your invitation," War muttered, as he swung and missed the warlock. "We maintain control in the light. Idiot, witch."

Grim recited an expulsion spell. He was powerful and had somehow overcome Pain, and he was now trying to expel the demon from his body. CJ thought if he could touch the warlock when the final word was spoken...

War wheeled his body away from the warlock and searched the grounds for another weapon. Forcing his body to move with only his mind, CJ managed to thrust toward the warlock.

He slapped his grip about Grim's neck as the last word of the expulsion spell was shouted. Pressing the fingers of his left hand over his heart and the entrance spell, he held on tight. Lightning sparked between the two witches. Rain showered them. Their bodies juddered, connected through a vile communion of dark and malefic magic. A tribal grunt emitted from CJ's core, dueling with Grim's scream.

And CJ felt War leave his body and sluice into Grim as if a dark mist seeping from his pores. No flesh torn, just a tug at his molecules. A simple exit.

He dropped the warlock and scrambled away. The demons were gone from him. He felt lightened. *Free.*

No time to rejoice, for they had taken up residence within Grim's soul. And he could not stand against War and Pain.

Vika. Where was she? Back in the tunnel.

As the yard light flashed in CJ's eyes, he staggered over Grim's prone body. The warlock was far from dead, but he'd lost this battle. Spitting to the side, CJ smacked a hand to his opponent's cheek. He was covered in blood, and not all of it was Grim's. War and Pain had served him well.

"You earned your reward."

"To kiss the red witch," Grim muttered weakly.

"Yes. But I won't grant it while you are sheltered within this disgusting warlock. Later, Grim."

Certainly ran out of the train station and toward the city. He had an idea where he was, and he sighted the Metro stop at the end of a triangular block. He raced toward the entry station, shoving aside passengers who scrambled to get out of his way when they saw the blood covering his hands and face. He ran down the concrete stairway and read the map along the tiled wall. She was five stops back. He jumped onto the train as the doors closed.

Half a dozen people stood or sat nearby. He kept his back to them, but he realized his shirt was torn and he was bleeding everywhere. Didn't matter what they thought. He'd left Vika alone with the Nacht März. Never should he have placed such a dangerous object in her hands. And not because he didn't think she could handle it, but because he didn't want to taint her any more than he already had merely by being in her presence.

He had changed Viktorie St. Charles. And he wasn't sure that was a good thing. Yet she had changed him, and he knew it was for the better.

"I'm sorry," he muttered, wishing the train would move faster. "I'm almost there. Hold on, lover."

Sweeping his tattooed hand over the healing sigil at his hip, he sucked in a breath as his skin knit in various places on his body. Now that the demons were gone, his magic worked smoothly. He laughed because his renewed strength felt immense. Back to his old self. And so powerful.

The train slid to a stop. CJ saw the red witch lying in a dark corner and jumped off the train, sealing the door behind him so those inside could not follow.

Racing to her, he knelt beside her and lifted her head. Garnet hair spilled over his hands and knees. "Vika?"

She murmured and winced. "You're…safe?"

"War and Pain are gone."

She touched his face then glided her fingers down to his neck, where the demon mark was—or had once been. "It's gone. You're demon-free?"

"Yes, but it doesn't matter right now. I'm sorry. I had to throw you to this side to get you away from Grim and the demons. Tell me you're not hurt. Please, Vika."

He nuzzled his cheek against her forehead. Her skin felt cool. He didn't see any bruises, but…something was different.

"The whistle is destroyed," she whispered, touching his bloodied lips and managing a smile. "Tossed it in front of the train."

"That's good. Smart of you."

Only, that wasn't good. As much as he'd been hoping to get by with a sleight of hand regarding the soul bringer, now the Nacht März call had not been issued. Vika's and Libby's souls were still in jeopardy. Could he find the pieces of the whistle and reassemble them before the forty-eight-hour deadline passed?

"He was here," she said on a breathless gasp. "Reichardt."

"What?" He lifted her into his arms and hugged her close. Why was she so cold? Humid air cloaked the tunnel depths. "You should have given him the whistle."

She shook her head vehemently. "Couldn't sacrifice all those mortals. Unthinkable. He took…my soul."

"No, no, Vika, no!"

"I will…survive." She coiled into him. "Take me home."

He'd failed her. He had only wanted to prevent the soul bringer from taking his lover's soul. And because of his idiot macho rivalry with the warlock, instead he'd handed Vika's soul to Reichardt on a silver platter.

He set her down on the couch in her living room and brushed aside the hair from her face. She'd walked up the front steps with him, but she was exhausted. She mumbled something about her mala beads in the bedroom, and CJ figured she wanted them. He rushed upstairs to claim the strand of jade beads from the vanity. He draped them over her fingers, and sleep took her as soon as she closed her eyes. He grabbed the red blanket from a nearby chair and covered her to the shoulders.

Salamander jumped onto the back of the couch. The cat mewled warningly at CJ.

"It was my fault," he said in agreement. "I'm sorry."

He touched Vika's pale cheek with his fingers. No rosy blush there. She was cold because she now had no soul.

"Misfortunate lover, mine. I will get it back for you," he vowed. "If I have to go to Above and Beneath and sort through the eternity of souls within. I promise you."

He kissed her forehead and stood.

The chandelier was lit, so he flicked it off. It was nearing morning but still dark. Hell, he didn't need the light anymore. He was free of demons. He should be celebrating. And yet, the inner triumph meant little to him.

He would take on a world of demons in trade for Vika's soul. And her sister's soul.

Wondering where Libby was, he pushed open the swinging kitchen door and saw the legs stretched out from beyond the counter.

"Oh, hell."

He rushed to find Libby on the floor, her hands spread open, eyes closed. Cold to the touch. "That bastard."

Lifting her, he carried her upstairs to her bedroom and laid her on the bed, covering her with a blanket and making her the same promise he had made to Vika.

"The soul bringer and I are going to come to terms."

And he suspected one of them wouldn't survive. But in his heart, he had no idea which of the two of them it would be.

Ian Grim opened his eyes and stared at the rising sun. Arms stretched out above him and legs sprawled across the gravel, he felt every painful ache, every broken bone and cut that abraded his skin. But it felt…great.

He was healing, slowly. Certainly Jones had taken a lot out of him. A fine match.

But the dark witch had also given him something he hadn't expected, and he would not begrudge this gift. For indeed, the two demons he felt roil within his soul had been gifts.

"War and Pain," he muttered, and chuckled at the back of his throat. "I can work with you two."

# Chapter 25

Vika woke in the cool morning light of her living room. The scent of spice welcomed her with a gentle slap to her senses. A rose-embellished porcelain tea-cup sat on the coffee table, steam wafting from the amber surface.

"You're awake," her lover's voice spoke from some-where nearby. He sat in the winged chair across the room where shadows yet reigned. "I thought clove and cinnamon would appeal."

"Thank you." She sat up and, almost dropping the jade beads, slipped the strand about her wrist, coiling it a few times. Having the prayer beads close gave her solace. She rubbed her palms up and down her arms, feeling inordinately chilled for the middle of summer. She sipped the sweet brew. That hit the spot. Her core felt frozen, stained by darkness. The tea warmed her a little— "The light!"

What sat across from her in the shadows, acting as if her lover?

CJ stood and approached her, his steps easy and demeanor calm. He didn't feel demonic, but Vika pressed her back to the couch and absently reached for her grandmother's nail.

"They're gone," he said quietly. "War and Pain. Grim took them out of me."

"As a favor?" she asked, not believing the warlock would do anything so kind.

"No, I had in mind to put them into Grim when I had opportunity. The demon initially resisted, but then, it was gone. Poof. Like that. I think Grim stole them for himself. All I know is I'm clean of demons for the first time in half a year, and it feels beyond amazing. So light. And now, sitting in the darkness? It's a comfort."

"But Grim. What will he do with them? It'll be nothing good."

"I'm sure not, *if* he can control them. Which he may have the ability to do. He's powerful, Vika. But I feel as though he's out of our lives for now." He clasped her hand and kissed it. "How are you?"

How *was* she? She felt the same as usual after one had been tossed about and through a tussle. And yet, not warm, or even whole. Empty.

"Soulless," she said, her heart stilling at the implications. "It had to be done. So let's not get into an argument about what I should or should not have done. It's over. The soul bringer got his due. The Nacht März was not issued. The world is as right as it can be. At least until you decide to steal another dangerous instrument from the place of all demons."

"Never," he rushed out. "I promise you that."

"What if Grim wants something?"

"I'll let him go at it. I swore to you I would not return to Daemonia, and I stand by that promise."

Did his eyes seem greener? Not so dark. Alive with warmth, they compelled her as had the beads about her wrist. Solace.

"I believe you," she said, and then tilted up her chin to kiss him at the corner of his mouth. "Thank you, dark one."

"You have nothing to thank me for. You are without a soul. I could have prevent—"

She put up her palm, and he understood to drop the subject. "Vika, I uh…I put your sister upstairs in her room. I found her in the kitchen."

"Libby? Ohmygoddess, I didn't think about her. She was…?"

CJ nodded. "The bastard took her soul, too. You should go to her."

"Yes." She handed him the teacup and rushed up the stairs to find her sister just waking on the bed. "Libby?"

Sitting on the middle of the bed, her sister took one look at her and started to cry. "Oh, Vika! I love him. How could he do that to me?" She pounded her breast with a fist. "It's gone. He took it without a care. After we'd…after… Oh!"

CJ crept into the room, put a hand to Vika's hip and

whispered in her ear, "I'm going to leave you two. You should be with your sister right now."

She clutched his shirt. "I don't want you to leave." She knew she sounded frantic, but hell, she was. After all they had been through, could he so easily walk away from her now?

"I have to. I have something to do at work."

"You're not going after Ian Grim. Tell me you're not."

"The warlock has nothing I want or need. But I won't stop until I get your souls back," he said. "I can't."

She gripped his shirt, stopping his retreat and wishing she had some kind of containment magic. "It's over, CJ. Leave it as it is. Because I know you'll offer your soul for ours, and what is that going to change? Nothing."

"My soul may be more valuable to the soul bringer than yours and Libby's together. I'm filled with knowledge of multitude magics—"

"No! I won't hear of it. This is not some one-upmanship between you and the warlock. This is me. And you. And I don't want a lover without a soul. Hell, you just got it clean of demons. Don't you want that?"

"I don't want a lover without a soul, either," he whispered. Brushing a kiss over her hair, he stepped back and shuffled down the stairs.

Vika clung to the door frame, following his retreat. Her heart shuddered against her rib cage, and her skin grew cold, so cold.

Of course. She was damaged now. Cold and soulless. How could any man want that? By tossing the bone whistle before the train, she had sacrificed not only her soul but also her relationship with CJ.

She looked to Libby and saw tears spilling silently from her sister's eyes. And Vika began to cry, too.

CJ sorted through the recent acquisitions the archives had received after the raid on Antonio del Gado's private lair. The vampire leader of the tribe Anakim had been determined to call the Fallen to this earth, with hope the angels would then find and impregnate their muses with a Nephilim. Anakim was a vampire tribe whose members could not withstand sunlight, yet with an infusion of Nephilim blood, their lineage would be strengthened. The leader, del Gado, had failed with his plot. And the spoils had been collected by Council member Ivan Drake and ordered stored in the archives.

The code for Final Days had been locked securely. Various angel ephemera still awaited filing. A notebook with angel sigils and another book handwritten by a muse listed a majority of the Fallen ones' names. Match the sigil to the name, and a person in the know could summon a Fallen to this realm. That was helpful, to a degree.

The soul bringer had fallen, but not purposefully, and CJ could not find his name on any list. Of course, he didn't know his angelic name. Reichardt had originally been an angel, expelled from Above to serve as ferryman of souls. He wasn't the same as a Fallen angel because he had either accepted the challenge to fall and become soul bringer, or he'd been shoved. No book detailed that stipulation. And though his origins were angelic, CJ wasn't sure if the man was still considered such, or if he was an entirely different beast.

He set the books of names and sigils aside and wandered into the grimoire storage room, knowing it boasted a whole section dealing with Above and all its native inhabitants. The dusty room made him sneeze, and once again he vowed to get an assistant.

Or a dedicated cleaner.

He'd hated to leave Vika, but he had known she and her sister needed to be alone. He regretted saying the thing about not wanting a lover without a soul. He hadn't meant she repulsed him, only that he felt responsible for her missing soul.

Hell, he wasn't as proficient in this relationship thing as he liked to believe.

And he had come from a tremendous battle against Grim so he was off-kilter, not completely in grasp of the finer talents of empathy.

No excuse. He'd avoided one disaster, only to create another. He should have called the demons to the march and let the chips fall where they may. Only problem with that was the chips were mortals. And he could not live with such a result on his conscience.

"I need a full name," he muttered, and headed toward the Angel section of the room. "On second thought." He pulled out his cell phone and dialed up Cinder.

Vika answered the phone only because Libby shoved her toward it. Feeling lethargic and wanting to sleep all day, she'd stared at the phone for three rings. As depressed as her sister was, Libby was still oddly chipper and had thought about making a batch of cookies. Until the sight of the chocolate chips had made her cry.

It was Vincent Lepore from the Council, requesting she clean up out by the ring road.

"I'm not sure," she said.

"Are you busy? Vika, you're the only cleaner available in the area, and this is on a mammoth scale."

"What's going on?"

"It's Ian Grim. Seems he's unleashed a war demon on the streets of Paris. There are five mortal casualties thus far, and dozens of vampires."

She gasped. "Mortals. Oh, no. Has Grim been contained?"

"We're working on that, but his magic is insurmountable."

"Certainly Jones," she blurted before thinking it through. "He can stand against Grim. I know he can."

"I didn't think of that. I believe he's in the archives right now. Thanks. You'll get on the job?"

She agreed then hung up. "Libby, we've a mess to clean up."

A mess she had somehow started.

## Chapter 26

Grim was out stalking the streets of Paris with War leading the way. Not good. CJ knew he couldn't stop the warlock, especially under the influence of War and Pain, but after some thought, he decided he may be able to steer War over to his side with an offer the demon couldn't refuse.

Unless, of course, War enjoyed occupying Ian Grim. Then CJ's plan would be shot to hell.

It didn't take long to find the warlock. The Council had been tracking him since the first mortal deaths had been reported. Yet the warlock ducked in and out of buildings, attempting stealth.

No demons made CJ a strong, alert witch. He was in complete control of his faculties—and his litany of spellcraft and magics. Using his black-bladed athame to prick the air before him, and whispering a sensory command, CJ drew up the sulfurous scent of War. His body recognized the demon and his muscles cringed, yet he stood strong, unwilling to flinch at a reunion with the powerful demon.

Turning a corner, CJ took a quick step when he spied Grim licking the blood from a knife blade and gurgling with delight. Both War and Grim would react the same, so CJ must be cautious until he knew who was in control of the body.

Shirt unbuttoned, he touched the entrance spell above his left nipple, closing it with a tap of his forefinger, and then enacted his wards without cloaking.

Grim whipped his head toward CJ and snickered in a deep, growling rumble CJ recognized all too well. The warlock was in control or, at the least, leading his wicked inhabitants.

"Grim," he said, approaching cautiously and keeping his blade in view at his side. "I see you're enjoying your new companions?"

"War is my bitch," the warlock said on a spatter of blood. "He likes to kill things. I will reap his tally and gain entrance to Daemonia."

"The Nacht März has been destroyed. What more could you want now?"

"Daemonia is rife with decadent tools of destruction. You know I like to possess impossible things." The warlock's body suddenly arched awkwardly, and he dragged his shoulder, revealed through his ripped shirt, down the brick wall, leaving a bloody stain. "Pain's an asshole, though," he said through gritted teeth, obviously fighting against the demon's control. "He's trying my healing spells."

"I want to speak to War," CJ demanded. "Now."

Grim growled, his voice echoing with sepulchral tones that could birth only from the place of all demons. With an unnatural twist of his head upon his neck, the warlock's face hardened and his cheekbones sharpened. Indeed, the demons had gained power inside the warlock's body.

"You miss me, dark witch?" War hissed.

"Not particularly. But I do need a favor of you."

The demon laughed so icily the sound would have cracked tombstones.

"I would have given you your freedom, your passage to Daemonia," CJ said, "but instead, you prefer to be this warlock's bitch?"

War lunged, snapping Grim's bloody maw at CJ. "Get me out of this warlock!"

"I can do that," CJ offered. "You should be easy enough to exorcise now you've entered a host while in the mortal realm. But I want something in exchange. Information."

"You are aware I know much. I like that about you, dark witch. This idiot tries to control..." The demon winced and smashed Grim's head aside the brick wall. "He is strong, but Pain keeps him in check. Heh, heh. What do you want to know?"

"What is of more value to a soul bringer than the souls he collects day and night?"

"Heh. Nothing. The angelic freaks are automatons. They want for nothing. They require nothing. Although…"

"I thought so." CJ spun the dagger smartly between his fingers. "One exorcism, ready to rock. You taking?"

War bristled, lifting Grim's chest and huffing out a hot breath that challenged CJ's determination to stand in the face of such rancid odor.

"The soul bringer would desire his own soul," War offered.

Interesting. CJ had no idea the angelic breed actually had souls. And yet, he was aware the Fallen lost their souls when plummeting to earth, so it made sense the others would have them, as well. "Where is it? Can it be found? Given to the soul bringer?"

"It lies where most forgotten things go," War said, following with a wicked laugh that pricked down CJ's spine like a spiked wheel.

"Daemonia," CJ guessed. Fuck. Why was everything in that accursed place? "I need that soul."

"I've given you information. Send me back."

"I want the soul bringer's soul."

"I can't give you what I have not access to. Give me what you promised, dark witch."

"Very well. You have served me admirably, War. But if I may humble myself and dare to request a favor, you would have my eternal gratitude."

"Gratitude is intangible. It is not as satisfying as broken bones."

"As are you intangible. In Daemonia you rule in corporeal form. I need that soul." He waited for the demon to get over his bad self and realize Daemonia truly was the place for him. Didn't take long.

Grim's bloodied face cracked a broken-toothed grin. "Bring the Nacht März to Daemonia, and I'll give you one soul ringer's soul in exchange."

CJ had promised Vika he would never return to Daemonia. And the damned whistle was broken. Did the demon want it in pieces? So much to consider, and not the time or place to do so when War stared him down.

"It must be a specific soul," CJ said. "One belonging to Reichardt Fallowgleam."

"His complete name?"

"Kryatron, Angel of the Seventh Soul." Cinder had been a member of the angelic ranks at one time; he had come through for CJ.

"Gratitude in the form of my release to Daemonia." He considered it. "Then we've a bargain. And I will have that promised kiss from the red witch."

CJ nodded. "Someday."

War spread out Grim's arms, lifting his head and closing his eyes. "Commence!"

Using the blade, CJ drew a pentacle in the air before the demon-possessed warlock and recited the Latin exorcism rites. The body took the force of his rede, plunging against the wall. Grim cried out as War was forced out and back to Daemonia. The warlock collapsed forward, catching his palms in a bloody smear across the cobbles before CJ's feet.

"No!" Grim cried as CJ strode away. "Get the other

out! I can't control it. It'll kill me to serve its desire for pain!"

"I doubt that," CJ called back. "It'll spare your life in order to use it over and over, even if it has to grind you to the core. You'd best get yourself to a Catholic church before Pain tears off all your skin. See you around, Grim. Next time, let's do this the gentleman's way and make it official dueling rules, yes?"

Veering toward the Metro station, CJ now had a new mission.

"You know, we're cleaning up your boyfriend's mess." Libby tossed a severed werewolf head into the black bag.

"It's not CJ's mess—nor is it his fault." How werewolves had gotten into the mix, Vika did not want to know.

"He let the warlock take the last demons from him. They, in turn, created this mess. Seems like it's the dark witch's fault to me."

Vika looked up from sweeping up a pile of vampire ash sodden with blood. She blew a strand of hair from her face that had escaped the Tyvek cap. "This, coming from the chick whose boyfriend stole my soul?"

Libby gaped. "He was only doing what he promised! What he was owed!"

"Seriously, Libby?"

Her sister's defensive posture deflated, and Libby knelt next to the werewolf's headless body. "I'm sorry. You're right. I just feel so—"

"Cranky?"

"Yes. And bitchy. That's so not like me. It's what not having a soul is like, isn't it?"

"I hope not. But I feel the same. Not right. And so cold."

"Me, too. I need a sweater and it's seventy degrees out. Hand me that foot. I'll stuff it in this bag."

Vika did so and shivered at contact with her sister's skin. If she had wondered what having no soul would mean to them, she had to look no further than Libby. Her sister was growing hard inside, adamantine. She was sinking, and Vika didn't know what to do to pull her to the surface. Because she was sinking right beside her, both failing to clutch on to the life raft neither could see.

She wondered, with futile hope, if CJ were having any luck contacting Reichardt. And then she cursed herself for wishing such a thing. She had meant it when she'd told CJ she would not tolerate him trading his soul for theirs. At least one of them in this relationship must retain a soul.

If it could be considered a relationship now. *I don't want a lover without a soul, either.*

He may be finished with her. She couldn't let that happen. She'd not had her say, a chance to fight for what she wanted. And what she wanted was Certainly Jones.

"Let's hurry," she said. "I suddenly need to know what CJ is up to."

"Hopefully, he's trying to get us out of this mess."

"Yes, but at a risk to his own soul? I couldn't abide such a thing."

Libby sighed. "True. He's suffered enough. And we did get ourselves in this mess by consorting with the soul bringer."

Vika lifted an eyebrow. The true meaning of her sister's statement soared completely over her head.

Libby gestured to the back of the hearse. "I can roll the vacuum over the vamp ash if you want to go."

"No, I'll help you finish. It'll be faster that way."

CJ located the place where he'd found Vika in the train station after he'd thrown her across the tracks. She'd tossed the Nacht März before the train, and it had been crushed.

But why had either of them believed it would stay crushed? Something forged from Lucifer's wing had to be indestructible.

He waited for the current train to pass by then leaped down onto the rail and scanned a flashlight over the darkened recesses within the iron rails and tie bars. The thing was small and white, and so were the pebbles between each tie. He should be able to sense it, having held it enough.

Spreading out his left hand, he invoked the entrance spell and opened his senses wide. A wicked zap of electricity tickled his palm, and he reached, blindly, and grasped the whistle. Darkness shimmered through him as if goose bumps pricked up his skin. "Gotcha."

Now to call his brother, TJ, and his best friend, Lucian Bellisario. He'd need Lucian to give blood to help him rescue the woman he loved.

# Chapter 27

Vika knocked on CJ's door and almost twisted the knob and barged in, but she held back. Anxiously twisting the mala beads about her wrist, she knew her urgency was probably false. CJ wouldn't actually jump into some kind of dark, dangerous magic without telling her. Would he?

"Yes, he would," she muttered, then smiled at Libby, who had begged to come along, only because she didn't want to sit home alone pondering over her missing soul.

"He'll be fine," Libby offered, but it wasn't her greatest effort at providing reassurance. "And we'll be fine, too. What's taking so long to answer a stupid door?"

Just as Vika made a grab for the doorknob, the door opened. "Oh, CJ." She put her arms around his neck, and when a kiss was imminent, his sage scent put her off. "You're not CJ."

The man who looked like her lover offered her a shrug and a friendly grin. "Sorry. I'm TJ. Thoroughly Jones."

"The twin brother?" Libby perked beside Vika.

"You two really are identical," Vika said. Except TJ was broader and more muscle-bound than CJ, she decided. Certainly's muscles were nothing to sneeze at, though. Give her hard and lean, the adventurous brother with the magic fingers, any day.

"Come in, Vika," CJ called.

She spotted him leaning against the kitchen counter, arms crossed over his bare chest, jeans slung low on his hips and a whimsical look on his face. Another man stood next to him, tall, dark and also handsome as sin.

"I see you've met my brother."

"Almost got a kiss," TJ said, but not in a teasing manner. He smiled at Vika and gestured she and Libby enter.

"Oh, my goddess." Libby's head tilted back and her mouth dropped open as she studied the constellation of crystals.

Passing beneath the chandeliers, which were not lit, felt eerie, but Vika knew it wasn't the lacking light that caused her skin to goose-bump and her senses to go on alert. The atmosphere was heavy with dark magic and testosterone. She could feel it ripple over her skin, and not in a good way.

"What are you doing here, Vika? I thought you and Libby were—"

"Busy cleaning up your mess?" she countered, hands

to hips. Then she couldn't hold up the standoffish front, and she put her arms over his shoulders and kissed him. "I couldn't stay away. I don't want you to do anything rash. Promise me you're not doing something crazy? I can feel it. Something is not right here."

The man next to CJ cleared his throat.

"This is my best friend, Lucian Bellisario," CJ said in introducing them. "Vampire and antiques dealer. He's a shop in the seventh quarter. And my friend since the nineteenth century."

"You managed to hang with this guy that long, eh?" she offered, and shook the vampire's hand. It was a strong grip, and she noted Lucian's eyes sparkled with charm.

"We're the only two who can stand one another's company for so long," the man offered with what she noted was an Italian accent. Lucian cast a glance over Vika's shoulder. "And the other lovely redhead is?"

"Oh, sorry." Vika tugged Libby up beside her. "This is Libby, my sister."

"Nice to meet you, Lucian." Libby shook his hand. "Very strong grip. You guys are all so...striking."

CJ and Lucian exchanged looks along with sheepish grins, and Vika couldn't help a roll of her eyes.

"Libby?" TJ called from the salt circle, where he had retreated. "You the one involved with the soul bringer?"

"Oh, yes. Well, I mean, you know, we're close."

"Close? Uh, didn't he take your soul?" TJ asked.

"Yes, but he was just doing his job." Libby's smile faded quickly as she realized how pitifully desperate that statement had sounded.

Vika caught Lucian's smirk. "What are you doing here?"

"I'm part of the necessary accoutrements for the evening's entertainment."

"Necessary...?" A vampire and two witches? She turned to CJ, unable to hide her displeasure. "What are you doing? I know you're up to something. You can't do it. I won't let you do it."

"It's already begun." He looked aside, and she followed his gaze to the massive salt circle on the floor. TJ walked around it, smudging the air with a smoking roll of sage. Consecrating the circle in turn with an athame. "I didn't tell you because I didn't want you to worry."

"Worry I might never see you again? How thoughtful of you. You're not going."

"Where do you think I'm going?"

"Obviously, to Daemonia." Vika caught Libby's gasping look. Yes, she'd said it again, named the awful, evil place she had sworn never to invoke. She didn't care anymore. Too much was at stake, namely, her lover's soul. "I don't know what you plan to do, but I can feel that is your goal. Our souls are gone, CJ. Just leave it at that. Libby and I will be—"

He gripped her head between his palms. "Not fine. Never fine without a soul, Vika. And don't try to convince yourself of that. I will not rest until you and your sister have back what is rightfully yours."

"It's a nice thought," Libby interjected, "but seriously, I don't know what you can do. Especially in Daemonia. The soul bringer never sets foot in that wicked place."

"Even if you could do something," Vika added, "it's

too dangerous. How— Why do you think it can happen in Daemonia?"

"Five minutes, CJ," his brother called from his position manning the circle. "Lucian, get that shank of silver tubing ready."

The vampire shook his head in morose acceptance and wandered over to the table near the sofa, where he picked up a long silver pipe. Studying the gleaming thin pipe, he winced then started to unbutton his shirt.

Vika couldn't guess what that was all about, but the shivers had not left her skin.

"You're not going to stop this, no matter what I have to say, are you?" she challenged.

CJ took her hands and held them in a clasp between them. Meeting his eyes, she wanted to do a soul gaze, to look deep within him and somehow convince him this was not worth it. *She* was not worth it. And now that he was no longer infested with demons, such a gaze would be possible.

But she had no soul. A soul gaze was impossible.

"Lover mine," he said. "Bright Star of My Heart. Witch of My Dreams. I'm bringing the Nacht März to Daemonia—"

"No, you— It was destroyed."

"Not for long. Something crafted from Lucifer's wing can never be destroyed. I returned to the Metro tunnel and found it." He slipped a hand in his pocket and pulled out the white bone whistle. Vika cringed from the horrible thing. "Before I exorcised War from Ian Grim, we made a deal."

"Another deal with a demon? Oh, Certainly. You… you promised you would never go back there."

"I did, and…if you cannot see to trusting me on this, and still want me to uphold that promise, then I will. I have to. My word is good, Vika, I mean it. But, hear me out before you decide. If I bring this to Daemonia, then War will hand me Reichardt Fallowgleam's soul in exchange."

"That's the soul bringer's name?" What a stupid question. Did it matter? But she'd never heard it before, and it struck her as a sidhe name. She looked to her sister. "Did you know that?"

Libby shrugged and offered a sheepish nod. What other things had she not told Vika about the soul bringer?

She turned to CJ. "Why is his soul in Daemonia?"

"According to War, any Fallen one who serves as soul bringer, their soul was taken to Daemonia after the fall."

Made no sense to her, but then she knew next to nothing about the angelic ranks. "Why *his* soul?"

"Because." He kissed her hand and rubbed his cheek aside her knuckles. The subtle magic in his hand tingled over her skin. "I'm going to offer it to Reichardt in exchange for the St. Charles sisters' souls."

Libby's gasp preceded Vika's blurted-out "He won't agree. What is a soul to Reichardt?"

"Won't it make him mortal?" Libby chimed in. "He wouldn't want that. Of course…I would."

"How do you know?" CJ countered.

"How do *you* know?" Vika challenged.

"I don't. But I'm willing to take the chance," he said. "For you. Both of you. I have to do this. Much as it kills me, and marks my soul blacker than it is now, I have to break the promise I made to you. If...you will allow it."

Vika's heart melted into a big mushy puddle. This man was willing to go to a literal hell and make a bargain with an unreliable demon to procure something that may have little value to the one person who could restore her soul. Because he loved her.

"I love you," she whispered, feeling a hot teardrop splash her nose. "You stupid, impractical, reckless, dark and dangerous witch, you."

"Sweet words like that are what make me love you so much. Can you give me permission?"

"To break your promise? Yes. Because you do it with a true heart. For actually going to Daemonia again? I think it's going to take some time to forgive you for that."

"I'm not actually going there. My doppelgänger will. It's hard to explain. You'll see what we've cooked up. Now, TJ is waiting. And I don't want Lucian to lose his courage."

"How is the vampire involved?"

"Vika, I told you there were things I had to do to go to Daemonia. Sacrifices I made." He glanced to the vampire, and she understood.

Vampire blood was commonly used in witchs' spells. Their hearts were the catalyst to the witch gaining another century of immortality. Powerful magic that. She could guess a vampire sacrifice could serve a catalyst to entrance into Daemonia. Surely, he had made many.

"That explains all the vampire deaths we've been called to clean up lately. Ian Grim?"

Certainly nodded. "I suspect he was trying to get to Daemonia even knowing I'd already been there. I've a carte blanche to entrance now, but will need blood to reopen the doors. Lucian has offered to assist. But we have to get rolling. There's a window we have."

She gripped his shirt. "What if you don't come back?"

He squeezed her hand. "I'm not leaving this realm. If all goes well, I'll be safe in the circle, and my doppelgänger will trek through Daemonia. TJ is going to hold me here. It'll work. I promise."

Vika sighed. It sounded reasonable. And not. Anytime a man—of any breed—involved himself in the workings of Daemonia, it could not end well. She gripped his hand as if to squeeze it tight enough would hold him to her.

"I love you," he whispered. "Your love will keep me here. I know it."

She nodded. "You have to do what feels right. But I'm staying here. I'll sit on the couch and stay out of your way. Libby will, too. You can't ask us to leave."

The brothers exchanged glances. Lucian shrugged, leaving the decision up to the witch in charge.

"Fine." CJ kissed her quickly. "But stay out of the way, witch, or I will spank you. And on second thought, Libby, you might want to keep an eye on Lucian. No matter what occurs, trust he will be fine. But take a look at him after his part is done, will you?"

Libby exchanged nervous gazes with the vampire, and nodded silently.

"Let's do this," TJ rallied.

# Chapter 28

A circle has no beginning and no end. There is, theoretically, no way in and no way out. The perfect means for protecting magic—and containing the vilest of evils.

It was amazing to watch the brothers work in tandem. Two masters of dark spellcraft who barely had to speak to one another and easily found a deep, harmonizing rhythm to their spell chant. CJ, stripped to but tattered jeans, stood barefoot in the center of the circle, the white-bone Nacht März in hand. He chanted low and bass to his brother's matching bellow.

Thoroughly Jones, clad in black and wearing a top hat that emphasized his darkness with a steampunkish touch of mischief, walked the circle with a bended knee and a spring to his step, almost as if an Indian fancy dance. He recited a spell Vika was not familiar with, but she understood they were summoning a doppelganger for CJ, a double who would emulate him in flesh, blood and even soul and who would remain connected to CJ via a fine astral cord that should run between them. An invisible cord of life—CJ's aura, if you will.

Vika had never seen the ceremony performed before, and she sat forward beside her sister, her elbows on her knees, fingers clutching the jade beads.

TJ nodded to Lucian, who had removed his shirt and wielded the steel pipe. Vika didn't want to imagine its use, but she had a good idea. Blood from the vampire's heart was the important ingredient.

"The things I do for friends." Lucian offered the sisters a smirk.

Stepping inside the salt circle, the vampire handed the pipe to CJ, and without a second thought or a verbal warning, CJ jammed the pipe into his best friend's chest.

Libby let out a chirp. They clasped hands, and Vika's shiver joined her sister's shaking. It wasn't like her to get frightened during spellcraft. They pulled one another into a hug.

Blood poured out the end of the pipe, over CJ's hands and onto his bare feet. The vampire braced himself against his friend's shoulders, wincing yet otherwise appearing to take the intrusion as nothing more than a prick from a pin. CJ, using his left hand, traced over the spell tattooed above his heart, leaving a pentacle drawn in blood dripping down his skin. He then touched his forehead, his eyelids and chin, marking the spell.

"Out of the circle, Lucian!" TJ commanded.

The vampire nodded to CJ, who gripped the steel rod, and then he jerked his chest away from the weapon and stepped backward, watching his steps so as not to muss the salt circle. Once outside, he staggered and dropped to his knees. CJ tossed the bloody pipe out behind him.

"That's my cue," Libby whispered. She scampered over to the vampire's side, catching him as he fell forward into her clutches.

Suddenly TJ shouted, "Harrahya!" and reached over the salt line to clasp his brother's right hand firmly. The brothers raised their hands high. The room grew ominously shadowed, and outside lightning flashed.

The air electrified, lifting the hairs on Vika's skin in a prickling tingle and bringing the various oils used in the spell to a heady perfume. Earthy vetiver filled the space, lemony sweet. Cinnamon and frankincense to access the psychic realm. Clary sage would attract and secure the doppelganger.

Inside the circle, CJ's body went stiff, his eyes closed and his jaw clamped tightly shut, as if he was being pierced through with a shock of electricity. He'd dragged his bloody hands over his abdomen, leaving a tribal marking down the side of his torso.

Vika crept forward on the couch, feeling the urge to rush in and help. But she would only destroy the spell. She must be patient and trust the Jones brothers knew what they were doing.

Libby cradled Lucian's head and shoulders in her lap, but the vampire observed the spell with keen eyes. He would be fine, the narrow pipe not wide enough to have made his heart burst. His healing should be complete within moments.

The brothers' chants rose in a bellowing wave and knocked at the veil between the realms. Baritone rhythms mastered the atmosphere. Vika felt their voices upon her skin, permeating, exploring, laying claim. With a tribal yell, CJ's body stiffened with a hand up in a triumphant clasp with his brother's hand.

A chill swept about Vika's shoulders as the claiming touch receded and she decided Daemonia had been breeched. CJ's torso arched forward, while his head and feet remained back. He looked as though he were being tugged by a rope about his waist. The fingers of the hand he clasped within TJ's stiffened, and she could see the struggle to unloose himself from the firm hold. Jaw tight, CJ fought against something.

When in Daemonia, Vika knew, the moments became days and hours turned to weeks or months. If the spell lasted only minutes on this side of the veil, CJ could well endure a week in the place of all demons.

She didn't want that for him. Why had she let him go through with this? What sort of man would return, should he return? He would be changed, altered, perhaps even inhabited with more demons. Could the doppelgänger bring back demons to CJ's soul?

Squeezing a pillow on her lap, she realized in her apprehension she'd torn the seam to expose the stuffing.

A glance to Libby found her sister riveted to the

center of the circle, along with the vampire, who held a palm over his wounded chest.

TJ turned, twisting at the waist, and tugged at CJ's hand, as if pulling on a tug-of-war rope. "He's struggling," he said to Vika.

"What can I do?"

The witch shook his head, dismissing her to focus his concentration on the task. He resumed chanting, deeply, rhythmically.

Standing, Vika spread out her fingers, but she had no magic to hand for she had no idea what her lover needed. She felt out of control, helpless. Her lover's body was beginning to arch backward, his head tilted over his shoulders and his chest lifted. He stood on his tiptoes, an impossible feat. Yet he remained in that position, despite his brother struggling to maintain hold on his hand.

"Please let the war demon stand good on the bargain," she whispered, and closed her eyes, whispering the same thing over and over as she began to mark out each bead on the strand of jade. Repetitive chanting would enforce the energies required to bolster the spell. The beads would keep her focused.

"He's pulling me in," TJ gasped. "I'm not sure I can hold him."

"Let me help!" Lucian shouted.

TJ shook his head negatively. Any interference now from a nonwitch would deplete the spell's strength.

She could see TJ's body sliding toward the salt line. The moment his boot cut through the line, the consequences could prove disastrous. He had to remain out-side the circle to keep hold of the spell.

Clasping the nail necklace, Vika winced. Just as the brothers' hands separated, she leaped toward the circle, straddling it with one foot. Dropping the beads, she slid her hand into CJ's and at the same time gripped TJ's hand. "I can be an extension."

"Yes, good." TJ's grip was sure in her hand. "So powerful," he noted with a look of surprise. And then he switched to business mode. "Hold him, Vika. Don't let him go!"

"Never."

But her lover's hand was hard and cold as ice, and it felt as if she'd laid her bare flesh against a frozen steel pole. The chill of Daemonia trickled through her veins, and she gasped in the incensed and blood-tainted air. She could feel his heartbeat, her lover's galloping rhythm of life, and she would not give it up.

Tugged abruptly, her other foot lost hold and she lifted it as it entered the circle. CJ grasped her across the back. Face-to-face, they held one another, while TJ maintained his grip on her hand. She wasn't sure if CJ was aware, conscious of what he was doing on this side of the connection, but she held his gaze in an at-tempt to keep him here. His clutch on her was strong, crushing out her breath.

"Libby, help!" she cried.

Libby dashed to her side yet remained outside the circle.

"Let her take CJ's hand," Vika called to his brother. "Our magic combined can hold him here."

With a nod, TJ grabbed Libby's hand and made the switch. Her sister grabbed CJ's other hand, then took hold of TJ's hand as he anchored himself, one leg bent and leaning forward to hold Libby to the safe side of the circle.

"Damn, your sister's powers are strong," TJ hissed. He tucked his head and focused.

Grandmother St. Charles's power focused between the two of them. Normally it took three from the family—Vika, Libby and their sister, Eternitie—to invoke such power, but combined with TJ's magic, it seemed to be doing the trick.

Vika felt the chill of Daemonia trickle through her veins, as if sluicing out to drip from her fingertips. The air grew humid, brewing up the cinnamon and frankincense. Blood cloyed at the back of her throat.

CJ's body went lax, falling out of her and Libby's grasps, and he collapsed on the floor, sprawled across the salt circle.

Vika teetered but did not fall, and she managed to stumble outside the circle. TJ caught Libby before she crashed in a sprawl on the floor.

Vika looked to TJ, who pointed to his brother's hand, the one lying out of the circle.

In it glowed a bright blue halo.

## *Chapter 29*

"**Y**ou did it!" Vika straddled CJ's inert body and bracketed his face. He didn't smile up at her or even move. "CJ?"

"What is it?" TJ asked from over her shoulder.

She pressed her fingers to his neck, over the vein. "No." Crawling down, she put her ear to his chest. His heart didn't beat.

"He's not breathing," TJ noted, and shoved her roughly aside. "He needs CPR!"

As TJ lifted his fisted hands above his brother's chest, Vika's world wavered to a blurry muddle of confusion. He couldn't be dead. He…loved her. She loved him. They were going to be together if she ever got her soul back. They'd share magic and make love every day. He couldn't be…

The thud of TJ attempting to revive CJ brought Vika back to the moment. And she remembered.

"No!" She shoved TJ away and grabbed CJ's hand from the floor, the one that didn't hold the halo. "Command central."

"What?" Lucian asked, as he'd joined them now.

"He needs a kick-start!"

"Yes," Lucian muttered, and he slapped TJ across the back. "You know about that?"

"He told me, but I'm not—"

"It's this hand." Vika dragged her lover's hand up to his chest. He was covered in the vampire's blood, and it was difficult to find the tiny battery tattoo. She wiped away the blood as best she could, then pulled up his little finger and placed it over the battery.

CJ's chest pulsed upward, his body flopping lifelessly.

"Do it again," TJ coached. "Hold it there."

She pressed his finger over the battery, having no idea how the ink magic worked but having faith it would. Again, his body pulsed upward, and again, he remained lifeless.

"No, this has to work," she cried, and spat frantically onto his chest to smear away more of the blood. "I need to clean the area. Hurry!"

A bottle of whiskey was slapped into her hand. Vika poured the alcohol over CJ's chest, and then she rubbed the small tattoo dry with the hem of her sleeve. With a glance to Libby, who held vigil with hands clasped to her mouth, Vika nodded once, then again placed the man's finger to the tattoo on his chest.

This time when his chest rose, he cried out and kicked the air, tumbling Vika from his chest.

\* \* \*

As CJ lay prone, Vika straddled him and pushed the hair from his face to kiss him. Her mouth was warm against his, giving so much. She kissed his eyelids and smoothed her lips along his cheek. Nothing felt more welcomed, so warm. He had landed home.

Though his body had remained within the circle, he'd experienced it all. The trip to Daemonia had taken a week, surely, though he'd known before going it would register only a short time in this realm. The landscape had been vicious. Razor winds, agonizing heat, combined with brutal cold and rivers of blood and souls. It was the closest he ever wanted to get to Beneath.

Surprisingly, War had stood good on his word. But the moment the demon had granted CJ the soul bringer's halo, the entirety of Daemonia had lifted their heads and sniffed out the intruder. He'd battled against claws, talons, fangs and bladed wings. Blood had run from his doppelgänger, and bones had cracked. He'd felt every break, every slashed muscle, every bite to tender flesh, and all the anger and relentless hatred that brewed the place of all demons to the nightmare it was.

And the whole time? He'd felt Vika's hand in his. Along with TJ's hand—and then suddenly Libby's hand. CJ had felt a connection to the people who meant the most to him. So he'd fought and withstood the masses of demons determined to claim a strip of his flesh as prize.

And he'd survived to return. Without any passen-

gers. He felt nothing had hitched a ride in his soul. He hoped that was so.

Setting aside the horror of the past week—or more likely, minutes—CJ fell into the warm, lush strength of Viktorie St. Charles's kiss. He wrapped his arms about her sleek body and pulled her onto his, connecting at hips, stomach, chest and mouth, reassuring she was real and he was alive and back. In her arms.

Never again would he lose days in the archives because it was important to fill his cranium with as much spellcraft as he could possibly fit in there. There were better things in life, such as smiling at a beautiful woman, gazing into her green eyes, kissing her soft mouth and holding her perfect body against his.

He would never let her go. And while his skin burned from the touch of the nail at his throat, he thanked her grandmother for the power that enabled Vika to love him.

Perhaps it had been the kick-start as well that made his flesh feel as though he'd been jolted with a few hundred thousand volts. Good girl that she'd remembered about the spell.

"Don't ever scare me like that again," she whispered and kissed his cheek. "I thought I'd lost you."

He kissed her back. "Never. You'd come after me though, right? Catch my corpse light and keep me?"

"Don't say that. I want you whole and in my arms, dark one."

A man cleared his throat, and CJ remembered it had also been his brother's presence that had been with him for the entire journey through Daemonia.

Vika sat up beside him, and he missed her warmth *like that*. He pushed up, and before he could pull her back to him, he noticed for the first time he held a halo in one hand. He turned it before him, and he and Vika looked it over. It was a thin piece of dull metal, looking beaten down by the elements over the years. It appeared easily bendable, but when he gave the thin circlet a try, he found it adamant.

"Doesn't look like much," she said. "That's the soul bringer's halo? His soul is contained within?"

"I guess so." He rapped it on the hardwood floor, producing a dull, most unangelic *clunk*. "Thanks, TJ. We did it."

"Yes, but if it hadn't been for Vika, we may have lost you forever." His brother offered his hand and CJ stood, bringing Vika up with him. "How long were you there?"

"Seemed like a week," CJ said, clutching Vika tightly against his side.

"More like fifteen minutes," TJ said. "You are never going back to that place if I have to lash you to a stone at the top of Everest to keep you away."

"Sounds extreme. I'll be a good boy and promise to stay in this realm from now on."

"I heard that," Lucian said.

"You have four witnesses to that statement," TJ said. "How are you, old man?" he said to the vampire, who approached and gave CJ's shoulder a slap.

"Fine. But don't they give out pins after you've donated a gallon of blood? I want my pin."

"Thanks, man." CJ pulled Lucian into a man hug

and the two clapped hands against one another's back. "You're always there when I need you."

"Someone's got to be a guinea pig for your magic, Brother."

Libby joined the group, sheepishly taking her sister's hand and observing the reunion.

"You'd better get some rest, Certainly," TJ said.

"Can't. I have to summon the soul bringer."

CJ took a step, but Vika caught him as his body wobbled. Maybe he was weak. Last time he'd returned from Daemonia, he'd slept for two weeks straight, rising only to eat and use the bathroom.

"I'll take care of him," Vika said to TJ. "He's not going anywhere until after I've gotten him in bed."

TJ and CJ shared a grin that said more than either were willing to detail.

"Yes, I mean that exactly," Vika said, figuring out their man code. "Libby, are you cool to go home alone?"

"Of course. Lucian, can I offer you a ride? And TJ? The hearse fits three."

"Hearse?" Lucian's brow tilted into a sexy chevron. "This I've got to see."

Vika wandered about CJ's loft, while over in bed, he slept. He actually snored, which she marked as a good thing, since it had to take a lot out of a person to journey to the place of all demons. He deserved the sleep. She'd do a little cleaning.

She used a broom to sweep up the salt circle, not wanting to wake her sleeping hero with the vacuum.

And after every last salt grain had been swept into a box for reuse, she then cleansed the area with a spell and wormwood smudge, using supplies from his work shelf.

Some reorganizing in the fridge, tossing out old vegetables and expired peanut butter, and some straightening in the cupboards, and she felt satisfied that she'd cleaned without intruding on the not-too-chaotic disorder CJ was accustomed to.

She would leave his spell area alone, because that would infringe on his personal things, but she couldn't resist snooping through the grimoires and his book of shadows. He was a powerful witch, and his power had been returned upon the exorcism of the final demons.

She couldn't wait to see Certainly Jones at his finest. It was what had initially attracted her to him. Yet she'd already seen into his heart, a fine and wondrous place. In turn, he respected her magic and allowed it to be what it should be. Not once had he asked her to remove the nail about her neck to make it easier to touch her, as other of her lovers had in the past. He respected her power.

Never had a man been so generously accepting. His was a true and impeccable heart she was glad to have touched.

And oh, his touch. Sitting on the high stool before his workshop bench, she imagined him kissing her and her growing languid and melty in his embrace. Never had she a lover who could do that to her, make her grow warm thinking about their connection.

And what of his magic fingers? That was something

new and worthy of much practice. Mastery may never be achieved, but he could try all he liked, although only on her. She intended to keep him all for herself.

So she'd fallen for a bad boy. She understood their appeal now. Not really bad, but the outer appearance, and CJ's alliance with dark magic, defined him as mysterious and dangerous.

She knew otherwise; he was good.

"So good," she whispered, and smiled as she caught her chin in hand and twirled her hair about a finger. "I love my dark one."

With a yawn, she got up and wandered over to the bed. He lay on his side, his face concealed by a swath of hematite hair. His bare chest rose and fell rhythmically. She wanted to touch him, to be near him, so she carefully slid onto the bed, put an arm over his hip and snuggled into a peaceful slumber.

Certainly stirred and felt the warmth against his back. He knew immediately it was Vika lying beside him. He wasn't sure if she was awake, so didn't move.

He was back. Alive. Free. All he'd hoped for was peace. Perhaps now he would have it.

Soft lips kissed a trail down his spine. "Did you have a good rest?"

He rolled to his back, and her hand slid over his chest and down his abs. He felt a familiar stirring, and his erection hardened. He had stripped off his bloodstained jeans before collapsing in an exhausted heap on the bed, and the sheet covered him to the hips.

"Yes. How long did I sleep?"

"Most of the afternoon."

"And you stayed the whole time?"

"I did some cleaning. Not much. And don't worry, I didn't mess with your spell stuff, though I did snoop a little."

"Find anything interesting?"

"Your expertise in magic dazzles me, dark one. I want to learn from you. Will you teach me?"

"The dark stuff?"

"I think so. While I've chosen to only practice the light, I think knowledge on the dark can only make me more rounded and to see beyond more than my viewpoint."

"I would love to teach you." He took her hand and kissed it, then placed it over his erection. "But not right now, for you are the Purveyor of Hard-Ons. If not a little cool. You in a hurry to get your soul back, or can we…?"

"We're not going anywhere until this guy—" she gave his cock a squeeze through the sheets, and CJ groaned at the teasing move "—sees some action. I should check it out, make sure he survived the strenuous journey to…that place."

"You probably should."

She sat up and tugged down her dress sleeves, her hair spilling liquidly over her soft skin.

Certainly said, "Allow me." He gestured at her dress and invoked transprojectionary dislocation, which pulled down the zipper at her back and slid the fabric to a puddle at her hips to reveal her tight, rosy nipples.

"My magic is stronger and faster now the infestation has been exorcised."

"You can do this with anyone?" she asked with a cautionary tone and a lift of brow. "Strip them?"

"Of course, but I'll only use it on you. Promise."

"Your promises are made to be broken."

"Only with your permission."

"Fair enough. Can you…move anything else around?"

He quirked a brow, taking her tease for the challenge it was. "Let's see what comes up."

After a few flicks of his fingers and a "Lero," CJ raised his hand and lifted Vika from the bed. She startled initially but quickly relaxed, allowing his magic to move her body. Sitting cross-legged, she hovered over his hips, the fabric of her dress dusting his thighs.

"Oh, this could be dangerous." Tugging off her dress, she put down her knees to straddle him. "Should I let you do all the work?"

"Yes. I've never tried this before. Let's see how well I do."

Another flick of his fingers pulled the sheet away from his torso and legs. His cock, hot and furious for her enveloping heat, sprang up against Vika's mons. She reached for it, but he reminded her he was doing it all, so she relented, placing her hands akimbo.

"A little warm-up, I think," he said, and gestured his forefinger up and down in a come-hither movement.

Vika tilted her head and moaned satisfaction. The sensation of touch landed on her clitoris; he directed it softly, evenly and then firmer. "Oh, yes, right there. I can't believe you can do that. Oh…Certainly."

"It's not as satisfying as actually touching you," he said, "but I do seem to have a talent for this." A twist of his finger and she bit her lip, spreading her legs wider in a brazen pose.

"You wet for me, lover?"

She nodded, lost in the pleasure of his invisible touch.

With a lift of his hand, he raised her body a few inches over his cock, and then slowly, gently, lowered her onto him. He hissed and swore as she enveloped him, as if entering a fiery, squeezing tunnel. Reaching back to clutch her ankles, Vika allowed him to control her, moving her body slowly up and down, and he in turn, pistoning his hips upward, rocking in and out. He wanted to touch her, to pull her to him, and—screw it, the magic was fun, but he needed the real thing.

Sitting up, Certainly spread his hands up Vika's back and bent to kiss her breasts. She pulled her fingers through his hair, slipping it over her mouth, and all the while they rocked together, joining, feeling one another, bonding.

"Blessed goddess, I've never felt such a connection to another person like this before," Vika said. "You own me, Certainly Jones."

"I don't want to own you. Well, maybe your heart."

"You have all of me." She tilted his chin up to kiss his mouth. "I am yours. And you are mine. I've claimed you. If you don't like it, then try and stop me."

"I like it fine."

He clutched her derriere, rammed himself deep within her and then surrendered to a shuddering orgasm. Her fingernails dug into his shoulders, bruising the flesh as she cried out. This wicked magic belonged to them, and only them. And he would protect it, heart and soul.

## Chapter 30

The threesome stood out in the garden behind the round white house in the center of the fourth arrondissement, under a full moon. Night jasmine perfumed the air, and lightning bugs stitched flickering hems through the darkness. The red witch ball gleamed with a captured butterfly soul, casting soft crimson light over the heliotrope petals.

The faery-tale evening gave Vika a surprising shiver as the breeze tickled her bare shoulders and brushed the loose hair across her back. She and Libby had dressed elegantly, she in tight-fitted black satin, segueing to black lace at her knees and angled to her heels. Libby wore curve-hugging purple, and she'd stuck rhinestone pins in her hair, which glittered with captured moonlight.

Oddly, CJ must have been feeling the same grand

mien, as he'd appeared at their front door clad in dark
trousers and shirt and a damask vest threaded through
with silver. He looked a marvel, and it was all Vika
could do not to clasp his hand and imagine them walking down the garden aisle to some greater connection
that would bond them through life.

Perhaps someday they would exchange vows with
one another. She would like that very much.

She and her sister spoke little while following CJ's
instructions, as their giddy expectations took away
their breath. Yet at the same time, they were unwilling to get too excited over the prospect of their returned souls. They might not be able to invoke the soul
bringer. And if they did? What's to say his own soul
would prove of value to him?

"Let's join hands," CJ directed. The threesome
formed a circle before a crop of queen's lace, directly
below a beam of moonlight glistening on the flagstone
tiles. "Follow my lead, and weave in your own vocal
magic to strengthen the summons."

He began to hum, which grew to a chant of nonsense
syllables, yet it didn't matter it was not words. It was
the tone and intention behind them.

Vika found a chant and wove it into CJ's, squeezing
Libby's hand briefly when her sister also joined them
at a higher, dulcet tone.

The vibrations of their intent shivered through
Vika's body, and she knew they three shared the incredible volume of magic their voices created. It felt
wondrous and vast. An edge of darkness rimmed the
tones; CJ's contribution. A glimmer of gaiety splashed

the sound with vibrant colors; that was Libby's doing. And holding it all together, Vika rounded the song and expanded it into the universe.

The power of three could not be disregarded. And with their grandmother's magic to bind it well, nothing could stop them.

And in the center of their circle appeared Reichardt.

They dropped hands and stepped back, giving the soul bringer space as he looked about, summing up what had happened. With a stern glance to Libby before he lifted his head imperiously, he then grunted out, "What now?"

Vika watched Libby try to contain her glee, hands clasping over her heart and eyes going dewy, but with a shake of her head, her sister nodded and dropped her hands to her sides, assuming as much calm neutrality as she was able.

"I want to offer a trade," CJ said to Reichardt, "for the sisters' souls."

"Yours?" Reichardt posited with interest.

Vika's heart thundered. She raked her fingers at her thighs.

"No, yours." CJ reached behind him and grabbed the halo he'd tucked at the back of his pants. He held it gripped in both hands, just out of the soul bringer's reach.

Reichardt didn't move to touch it, nor did he exhibit the slightest increase in interest. "You've been industrious, dark witch."

"Two trips to Daemonia is enough for me," CJ replied. "But well worth it if you agree to the exchange."

"I've no use for a soul. That bit of tin is worthless to me."

"But you could—" With a castigating look from CJ, Libby cut off her protest. She nodded and looked aside, avoiding eye contact with her infatuation.

"Soul bringer, I realize you have walked this earth for millennia," CJ said. "Your life consists of ferrying souls. Back and forth. Up and down. Day and night. Ever the same. No need for connection, for conversation, for…cookies."

Vika pressed her lips together, preventing a smile. Her man knew all the right things to say.

"And should you accept this soul you would become a mere mortal," CJ continued. "Pitiful condition, if you ask me. Unable to remember your life as a psychopomp, visiting the gates to Above, yet never being allowed entrance through them. Stomping on the steps before Beneath, getting but a glimpse of devastation. It all means little to you, because your heart is glass."

"Exactly," Reichardt answered as means to put an end to the ridiculous offer. He glanced Libby's way.

Libby lifted her eyes, and they absolutely glittered at Reichardt. A deep blush rosed her cheeks, as well.

Work it, Vika thought. They needed all the help they could get.

"You cannot understand the concept of having one care for you," CJ continued. "Though, let me tell you, it is like nothing on this realm." He glanced to Vika, and winked. "Of knowing should you gain mortality, you would be loved."

Reichardt tilted his head, and while he was attempting to not look at Libby, Vika saw he failed. Some interest there. But was it enough?

"No," the soul bringer said abruptly, and dematerialized from within their circle.

A whoosh of cold air crept over their shoulders. Libby grasped the air before her. CJ dropped his hand, the halo brushing his thigh.

"No," Libby gasped.

Vika could feel her sister's disillusionment. Not only had she lost her soul, but as well she'd lost her heart to the cold, emotionless man. Talk about unrequited love.

Just as Vika summoned a consolation and went to embrace her sister, the soul bringer reappeared.

"Yes," Reichardt said. "I agree to the exchange." He winked at Libby.

*Winked.*

Libby clutched Vika's hands and tittered on her feet.

"Excellent." CJ gestured Vika and Libby stand beside one another. "Return their souls, and then you can have yours."

"Very well." Reichardt held up his palms before the sisters.

Libby leaned toward Vika and whispered, "Don't we have to get naked for this part?"

Smirking, Vika shook her head. "I think we're fine like this."

The soul bringer closed his eyes and pressed his hands to Libby and Vika low on their chests. It happened quickly. Her body jolted, her shoulders jerking back, and her chest lifted and burned bold and warm. The warmth radiated out through her extremities and filled her, finding home. Must be what Certainly felt when she'd blasted the souls through him. What a wondrous feeling. Her soul had returned.

She and Libby had joined hands, and now she hugged her sister. "We're back."

"Thank you, Reichardt," Libby offered, yet wisely not leaping in for a hug. He wouldn't know how to accept that yet. Maybe.

"And now?" Reichardt looked to CJ, who wielded the halo.

"Now I honor my part of the bargain." As he approached the soul bringer, CJ paused. He tapped the halo against his palm, considering. Turning, he placed the halo in Libby's hand. "You should do it."

"Really? But I don't know how."

"Just…place it above his head, where it would have normally resided when once he walked the heavens."

"The heavens," Libby said in awe.

"And you must recite his angelic name." CJ leaned next to Libby's ear and whispered the name.

With a nod, Libby asked, "Are you sure about this, Reichardt?"

The soul bringer studied Libby's inquiring eyes. "With my earthbound soul I will lose all knowledge of this life I have led for millennia. I will become lost in this world. An infant in a man's shape, possessed with the knowledge of the world, yet unfamiliar with common emotions."

"You won't be lost, because you'll have me," Libby encouraged.

Reichardt nodded and clasped his hands before him. "Then I am sure."

"Okay." Libby glanced to Vika, giddiness making her bounce on her toes. She turned and approached Reichardt. "It's a wondrous thing, having a soul. Here's to much magic and wonder in your new life, Reichardt Fallowgleam, Kryatron, Angel of the Seventh Soul."

Tilting up onto her tiptoes, Libby moved the halo above Reichardt's head. It fixed and remained in one particular spot, and Libby was able to step back and join Vika's side. Hugged by Certainly on one side and her sister on the other, Vika watched as the soul bringer's body suddenly stiffened, his arms jutting out and head tilting back to face the heavens.

The halo flashed a brilliant blue and then a medley of colors, such as an aurora borealis. The soul bringer's body lifted from the earth and floated upward a few feet.

Vika hugged her sister tightly while she clasped CJ's hand. The garden had gone so still the grasses did not sway nor did a single cricket chirp.

With a whoosh of perfumed air, massive wings suddenly swept out behind Reichardt's shoulders, spanning the small garden. Gorgeous, they were fashioned of an eerie blue smoky substance, yet formed as feathers. All angels' wings were in the form of their original occupation. Vika couldn't decide what the blue smoke signified for Reichardt. The Seventh Soul? She had no clue.

The soul bringer cried out. His body glowed all over blue, shimmering and dazzling so all three looked aside from the brilliance. Behind her, the witch ball suddenly shattered, releasing the butterfly soul to the universe. And Reichardt's wings suddenly dispersed into glistening bits of crystal, dropping at once to the ground at their feet.

The soul bringer's body followed, collapsing upon the crystal angel dust. The halo was gone. A single blue feather lay tucked amidst the dust.

"Was that it?" Vika whispered.

"I think so." Certainly kissed her aside the neck. "That was beautiful."

"Is he okay?" Libby plunged to kneel beside Reichardt. She stroked his thick, dark hair, and he groaned, coming to. "Reichardt?"

"I can feel…." He smiled at Libby. "I can *feel*."

"He'll quickly lose memory of all his interactions in this realm and be left as if a newborn in this world," Certainly said. "Let's get him inside and— Vika, can you sweep up the angel dust? It might come in handy someday."

"You don't have to tell me that. Dust and broom, coming right up!"

As Libby led Reichardt into the house, Vika was swept into Certainly's arms. He kissed her then leaned back, swaying with her beneath the moonlight. "We did good tonight."

"I think so. We make an interesting team, dark witch."

"Interesting?"

"Yes, and I'd rather that than perfect, or made-for-one-another, or even cute."

"Never cute, my Moonlit Soul Vestibule. You absolutely beam now. You're not cold, either."

"It feels good to be me again. Thank you, Certainly. You think Libby's got a new boyfriend now?"

"He'll make an interesting one, for sure. A two-thousand-year-old virgin who will soon have no grasp on his past?"

"She could so mold that guy to her will. But she won't. She'll be good for him."

"I suspect you'll have a new boarder. Unless we can learn where he lives before his memory leaves."

"I should go pry that out of him sooner rather than later." She kissed him quickly then promised she'd return with a broom.

Certainly squatted before the angel dust. Gorgeous stuff. It was valued by vampires and angels, and hell, any paranormal breed could find a use for it, both good or evil. He picked up the blue feather, which was as large as an ostrich plume but with tight vanes that felt liquid under his touch.

"From Above," he said. "A piece of the divine."

The value of this feather was astronomical, and he knew exactly where he could store it for later use in a spell.

On second thought…

"No. This belongs to Reichardt. He'll need a souvenir, whether or not it means anything to him now."

Tucking the feather in his shirt pocket, he stood and glanced to the moon. "Blessed be," he said. "And all will be well."

## Chapter 31

A week later the world was well. Dark witches were staying out of Daemonia. The occasional werewolf body required removal before mortals stumbled onto the mess. The local hotels were receiving strange but welcome donations of chandeliers.

And a former soul bringer was learning to vacuum.

Vika followed Reichardt's careful path as he pushed the vacuum cleaner around in the living room beneath the chandelier. They'd discovered he did keep an apartment in Paris, but it was empty, with but a bed and a chair, and a few odd knickknacks. They'd decided to keep the place until Reichardt could decide for himself if he preferred the bachelor's lifestyle or to share the St. Charleses' home.

"Really, Libby?"

Libby stood proudly watching her man fit the vacuum into a corner behind the couch. "He enjoys it. Says it gives him a sense of purpose. Hell, the man is a babe in the world, Vika. He's curious about everything, but an afternoon at the park is like overload to his emotions. We have to take things slow. Besides, I reward him with cookies."

"I see great things for the two of you."

"Do you really?"

Vika wasn't sure about that. But if anyone could make a relationship of what they had been given, it was Libby.

"How's your hip?" Libby asked.

"Sore. I'm headed to CJ's place now. Sayne told me earlier he had an appointment with him this afternoon."

"Matching love tattoos?" Libby said with a flutter of her lashes.

"I don't know. He's probably getting another spell tattoo. I'm staying at CJ's tonight, so I'll see you tomorrow. Don't make him work too hard."

"Vika, please. After the work, the guy earns a massage."

"I see." Oh, yes, their relationship definitely held promise.

When Vika arrived at CJ's loft, yet another delivery team was carrying out a chandelier that had been carefully packed and shrink-wrapped. CJ wanted to keep a dozen of the fixtures. And Vika loved the ones with black and red crystals, so she had suggested those remain, as well. CJ had invited her to live with him, and while she loved her round white house, the idea of hanging around while Libby and Reichardt started whatever it was they intended to begin had been all she'd needed to agree. She intended to gradually move in over the next few weeks.

Caught about the waist from behind, she twirled in her lover's arms. "Sayne gone already?"

"An hour ago," he said. "Where have you been?"

"At home. Libby is teaching Reichardt to vacuum."

His lifted brow got an agreeing nod from her. "I know, right? Strange as it may seem, I have hope for that pair. Though he's lost all his former powers and Libby says he's physically quite weak, despite the six-pack and huge biceps he sports."

"The man is completely mortal now. Stripping his immortality from him probably played a real number on his body. And he was told about his past. Don't you think that's going to screw with his brain? Knowing how powerful he once was?"

"Libby will see him through it. She, and her chocolate chip cookies. She sent some along for you." He took the zip bag and set it on the kitchen counter. "So let me see the artwork," she said, drawing her fingers down his unbuttoned shirt and teasing at his bare chest. "Where is it?"

He tugged up his sleeve and revealed his wrist. Above the barbed rose sat a thick black checkmark with fresh red edges.

She tilted her head to study it but couldn't figure what it meant.

"It's a *V*," he finally said.

"Oh. For Vika?"

"For Viktorie. For my Vivacious Vixen. For us."

"Oh, that's so sweet. No magic?"

"All the magic required is right here." He kissed her, spreading his hands through her hair and pulling her in close. "And here." He planted a kiss on her nose. "And here." Her forehead, her chin and down her neck. "No more visitors or pickups today. Let's get naked."

"Yes." She strolled toward the bed, unzipping the back of her dress and letting it fall to her hips. "Then you can see what I had Sayne do this morning."

"You— You got a tattoo? He didn't mention— Vika?"

She shimmied her hips, and her dress slid down to puddle in black waves on the floor. Certainly's hands slid up her thigh and stopped at the top of her derriere. She felt his kiss there, beside the sweet ache lingering from the tattoo needle.

"My name," he said. "Oh, witch, this is…"

"You like it? It means I'm yours. Or you're mine. Or—"

"It means you can't ever get rid of me now. How many other Certainlys are there out there?"

"I can always change it to Certainly Mine."

"Vixen. We'd better not put you on your back until it's healed." He stood and pressed her stomach and chest against the bed poster. "Guess we'll have to do it standing up."

"Or in the air?" she suggested, tapping his left hand.

Her lover wrapped his arms about her, and together they twirled up from the floor to float near the dazzle of a red chandelier. Bodies painted with crimson light, they forged the night with sexmagic and a true love that ran deep into their souls. The darkness had receded, and together they now shared the light.

\* \* \* \* \*

*A sneaky peek at next month…*

# NOCTURNE™

**BEYOND DARKNESS…BEYOND DESIRE**

## *My wish list for next month's titles…*

In stores from 21st June 2013:

❏ Keeper of the Shadows – Alexandra Sokoloff

❏ Beautiful Danger – Michele Hauf

In stores from 5th July 2013:

❏ Lord of Sin – Susan Krinard

Available at WHSmith, Tesco, Asda, Eason, Amazon and Apple

## *Just can't wait?*

# *Special Offers*

very month we put together collections and
nger reads written by your favourite authors.

ere are some of next month's highlights—
nd don't miss our fabulous discount online!

ANDRA MARTON

THE
SCANDALOUS
*Orsinis*

*The Sheikh*
WHO LOVED HER

SUSAN
STEPHENS   KATE
HARDY   LIZ
FIELDING

THE
CORRETTIS
*Secrets*

SHARON KENDRICK
LYNN RAYE HARRIS

n sale 21st June          On sale 5th July          On sale 5th July

# *Save 20%*
## *on all Special Releases*

# *Join the Mills & Boon Book Club*

Want to read more **Nocturne**™ books?
We're offering you **1** more absolutely **FREE!**

We'll also treat you to these fabulous extras:

- 🌹 **Exclusive offers and much more!**

- 🌹 **FREE home delivery**

- 🌹 **FREE books and gifts with our special rewards scheme**

*Get your free books now!*

## visit www.millsandboon.co.uk/bookclub
## or call Customer Relations on 020 8288 2888

# *Mills & Boon® Online*

Discover more romance at
**www.millsandboon.co.uk**

- 🌹 **FREE** online reads
- 🌹 **Books** up to one
  month before shops
- 🌹 **Browse our books**
  before you buy

  *...and much more!*

---